I0734388

THE CHANGE

The story within is a work of fiction. Names, characters, businesses, places, events, and incidents are either the products of the author's imagination or used in a fictitious manner. Any resemblance to actual persons, living or dead, or actual events, is purely coincidental.

The Change is
Copyright @ 2025 Oddity Prodigy Productions, LLC

All rights reserved.
No part of this book may be reproduced or used in any manner without the prior written permission of the copyright owner, except for the use of brief quotations in a book review.

ISBN 978-1-7333938-5-0 (paperback)

Author: Jacob Jones-Goldstein
Copyediting: Greg Schauer
Cover art and Interior Layout: Jennifer Marang
OPP logo: Steve Myers

Published by
Oddity Prodigy Productions, LLC
302 Arbour Drive
Newark, DE 19713

www.oddityprodigy.com

THE CHANGE

By Jacob Jones-Goldstein

DEDICATION

For Woody and Bob,
who knew that a song could change the world.

"WHERE WAS GOD?"

by Trapper Schoepp and Jacob Jones-Goldstein

A change is coming
In the land they call free
From the old French Quarter
Up to Little Italy

The Great Plains vacant
The cities crumble
Highways torn up
A nation was humbled

Where was God?
Where was He?
Hear people praying
Holding rosaries
Where was God?
Where was he?
All boxed in
In the land of the free

Years pass
See new walls
Baby, we just made it
But he still hasn't answered the call
Had we forgotten
'Bout the four horseman running?
I think it was in Revelations
I just hear guitar strumming

Where was God?
Where was He?
Hear people praying
Holding rosaries
Where was God?
Where was He?
We're all boxed in
In the land of the free

PART ONE

CHAPTER ONE

I was seven years old the day I first met Dylan Droge. This would have been about 15 years ago. I lived on a small farm with my brother and my mom. We grew enough to feed ourselves, and always had some left over to sell. The money we made wasn't much, but it kept us in generator fuel, and that was all we really needed.

My mom had a cheerful way about her that had men from town knocking on our door. Despite their many attempts, she never so much as went on a date with any of them. Whenever I asked about it, she would tell me that she had fallen in love once, and that was enough for her. She had been raised on a farm and had the strong arms and deep tan to prove it. Our family had always been farmers, she said, even before the Change. We had a photo album that had some old color pictures in it of the farm she had grown up on, and it was a beautiful place. It was out in the Kansas territories, not far from Silver City. She left when she married my father. Apparently, my grandfather never really took to my dad, and it caused a bit of a rift. Mom never talked about it much, but I think that's why we ended up where we did.

My brother, James, was twelve at the time and had begun to travel outside our farm compound some. Mom didn't much like him going out on his own, but he had a knack for hunting and scavenging so she let him go. That didn't stop her from waiting by the gate for him to come home. I will always remember seeing that look of fear in her eyes every time the sun started to set, and he wasn't home yet. He always cut it too close for her comfort.

When people tell stories about big days in their lives, they always seem to preface them with details that imply that they knew something was in the air, like they had some kind of sixth sense about it. You know the kind of stories. "When I was walking home that day, a black cat crossed my path, so I knew something was going to happen" and the like. I don't remember any kind of premonition like that. My brother left at dawn to go hunting and to check out a cave he'd found late the previous afternoon. He seemed to think there was some good usable metal there. Mom and I spent the early morning working in the field. The first time I saw her go to the gate and look for him was when we broke for lunch. I remember the meal was a tomato and some cornbread. We ate pretty simply in those days. As the day progressed, she began to spend more time looking out from the gate. This was normal for days he went out, but she seemed extra agitated because of his discovery. Caves weren't the safest places in the world even before the Change; these days they could be absolutely deadly.

Evening approached, and my brother still hadn't returned home. I went out and sat by the gate with my mother. She leaned on the post where the button to close it was. I was sitting next to her drawing pictures in the dirt with a stick when we heard the first moan. My mother went rigid. It didn't sound like it was that close by, but anytime you hear a moan, you don't want to be standing there with your gate open.

"Go get the gun. Hurry," she said in a tone that I had never heard before. All the good humor had drained from her. Even as a seven-year-old, I could sense that she was scared. We didn't get a lot of traffic where we lived. Too far from any real population center to attract much. Because of that, I had never seen a Changed. I knew what the fence was for and why we didn't travel at night. I had heard them - you can't not when it gets quiet at night - but I wasn't really scared of them. Not as scared as I should have been. Even so, I ran to the house and got the gun from over the bookshelf and came running back. I handed it to my mom, who did a quick check that it was loaded. She then did something that I had always been told you shouldn't do. She called for my brother as loud as she could. One of the things they teach you is to keep quiet once you hear the moans. The Changed can't see or hear all that well, so sometimes, if you're quiet and still, they have trouble finding you. However, if you start yelling, they can hone in like a shark who senses blood in the water.

The only response to my mother's call was a second moan from the direction we'd heard the first one and then another from the opposite direction. The second moan was even closer than the first. Mom stepped outside the gate and looked around. The sky was getting very red, and the sun would set soon. She shouted again, and it was returned by still more moans. I think even if my brother had been within earshot, he would have been smart enough to not respond. He knew to be quiet when you were out in the open, especially at sunset.

At the age of seven, I knew the dilemma that would be facing my mother. We couldn't leave the gate open and the fence turned off after dark. She also knew my brother hadn't brought a lantern or a flashlight with him, which meant she would have to turn on the floodlights for him to find his way home in full dark, but if she did that, the farm would be surrounded within an hour of the Sun setting. There weren't a lot of Changed in the area, but if we put on the lights, every single one within miles would move toward it like moths.

Sensing my mother's fear, I remember I started to cry. She began to say things like 'It'll be ok, he'll make it home, don't worry, honey,' in a voice that attempted comfort, but didn't really hide her fear. That voice terrified me more than the moans, which were getting louder and more frequent.

By that point, the Sun had become a very small point on the horizon. Full dark would be upon us, and my mother would have to close the gate soon. Just as the last bit of sunlight winked out, we heard running footsteps. The Changed didn't run. They were coming from the same direction the first moans had come from. My mother switched on the floodlights as soon as she realized what she was hearing.

My brother came into view as he crested the hill that was at the north end of the field outside our gate. He was running as fast as he could. Seconds after we saw him, we saw the first of the Changed. It came out of a copse of trees on the west side of the field. It was moving slow, but my brother was still far enough away that it was a toss-up who would reach the gate first.

The retort from the rifle firing was the loudest thing I had ever heard in my life up to that point. My mother was a good shot and hit the Changed, but it wasn't a kill shot. It stopped the thing from shambling for a moment, but it just started up again. Changed began to come over the hill and emerge from the trees to the east. This was going to be a very close race. My mother took another shot at the closest Changed, this time hitting it in the leg and knocking it over.

"Get ready to press the button as soon as he gets through the gate," my mother said. I was just tall enough to reach the button at that age and ran over to the post. I put my hand on it, ready to press. I couldn't see through the gate from that vantage point, so I'm not entirely sure what happened next, but my mother fired twice more, and then both her and my brother came rolling through the gate. It looked like my brother had tackled my mom. She shouted, "Now!" I didn't hesitate, pressing it as hard as I could. Immediately, I could hear the familiar rumble of the gears, and the whine, as the metal of the gate scraped on its track and began to close.

I ran over to my brother and hugged him. My mother had recovered from being tackled and was aiming the rifle at the ever-shrinking gap between us, and the nightmare outside the fence. Her shoulders relaxed a little as she let out the deep breath she had probably been holding for several minutes now.

That was when there was a loud sizzling sound from the generator, the gate stopped moving, and the floodlight went out.

For a brief moment, it was impossibly quiet, and then everything seemed to happen at once. There was a very loud moan right from where the gate should have been. My mother fired the rifle again, and in the muzzle flash, I got my first real good look at a Changed. The flash drained all the color from the world, so the vision I still see in my nightmares was black and white. It was human-looking, but the skin on its face had a stretched look to it like someone was pulling it from behind. The eyes were sunken, empty things. It was impossibly skinny and stretched its arms out towards us. The gauntness made the arms look too long. It had no skin on its fingertips, so its fingers looked like claws.

"Get to the shed," my mother yelled. Without the generator, it would take all three of us to push the gate closed and we didn't have time. Her bullet had knocked the Changed backward, but there were more right behind it. We had to fall back.

The house had too many doors and windows, but the shed was basically a corrugated steel box. The walls were thinner than that of the house, but it would be easier to defend with only one entrance. I started to run and stumbled. James picked me up and slung me over his shoulder. He was considerably bigger than I was, even at age 12. My mother was right behind us as we got to the shed. She slammed the door closed, and we all pushed the workbench over to barricade it.

Once the door was braced, we all huddled together with our backs to the bench. The Changed weren't strong or smart, but they were numerous and relentless. As we huddled there, we had to hope there weren't enough in the area that they would swarm. If enough Changed began to press on the door trying to get in, there was nothing we would be able to do to stop it.

It wasn't long before the banging started. The Changed had surrounded the shed and were trying to get in. The noise of their hands on the metal walls was terrible. I will never forget that cacophony for as long as I live. It went on for hours. I lost track of time as we huddled together in that small metal room with death on all sides, banging and scraping against the thin walls.

None of us noticed it at first, but after a few hours, the banging started to lessen. The sound had been so constant and the change so gradual, that there was no real way to notice until we heard the guitar. I think we all thought we were imagining things. It wasn't until my brother said, "Is that music?" that we acknowledged that we all heard the sound. As the banging slowed and then stopped altogether, the guitar got louder, and we heard a man singing. Soon, I was able to make out the words. It was something about walking down some street named Ventura.

We sat, entranced. The Changed creating a din trying to get in the shed was a sound that made sense. The horrible moaning made sense. The sound of singing and a guitar didn't make any sense. I don't think any of us moved or even breathed.

"I'm freeeeeee!"

After a few moments, the singing stopped. We held our breath, not knowing what would happen next, expecting screams or the banging to start again. Instead, we heard the tell-tale grumble of the generator starting, followed shortly by the loud clang of the gate closing.

Another minute passed, and then we heard a knocking on the door of the shed.

"It's safe to come out now," a man's voice said. "They're all gone."

"Who...who are you?" my mother said.

"Name's Dylan."

Not knowing what else to do and hoping beyond hope that this nightmare might be over, my mother and brother moved the workbench. She leveled her gun at the door and gestured for my brother to open it. I stood behind my mother.

Standing there on the other side of the door was a young man with his hands raised, and a guitar slung over his back. He was about six feet tall, wearing ragged denim jeans and well-worn trail boots. He had a blue denim jacket that looked like it had seen a lot of the world. It had colorful patches sewn on it in random places. He wore a dusty fedora and had long blonde hair. He was grinning at us in a way that implied he had never been happier to see anyone in his life.

"I don't suppose you'd have some supper left over for a weary traveler?"

"We might have something left on the stove if those monsters didn't get into the house," my mom replied. Her voice was a combination of weariness, hope, and bafflement.

"That would be wonderful."

"Who are you?" my brother asked.

"My name is Dylan Droge. Pleased as hell to meet you!"

CHAPTER TWO

It turned out that none of the Changed had gone into the house. They stomped up the vegetable garden pretty good, though. Despite Dylan saying they were all gone, mom insisted on checking the whole farm. We didn't have much land, but there were lots of places a Changed could hide. We checked every nook and cranny in the property and walked down all the rows in the cornfield. Mom wouldn't let my brother or me out of her sight, so it took a while to check everywhere. Once we were done, we found Dylan sitting on our front porch, strumming his guitar. I was in awe of the instrument.

I'd seen homemade guitars before. People always gathered in the town center after the sun went down on market days. It was dark out by then, so no one was allowed to go outside the fence. Most of the sellers lived on small isolated farms like us, so we had no homes to go to in town. Everyone brought cots or blankets to sleep on, but before setting up for bed, there was always a party. People danced and sang and courted and basically kept the darkness at bay by enjoying being together. Things were pretty lonely most of the time for those folks and for us. There weren't schools or jobs really. Not out on the plains. You couldn't be outside of a complex after dark, and you had to somehow feed yourself. Fence repairs and fuel for generators weren't cheap, so you always had to grow enough to eat as well as to sell. It was a tough way to live. The music and happiness of those after-market parties had a way of making things better for a little while. It was just enough life to keep you going for another few weeks.

I remember watching my mother dance. She was graceful despite her farm-earned muscles. She had a natural rhythm that was infectious. It wouldn't surprise me if a few of the local farmers fell in love with her every couple of weeks. She never encouraged any of them, of course, but I'm sure she had her hands full keeping them at bay.

I spent most of those nights running around and playing games with the other kids. My brother didn't really join in either the kid's games or the adults dancing. He would usually wander over to the town library and read on the nights we spent in town. He was always solitary. Once in a while, my mother would force him to join the dance, but it never lasted long. I think he was just uncomfortable around people. One of my only regrets from my childhood was never really getting to know him. He was only five years older than me, but it might as well have been a million years.

In some ways, having such a solitary brother made my childhood on the farm that much more lonely. As a family, all we really had were each other. He and I should have spent our days together playing and running around after the chores were done, but we never really did. He would mostly read or play with my father's telescope.

I think he was suspicious of Dylan at first. He stayed back from him and spent a good portion of that evening eyeing him up. I was too young to be overly suspicious of anyone, and there was that guitar. That magnificent guitar. It had a spruce top that was covered in a finish that made it shiny. Even though it was pretty scratched up, the light still danced off of it. The back looked like rosewood, and the fingerboard looked like onyx. The frets were white, like long straight pearls. Even the gears looked shiny to my seven-year-old eyes. It was a bit beat up and had undoubtedly seen a lot of miles but, besides my mother, I had never seen anything as beautiful. That day, looking at that guitar and hearing Dylan play, was the first day when I truly believed in magic.

"Pretty ain't she?" he said to me as he saw me admiring it.

He started playing it in earnest again. This time it was a different tune. It was a bit faster than the other one. As the music began to build, he looked like he was about to sing when my mother cut him off.

"Do you want them to come back? Hush up. Let's go inside and see if we have enough stew to feed you."

He smiled at my mother with that innocent grin that I would get used to seeing whenever someone around him was afraid. He stopped playing, slung the guitar over his shoulder, and opened the door for her. They went inside, and I followed. As I got to the door, I turned around and saw that my brother was staring at the fence. I watched him for a moment, holding the door open. Eventually, he turned around and came inside. My brother spent a lot of time looking off into the distance. My mother knew he wouldn't stick around the farm for very long and that was why she was always waiting by the fence for him to come back. I think every morning he went out scavenging a small piece of her believed that she would never see him again.

My mother put on some coffee. Coffee was one of the few luxuries she allowed herself. It wasn't something you could grow in Kansas. It came to town with merchant caravans from California and wasn't cheap. For her to put on a whole pot was unheard of. Even at my young age, I thought the night warranted an entire pot of coffee.

"That smells delicious, ma'am. I don't remember the last time I had coffee."

"How did you get them to leave?" my brother blurted out, cutting off my mother before she had a chance to reply.

"I just sang them a song and asked them to go," he replied without the slightest hint of guile or sarcasm. My brother glared at him. My mother, having seen that look from my brother before, interjected, "Now, now, let's not get to questions until we've had our fill. It has been an awfully long night, and I, for one, would like to eat something." The unease in her voice silenced my brother from further inquiry. I don't think my mother really wanted to know how he had done it. At that moment, she was simply glad that the Changed were gone, and both of her sons were alive.

We ate in silence. Not the kind of silence that you get when people are scared or angry. It was the kind of silence that people make when they are busy counting their blessings and thanking God they are still alive. After dinner, my mother poured coffee for Dylan, my brother, and herself.

"That was wonderful, ma'am. Thank you very much for your hospitality," Dylan said.

"You're welcome. I'm not sure I can ever really repay you, but you have my thanks for saving us tonight."

He smiled that smile again. "Wasn't anything, Ma'am. Like I said, all I did was sing them a song and ask them to leave."

"That's bullshit. They don't have any minds. You can't ask them to do things. All they want to do is kill people!" my brother shouted. He was obviously annoyed at this stranger sitting in his kitchen, telling what he thought were tall tales.

"Watch your language!" my mother responded before turning to Dylan. "He has a point, though. The Changed don't think. They're more mindless than a blade of grass."

"Wish I had a better answer for you, ma'am, but that's the truth. They just seem to listen to me. Not always, but most of the time, anyways. Usually, if I play them something, they don't put up much of a fuss."

"Well, however you did it, you have our thanks. We don't have much, but we can give you a bed to sleep on and some provisions for the road in the morning. It's been a long day for all of us, and I think it's time we all got some rest."

She wasn't much for conversation.

"Once again, I appreciate it, ma'am."

Before my mother had a chance to get up, he picked up his guitar and started to play again. He strummed out a beautiful melody for a few moments and then began to sing. The words were about taking a sad song and making it happy.

It was the most wonderful music I had ever heard. I sat entranced. Even my brother seemed ensorcelled by his voice and music. I'm not sure how long the song went on for, but it could have gone on forever and I would have been happy.

When he was done, I saw my mother openly weeping. My brother's eyes were glistening as well. Eventually, the spell was broken, and my mother stood up.

"Thank you," she said in a near whisper.

My brother left the room in a hurry. I heard him go upstairs to the room we shared and close the door.

"I'll get some blankets for you," she said and left to get some bedding for him.

He turned to me after they had left the room and smiled at me. I remember thinking that his smile seemed sad that time.

"You don't remember your father, do you?" he asked.

I was caught off guard by the question and just shook my head. My father had disappeared one day when I was very young. He had gone off scavenging when things were a bit leaner than they were now. He never came back. I don't remember what he looked like other than in pictures, but sometimes I'll smell something, usually leather, and I'm almost able to recall him.

"Your mother and your brother remember him. Hopefully, tonight they'll be able to forget missing him long enough to have a good rest."

"How...how did you know about my Dad?" I asked.

"Sometimes, I can just sense these things," he replied and winked at me. My mother came back into the room and took Dylan to the spare room with the cot.

The night I first met Dylan Droge was a very strange night.

CHAPTER THREE

When morning came, my mother had Changed her mind about sending Dylan on his way. She was usually very wary of anyone she didn't know who came to the farm. This was typically justified. There were many people who wandered the plains who needed shelter at night. Most were looking for a bed and some food, but many more were looking to take whatever they needed and move on.

We'd had an incident a few months prior to Dylan arriving where a drifter had come to the farm very late in the evening. Knowing that to turn him away was a death sentence, my mother let him in. She offered to let him sleep in the shed and gave him some food. Late in the night, he came into the house. My mother, being no fool, had stayed awake and prepared for such a situation. She told me later than she had intended to simply keep him at gunpoint until dawn. Unfortunately, the drifter decided to try his luck and ended up buried out near the forest. Not everyone was untrustworthy, but a woman with two young children living on a farm alone couldn't be too careful.

I believe it was the song that had convinced her about Dylan. She was as unnerved as my brother by Dylan's getting the Changed to leave, but after listening to him sing and play in our kitchen, she knew on an instinctual level that she could trust him. She offered to let him stay till market day and accompany us to town. Market day was only a few days away, and so Dylan accepted. He earned his keep by helping us work the fields and singing and playing at night.

He wasn't a very good farmer, but that didn't matter. Hearing him sing on those quiet nights was like knowing everything was going to be alright, at least for a little while. His voice drifted out and surrounded you like he was taking you into his hands and comforting you. Each night my mother was moved to tears, as was my brother. I think I was too young for melancholy, so it affected me in a different way, speaking directly to my need to be safe and loved.

I didn't know any of the songs he played. My mother thought some of them she had heard sung in her childhood. He said he learned the songs from people he'd met on the road and at places he stayed. All I knew was that as a kid, that guitar and those songs were the sweetest things I had ever heard.

Those days leading up to market day were the happiest of my childhood. My brother even seemed to thaw out for once. He didn't go wandering at all or even spend a lot of time staring out over the fence. At night he showed Dylan his telescope, and together they looked at the stars. I remember being jealous since he never let me touch it. My mother told me that the telescope had been my father's and that he and my brother would spend half their nights looking at the stars together. I think he was afraid that if I touched it, it would somehow be less special. Somehow my defiling it would make it just a telescope and not a connection between him and my father.

Dylan asked my mother about my father the last night before market day. He did this after my brother, and I were supposed to have gone to bed. I had woken up to use the outhouse and was coming back in when I heard them talking. Up until that night, I hadn't really known what had happened to my father, just that he had gone away. As I listened, she told him about how he had been restless like my brother, and one night simply didn't come back. That much I knew, but what I hadn't known is that he had returned on several occasions.

I didn't really know what the Changed were then. They were simply the boogeyman who came out at night and were the reason we had to have electric fences and gates that locked. It never occurred to my seven-year-old mind that the Changed used to be people. In telling Dylan about my father, my mother explained that he had gotten caught by the Changed and had become one of them. Three days after he didn't come home, my mother was still standing vigil by the gate in case he arrived and was being chased. She still had hope. On that third night, several of the Changed had wandered up to the gate and just stood there. Even though his skin had taken on the yellow pallor that the Changed have, he hadn't become emaciated or lost his hair like so many of them do. She recognized him.

Dylan asked if she had put him out of his misery. She responded that she couldn't. Even though he was one of the monsters now, she still hoped that someday they would be able to cure them. She laughed and said it was silly, but she still believed that. She commented on how Dylan must think that she was foolish. He didn't say anything for a really long time. Long enough that when he did speak, I nearly jumped. All he said was, 'It isn't foolish. Hope is the most important thing we can have in this world. Don't ever let go of that hope.' I couldn't hear my mother's answer to that, but I could tell she had begun to cry. He walked across the room, got his guitar, and began to play. It was a sweet, quiet song that he hadn't played before, and it began:

"I will remember you..."

CHAPTER FOUR

We packed up the next day and set off for town. I was too small to help pull the cart and young enough that the five-mile walk tired me out, so I usually rode in the cart with the vegetables. My mother and brother would take turns pulling. This trip, Dylan helped as well. In fact, he ended up pulling it most of the way.

We lived in the foothills on the edge of the Great Plains. Our town was right at the very base of the hills where everything flattened out. This always made the first part of the trip more difficult than the end. Hauling a cart full of vegetables and a seven-year-old up and down hills wasn't the easiest thing on anyone.

The Changed never came out during the day. The sunlight seemed to hurt them. Not in the burst into ashes sort of way that vampires in stories do but enough to keep them away. Whether or not they felt pain was always one of the leading debates among the groups that tried to keep people from killing them. The argument never did much to sway folks, though. People thought of them the same way people thought of rabid dogs. Sometimes a bullet is the only solution. I guess if people understood the plague a bit better then maybe things would have been different.

When it all started, people thought they were zombies. That's not that far from the truth, really. They were mindless. They moaned. They killed people. If they bit you, you would eventually turn into one. They were, for all intents and purposes, the living dead. The only thing was they weren't dead. People didn't die and then become a Changed; you just changed. The scariest part is that you could turn without being bitten, at least at first. For the first couple of years, people would wake up and find a loved one had changed. No one understood why, but that doesn't happen much anymore. Gradually people just stopped changing on their own. It still happens from time to time according to stories that get passed around but only in the larger cities. Silver City apparently has a weekly sweep that usually nets two or three. In the beginning, though, it happened a lot.

These were the kind of things you would think about out on the road. During the day, you may not have to worry about the Changed, but you never wanted to travel further than you could get before sundown. You had to worry about animals too. The Changed mostly left the animals alone, but in the years since things broke down, wildlife flourished. Without the vast population pressing in on their territory, animals spread out again. Deer where everywhere, and because of the abundance of deer, there were more predators. Fewer people around meant the predators could be bolder. Any trip had to take into account wolves and bears as well as Changed. The foothills we lived in were mostly grazing territory for deer and buffalo, so wolves were always a concern.

That journey was different than other trips. Having Dylan with us made all the difference. My mother was a capable woman and good with a gun but having another adult along meant that brigands and drifters would be less likely to bother us. Dylan's spirit of playfulness and joy made a difference too. We walked along and sang and laughed and played. Rather than a dangerous chore, it felt like a picnic. It was the first time in my life I understood the phrase 'getting there is half the fun.'

We didn't run into anyone on the trip until we got within sight of town. Another of the local farmers was bringing his goods in as well. He had pulled his cart to the side of the road to wait for us. He said he heard us singing. We walked the last mile together, singing the whole way. After a few songs, Dylan asked the farmer to teach him a song. I remember because he seemed to get very intense when he asked as if it was the most important question in the whole world. Dylan had asked my mother earlier, and my mother told him all the songs she knew. The farmer said he had one and sang a song I didn't understand about walking a line.

As he sang the first few lines, Dylan listened very intently. He played a few tentative chords on his guitar, then a few more that were less tentative. By the time the farmer had gotten to the chorus, Dylan was playing along and smiling again. The second time through the song, he sang and strummed along perfectly to my young ears. The farmer was clearly overjoyed. We all joined in the third time through and kept singing all the way to the town gates.

CHAPTER FIVE

The gates to town were open when we arrived. Two sheriff's deputies were keeping an eye on things as per usual. Guard duty during the day wasn't very exciting. They were really there for keeping track of who came in and out. Most towns tried to keep a headcount at all times in case people succumbed to the Change. A single person Changing in the middle of the night could cause trouble for the whole town if it wasn't brought under control quickly. The deputies also kept out any of the wrong sort of person who showed up. There were drifters and gangs who wandered the land and could cause a lot of trouble for a small town like ours.

I recognized both the deputies and waved to them from the cart. They smiled and waved back. We didn't come to town all that often, but it was a small community and most everyone knew each other. My mother introduced Dylan to the deputies so that they could put him in the count. They made some polite conversation before waving us through.

The town was built in a circular fashion with a bandstand and small park at the very center. We would set up shop somewhere around the edge of the park and pitch our tent right next to the cart. We had a small table and chair that we would put our produce on. It didn't take long to set up, and once we had our spot and the table up, my brother left to go to the library. I remember my mother telling him explicitly to be back at dusk to help clean up and join in the festivities. My ordinarily stoic brother would always whine and complain about being forced to take part in the singing and dancing. For my part, I was anxious to take off and find some of the other kids to play with. My brother asked me to introduce Dylan around a bit before I ran off. I remember there seemed to be a larger than average number of people there that market day. It was always a bit crowded since the town wasn't very big, only around a hundred full-time residents. That number doubled as people from all the local settlements and farms came to town. There were more that day because it was the first market for a group of about twenty-five people from a new settlement in the area.

I went around and introduced Dylan to the people whose names I could remember and the people who happened to be selling treats. He smiled and was very friendly to everyone. Almost everyone inquired about his guitar and where he was from. He never really answered the latter question, saying only that he was from here and there and had been on the road for a while. People were still setting up and getting settled in, so no one pushed him on it. The last person I introduced him to was our nearest neighbor. He lived on his own since his wife died and apparently had been in town for a few days. He told me to go back and warn my mother about the new folks. He said they were a church group and had the look of people getting ready to proselytize. My seven-year-old tongue had some trouble with that last word, but I dutifully hurried back to my mother to let her know.

When I got back, my mother said she had already noticed them and had them pegged as religious types. People in our town weren't as anti-religion as some other places, but they weren't altogether welcoming either. Too many folks were still bitter over some of the stuff that happened in the early and middle days of the Change. We owned a bible, and my mother read from it. She taught us parts, but it wasn't a big part of our upbringing. The town had a church, but it was mostly for weddings and funerals. There weren't Sunday services or any of the other stuff you read about in books. There was a local glassblower, and he doubled as the officiant for everything, as opposed to a real minister.

Dylan had stayed to talk with our neighbor when I ran back to my mother, so I was free to wander off and play. It didn't take me long to find a group of kids. I spent the rest of the day running around town playing while my brother read in the library, and my mother minded the table selling our small crop to townsfolk and other farmers. I'm not sure what Dylan did, but I never once heard him play during the day, so I guess he was just talking with folks and saving his music for that evening. I remember it was a beautiful summer day, warm with just enough breeze to make it pleasant and not uncomfortable. There were no clouds in the sky, so the night promised to be bright and full of stars.

As the day gave ground to evening, I made my way back to our table to help my mother pack up whatever wasn't sold and set up the tent to sleep in. When I arrived, I saw that she had sold most of what we brought and seemed in high spirits. She told me to go fetch my brother so that we could eat dinner. She was fine setting up the tent on her own.

I ran off to the library. It was a small, simple-looking building. Most of the buildings in town were basic structures with little ornamentation. The library looked plain even amongst all the other no-frills buildings around it. The only thing that marked it as the library was a small sign saying as much by the main door and a little carved wooden lion that sat next to the sign. The door wasn't locked so I went in.

The noise from outside always disappeared once you entered. The main room was so packed with books that they seemed to absorb sound. I knew there were reading rooms towards the back, and that was where I would find my brother. I told him Mom wanted him to come back to camp for dinner. He said he wasn't hungry and that the librarian had told him he was okay to stay late at the library as long as he locked the door when he left. I argued with him a bit, but ultimately I was seven, and he was going to do as he pleased.

I ran back and informed my mom of my brother's decision, and she sighed and shrugged. She knew it was a hard life for my brother out on the farm and didn't want to pull him away from the books if that was where he wanted to be. I asked if Dylan would eat with us, and she said he was busy chatting.

The new folks turned out to be a church that had left Silver City and made its way out to our area, hoping for a more receptive audience to their words. They had a group of tents on the far side of the mall and appeared to be setting up a small stage. My mom said that they had been trying to recruit folks and were going to hold a service soon. She hoped they didn't attempt to interfere with the festivities that evening. She was really looking forward to hearing Dylan sing with other people.

We sat down on a blanket to eat a simple supper of dried fruit and fresh vegetables. She had also traded for some beef jerky as a treat. We didn't eat a lot of meat in those days. Animals were more valuable for their ability to pull a plow than their ability to fill our bellies, my mother always said. I think she missed beef, though. She talked about steak a lot when she got sad.

As we ate, the church folk started in. We were too far away to hear much other than the general tone and the occasional shouted word, usually 'damnation' or 'repent.' This went on for our meal and kept going once we finished. The people in the group would occasionally stand up and shout 'amen' or wave their arms around. The whole time this was going on, the people around us started to become more and more agitated. Eventually, a crowd began to gather around the church people. My mother and I got up and followed them over to see what was going on. Townsfolk were loudly imploring the man doing the preaching to stop. The congregation and the preacher seemed totally oblivious to the townsfolk's requests. He continued on with his sermon, although he seemed to get angrier at the interruptions and more frequent catcalls.

The townsfolk were more open than most to religious people, but only to a point. People in town believed in God. Some believed in Jesus. One family that was seen on occasion on harvest days had a kid who told me they were Islamic. My mother didn't know much about what that was when I asked her, but she thought it had to do with Abraham. That family was just as welcome as everyone else in town. The problem was that people had long memories, and it was generally accepted that if not for the reactions of the Church during the beginning of the Change, things would have gone much better than they had. My mother had once told me that millions of people had died because of churches and that's why we didn't go to one.

The preacher eventually got around to saying that the Change was because of our 'Godless ways.' People had had enough at that point, and the mayor stepped in to stop any potential unpleasantness. He told everyone to simmer down and walked right up to the preacher. Stood in front of him and stared him right in the eye until the preacher faltered. The mayor was a massive man with farmer's muscles and a six-foot-four frame to back up his words. Most folks would have backed down. The preacher, by this time, had worked himself up. After a brief pause, he simply started shouting directly at the mayor. He then turned around and started yelling at the gathered crowd. The congregation, now behind him, stood up as one and started shouting along with him. Things like 'hallelujah' and 'amen' and 'praise the Lord'. A lot of them just seemed to be shouting streams of nonsense words. I remember feeling as scared as I was in the shed with the Changed banging on the door.

The mayor stepped back from the preacher, clearly a bit surprised. Most people listened to what he had to say. I was looking at him rather than the preacher who was nearly screaming about our souls now when I saw his eyes go wide. Then I heard a collective intake of breath from the crowd. Almost immediately, my mother grabbed me and pulled me into her arms and started to back up. I struggled in my mother's arms to see what was happening when I realized that things had gone quiet. The preacher had stopped. I was able to turn just enough to get a look at what was happening.

The preacher was on his knees. He had a look of pure anger on his face, or what had become his face. He had been a large heavyset man, but now his face looked like it had been pulled back, his eyes seemed to have fallen in on themselves, and his skin had gone from bright red to a yellowish gray. He was silent for a moment as everyone stared and then let out a low moan and lurched to his feet.

He had changed.

I had never seen it happen before. I don't think anybody else had either, at least not spontaneously. The whole crowd, including the congregants, slowly backed away. No one really knew what caused the Change, but bites from them could cause other people to Change. That was part of what made them so dangerous. The Changed preacher looked around and took a few lurching steps. It clearly hadn't gotten used to its newly Changed body. One or two people in the crowd regained their wits and rushed off to get weapons. The preacher let out a much louder moan and began to move more quickly right at where my mother and I were standing.

It let out another moan and then stopped dead in its tracks. It was a few seconds before I realized that what had stopped it was the sound of a guitar.

Dylan emerged from the crowd strumming his guitar and singing very softly. He was walking toward the Changed. Someone from the group went to grab him and pull him back, but my mother dropped me and stopped the person from halting Dylan. Everyone was transfixed.

He started singing a bit more loudly and strummed the guitar a bit more confidently as he got closer. It looked as if he had been looking for a sound and found it. I could make out the words at that point. They were about how you couldn't always get what you wanted, but you should keep trying.

The preacher just stared at him with hollow eyes. Normally the Changed will lunge at the closest person. They don't spend much time in contemplation. Dylan kept walking toward him and stopped when he got within about three feet. The preacher took one halting step toward him and moaned again. This time the moan almost sounded like a question. No one had ever heard anything like it. Changed moans were more or less a uniform sound. There weren't any variations. It was the sound made by something mindless. This moan was the sound of something that had enough consciousness to be confused.

Dylan kept on playing and singing, but rather than focusing on the preacher, he began to look around at the gathered people. He made a gesture with his shoulders and rolled his eyes in a way that everyone knew meant 'sing-along,' and people did.

Some of the people knew the words and started to sing the verses.

When the chorus came around, a hundred people began to sing along. The preacher started to look around at the voices. It almost looked frightened.

People began to sing louder and with more conviction. Every eye was on the preacher, and so everyone saw as the clouds lifted from his eyes, and the color returned to his skin. The muscles that had pulled taught began to loosen, and he dropped to his knees. He looked around and the singing stopped. There was just the sound of Dylan gently strumming his guitar.

"What....what happened?" the preacher asked.

He had Changed back.

The mayor was the first to break the silence.

"It's a miracle," he said. That was precisely what it was. The Changed never changed back to human. It wasn't possible. They became mindless monsters and were a plague on the land. The advent of the Changed had destroyed the old world and reshaped society into a land of fences and guns and subsistence farms. Millions had died. The modern world had died. We lived in a world where traveling by night meant death. We lived in a world where we were a second-class species living in pockets around the world. The Changed had taken all the in-between places.

And now we had witnessed a miracle.

No one knew what to do or what to say. One of the congregants rushed up and embraced the preacher in a hug. And then we heard the shouting.

The gathered crowd turned as one of the gate guards came rushing at us, yelling for the Mayor.

"Someone opened the gate and ran out, Mayor. We closed the gate, but the moaning started already."

"Who was it?" the Mayor asked.

"That farm kid - James," responded the guard.

James. My brother.

My mom didn't say anything. She simply turned and took off for the gate. I had never seen her move so fast. I started to run after her but tripped. People had begun to run toward the door. I was scooped up by my neighbor, who had been standing next to my mother.

"Hang on kiddo; you'll get trampled," he said and held tight as I tried to squirm free.

Dylan was still standing next to the preacher strumming his guitar. He was staring intently at the preacher, oblivious to what had just happened. I shouted his name. He turned and looked at me as if he had just woken from a dream. He looked around and realized that people were running for the gate. I told him to go help my Mom. He slung his guitar over his back and took off running after her.

My neighbor started to walk toward the gate carrying me. He was a farmer and almost as big as the mayor. I had no chance to squirm free. When we got to the gate, he went to the mayor and asked what happened. The mayor didn't turn to answer as he was looking out through the fence at the Changed that had begun to gather.

"The kid's mother ran out after the kid. She ran away from those Changed out there, but some of them followed after her. I didn't see the kid, but they're both as good as dead out there."

The gate hadn't been full closed, but there were two guards with their guns standing in the opening. They were aiming at the few Changed but not shooting yet.

I started to cry and scream. The mayor turned at the sound and realized what he said. Before he could formulate a response, I felt a hand on my shoulder. It was Dylan.

"I'll find them," he said and walked towards the gate.

He then walked past the guards at the gate and ran off into the night.

I've never seen any of them since.

PART TWO

CHAPTER ONE

"So what you're telling me is that not only were you there when Father Jordan was resurrected but that it was done by some guy singing at him? Pull the other one kiddo. It rings."

"Believe what you want, pal. I told you my story, and now you owe me a drink."

"Hah! I think maybe you've had too many already, but a deal's a deal. What'd you say your name was again?"

"Jesse. Jesse Chapin."

They were sitting in a dingy bar in one of the more rundown sections of Silver City. The walls were nothing more than corrugated aluminum sheets held together with fond wishes and hope. The ceiling was canvas fixed to tent poles in the corners. The only light came from bulbs strung from the poles. The bar itself was a patchwork of wooden crates, rusted barrels, and sheet metal. It was the kind of place that attracted people who were all business about their drinking.

Jesse liked it because it looked post-apocalyptic. The apocalypse had come and gone before he was born, and humanity had gotten back on its feet. Silver City was evidence of that. Most of the big pre-Change cities were uninhabitable as they were either overrun with Changed or destroyed by the chaos during of the early days of the Change. Silver City was one of the first places to recognize what was happening. They built a wall to defend themselves against the vast hordes of Changed that cut a swath across the country. People flooded into the city from the surrounding areas. Eventually, it grew too big to hold them all and a second wall was built. Then a third. Then a fourth. There were currently seven walls that contained the entirety of Silver City.

Each time a new wall was built, the city's refugees and lower classes were pushed out to the outer ring. Anyone who couldn't afford property or a permanent place to live was forced further from the center of the city. They lived in bedraggled tent and box communities. Most left the city to find work on farms outside the walls during the day, although some went inwards looking for whatever odd jobs people needed. They spent their nights in places like the bar Jesse found himself in. People old enough to remember the times before the Change, drinking to forget what they had lost, and people too young to remember, drinking to forget what they would never have.

It was the perfect spot for Jesse. After his family had disappeared, he lost the farm he grew up on. He was raised in a small town named Schoepp a few hours from Silver City until he was 15, and then he came to the city to look for work. At the age of 22, he was six-foot tall and thin. He was still strong, although he hadn't found much work lately, and his muscles were withering from lack of use. He mostly looked for jobs inside the city walls. He didn't like being on the outside, and he didn't like farm work. Memories of his childhood always threatened to overwhelm him when he plowed fields or picked crops.

He spent his time drinking and telling everyone that would listen that Father Jordan was a fraud, and the resurrection that had made him famous wasn't his doing. Instead, he told the story of Dylan Droge and his guitar. People usually just laughed at him and would buy him the occasional drink since the story was entertaining. No one had ever heard of a man named Dylan Droge who could heal the Changed with his guitar. Even the people in the town where the resurrection had happened told the story differently. Some would say they vaguely remembered a vagabond who sang that day but would never admit that the singer had anything to do with the 'Miracle at Wellersville' as it had come to be known. The story of Father Jordan undergoing the Change and then healing himself through the power of his faith was well known everywhere. Jesse's version was told only by Jesse. Sometimes, at night, he wondered if it really happened the way he remembered.

He told the story tonight in hopes that some new person in the place would buy him a drink. It had worked. Jesse nursed the beer for a long while hoping another transient would wander in, and he could earn another drink. Work had been scarce lately, and he was about as broke as he could ever remember being.

An hour later, Jesse had all but given up hope of anyone buying him a beer and got up to leave. As he did someone he'd never seen came in the door and looked around. The man was about six foot two and had an athlete's build. His blond hair was close-cropped and his clothes well-pressed. He didn't come from this part of town. Of that Jesse was certain. Once the man's eyes settled on Jesse, he smiled and walked over.

"Evening, sir. Are you the gentleman who tells the tale about the Miracle at Wellersville?" he asked with an earnestness that Jesse did not believe could be faked.

"That depends."

"Depends on what?" he asked again with more innocence that you would typically find in this part of town without paying a premium.

"On whether you're going to buy me a drink. Stories ain't free." Jesse replied.

"Oh! Absolutely! What'll you have?" the man replied taking the seat next to Jesse.

Jesse waved at the bartender, who sighed. He had heard Jesse's story a couple of dozen times and wasn't relishing listening to it again. He pulled a beer and brought it over.

Jesse took a long pull from the glass and launched into his tale. He was tired and soberer than he cared to be, so he mostly kept it short. Halfway through, he finished his beer and gestured for another. The bartender rolled his eyes, but the blond man just smiled and dropped a few more coins on the bar. Jesse hadn't noticed it at first, but the man was wearing white gloves. It made Jesse a bit wary but not enough to care. Eventually, he got to the part in the telling where Father Jordan shows up, and the stranger's eyes lit up.

Jesse had suspected as much. The stranger buying him beer was a member of the Church of the Risen as Father Jordan had taken to calling his flock. He'd grown up around the glassy-eyed believers and generally disliked them. They had flocked to Wellersville in the years after the incident. The town grew some and began to play up the so-called miracle. Jesse's refusal to change the story hadn't made him many friends.

He had gone to live with the librarian after his family had disappeared. The mayor bought his farm, and the money was used to keep Jesse clothed and fed. He liked the librarian who was always kind to him and instilled in him a love of reading similar to his brothers. Jesse read through most of the library during those long, lonely years. As he grew up, he spent the daylight hours searching the surrounding countryside for any sign of his family, and the night hours reading and trying to figure out what caused his brother to run off. Once he was old enough, he left Wellersville. He couldn't stand the town's capitulation to the phony Father Jordan. They weren't sad to see him go.

The blonde gentleman kept the rapturous look on his face right up until Jesse got to the part about Dylan's singing appearing to be the cause of Father Jordan's transformation back. Slowly it dawned on the man that this wasn't the telling he knew. He had heard that a witness to the miracle lived here and hoped for a first-hand account. This happened once in a while to Jesse. People wanting to touch a bit of history he supposed. They never left happy. Sometimes they would argue with him or call him a blasphemer. Usually, they just harrumphed and left. Having been in this situation a number of times, he didn't feel the need to put his guard up. Had he done so, he probably still couldn't have done anything about the punch that knocked him off his chair.

"How dare you?" the blonde man shouted. "How dare you spread lies about Father Jordan. You should be locked up!"

"Hey! None of that in here, pal!" the Bartender shouted, grabbing a baseball bat from under the bar.

Jesse shook it off and looked up at the man, taking in how big he was for the first time. He smiled.

"Sorry friend, I just tell it how it happened. You can believe what you want, but I'm not going to lie to you. "

The man glared at the bartender and then back at Jesse. To Jesse's surprise, the anger left the man's face and was replaced by a sneer.

"People like you," he stared at Jesse, "and people like you," he continued, shifting his gaze to the bartender, "aren't going to be tolerated for much longer. Father Jordan has been through the Change and come back, and he will heal the scars on earth. That is his purpose. Sniveling liars and peddlers of poison will have no place in our new world of love and peace."

The absolute belief behind the statement and the growling sneer with which it was delivered unnerved Jesse. He'd met his fair share of fanatics, but something about this one scared him. This was the kind of believer who didn't question what he was told, and he certainly wouldn't question orders. He was the kind of guy that made a great soldier.

The man spat on the ground and stormed out of the bar.

"Hey, listen kid, I appreciate that you're basically the only entertainment in the place, but I don't really need goons like that coming in here," the bartender said as he helped Jesse pick himself up. "I try to run a peaceful place, ya know? How about you find someplace else to drown yourself?".

"Yeah, yeah, fine. How about one for the road?"

The Bartender sighed but got Jessie another beer.

"Last one is on the house. Finish that, and then I don't want to see you again."

Jesse drank it in one go, tipped his hat, and stumbled out into the night. He started singing as he left. It was the same song that Dylan had played that awful night. It was always fresh in Jesse's mind.

Jesse stumbled down the street towards the tent he currently called home. He had set up on the outskirts of one of the larger squatter settlements—lots of tents and a lot of people who didn't have anywhere else to go. Most of them were refugees from towns overrun by the Changed or towns where food got too scarce. With no place else to go, they came here. Jesse felt more at home here among the people here than anywhere else.

The streets were dark and dusty as he headed home. There wasn't much noise this late. Despite the quiet, he never heard the people come up behind him and put a bag over his head. He felt the first couple of blows before losing consciousness. Before he passed out, he heard the blonde man call him a filthy blasphemer.

CHAPTER TWO

Jesse woke up in total darkness. It took him a moment to realize he still had the bag over his head. He tried to move but couldn't. His hands were tied behind his back and his feet to the chair he was sitting in. He tried to call out but realized he'd been gagged. Unable to make any articulate sound, he settled for a loud moan.

It seemed like an eternity before someone came near. Unceremoniously the bag was removed from his head and he was immediately blinded by the light in the room around him. He blinked trying to get a better idea of his situation. When was finally able to focus, he realized he was in what looked like a store room. Standing over him was the blonde man from the bar.

"About time you woke up," he said. "Father Jordan wants to talk to you."

"All he had to do was ask you know."

"You needed to be taught a lesson. If it were up to me, you and all your kind would be turned out of civilization and shunned. See how you do with no fence at night."

"My kind? I wasn't aware that I had a kind," Jesse replied. He was certain that provoking the blond man would earn him another beating, but he couldn't resist. He didn't respond well to zealots.

"Unbelievers. Blasphemers. Heathen. And you. You are the lowest of them all. You witnessed the miracle and still you don't believe. You spread your lies to anyone degenerate enough to buy you a beer."

"Lies? Buddy, I was there. I know what happened. You and the rest of 'em can swallow whatever story you want, but I know the truth. Your Father Jordan is a fraud and-"

The blonde man punched him in the jaw. He was rearing back for another blow when the door opened.

"Peace, Brother Lydon, this is no way to treat our guest. Especially not a lost soul such as this. Please, untie him, if you would."

Brother Lydon stared at Father Jordan for a moment then begged forgiveness and moved behind the chair Jesse was tied to. Jesse felt the ropes tighten painfully before loosening. The man whispered in his ear, "Father Jordan is more forgiving than I am. Your time will come, scum." Once Jesse's hands were untied Brother Lydon moved across the small room and stood behind Father Jordan.

"Please wait outside, Brother Lydon, I would like to speak with our guest alone."

"As you wish," Lydon replied, sneering at Jesse one last time before stepping out.

"I apologize for the way you have been treated, Mr. Chapin. I assure you I did not mean for violence to be done to your person when I asked Brother Lydon to bring you here."

Jesse looked at the older man. He hadn't seen Father Jordan in a few years. The last time had been right before he left Wellersville for Silver City. He hadn't aged much since then. He was about 5'10" with thinning blond hair. He wasn't fat but certainly wasn't starving, carrying the paunch of a middle-aged man who didn't exercise much. He wore an ancient looking pair of bifocals that, coupled with his full salt and pepper beard, gave the impression of a professor more than a preacher. He wore a simple black robe cinched at the waist with a gold colored rope. The only real change that Jesse noticed were a few more wrinkles and worry lines etched into his face. Jesse couldn't help but remember the rage on the man's face right before he Changed and how it had distorted his otherwise pleasant features.

"Yeah, that guy seems like the kind to take the initiative. You should keep an eye on him. He'll go far."

"Indeed. The church would barely function without him. He's a great help."

"I'm sure." Jesse glared at the preacher. He didn't like him when he was younger, and he didn't like him any more now. Every time he looked into the preacher's eyes, he saw a man who was very interested in power and control. The kind of person who didn't mind breaking a few eggs as long as the omelet came out the way he wanted it.

"Enough about Brother Lydon's merits. How are you doing, Jesse? You don't look like you're eating well."

"That's ok it looks like you're eating enough for both of us."

Father Jordan barked a laugh.

"Perhaps I am, Perhaps I am. I see you haven't changed much despite your descent into alcohol and poverty."

"If you mean I'm still not ready to bend a knee to you and start telling your version of what happened, then no. I haven't changed much since my descent." He spat out the last word. He knew who Father Jordan really was and didn't have much interest in playing games.

"No, I hadn't imagined you would. Some people refuse to see the light of truth and accept God's love and nothing on Earth can change their minds. You have always struck me as a good young man, Jesse, I hate to see you on the path to ruin."

"So, what do you want?" Jesse replied. He was used to being told he was crazy. He was even used to being called a liar. But it really got to him when people treated him like a wayward child. Father Jordan's condescending tone made him want to scream.

"I was actually hoping you would regale me with your version of the story. In fact, I was hoping you would be able to tell me more about this wandering minstrel that you claim saved me from the Change. I know your usual price is a mug of ale but perhaps we could offer you a good meal and a warm bed instead?"

That caught Jesse off guard. He had been hassled for years by Father Jordan's followers to renounce his version of the events. This was different. He was immediately suspicious.

"Why?"

"Nothing more than curiosity. I have been wondering of late why you alone have held so fast to the fiction that it was someone other than the Lord my God that saved me. I have spoken with other witnesses and none of them speak of this minstrel. Most simply tell me the story as it is told in our tracts. The only thing I can think is that you spent time with this musician before the events of that day and that has somehow confused you. Have you spoken with this man since?"

Jesse looked at him for a long while. He was holding something back, that much was obvious. Jesse had no idea what that might be or why after all these years he would suddenly care about Dylan. Jesse wasn't too proud to accept a warm meal when offered, even from these people, but he wanted to know why it was being offered.

"Bullshit."

"Mind your language, young man."

"Sorry. Bullshit, Father."

Father Jordan sighed.

"Jesse, I am a man of God. My mission in this life is to spread the good word and to try and bring comfort to people who are struggling in a world filled with monsters, a world where food is scarce and despair is common. We have reclaimed some of the life we had before the Change but mostly it is a lie we tell ourselves. Everyday another homestead is overrun by monsters. Each week the world controlled by the sons and daughters of Adam and Eve shrinks. We like to think that we have won the battle and that we have taken control but that is a fairy tale told so we can sleep at night."

"And you think you can save the world?"

"Of course not, Jesse. I believe Jesus will save the world. I am simply his vessel. I have experienced a miracle that was designed to show me the way, to show me my destiny. The world has turned its back on Jesus and my mission is to bring people back into the fold. The only way back from the nightmare in which we live is through Jesus, and Jesus is acting through me. This is the mission that your lies hinder, Jesse. I am not acting for my own glory but for the glory of the Lord Almighty!"

Jesse wasn't going to back down. He'd heard this sermon before. He didn't believe it then and he didn't believe it now.

"Yeah, the world turned away from Jesus when your kind led millions to their deaths during the Change. MILLIONS! Where was your

Jesus then?" he shouted back.

Father Jordan paused and took a deep breath to calm himself before continuing.

"Those millions whose demise you lament were brought into the loving arms of their waiting Lord, Jesse. Those faithful souls went to paradise. They left behind their mortal shells so that those of us remaining could find redemption in our time of tribulation. The Changed are a test from God to prove our faith."

"You're kidding? That's what you're selling now? A theology based on a fever dream and a bunch of old novels written for five-year-olds? Is that why I'm here? You think I'm the Antichrist?"

Father Jordan sneered at Jesse.

"Of course not, Jesse. The Antichrist will come in the personage of someone that people will follow. Someone that can inspire people. Someone so charming and persuasive that he could convince people that he performed a miracle rather than God Almighty. As for a theology based on 'a fever dream and novels written for children' it is much more than that. Certainly we are living in a time of tribulation. Even you must see that. We that remain are being tested. Our souls are impure, our faith has fled. Our only salvation is remembering the faith of our fathers."

Slowly it dawned on Jesse.

"You think Dylan is the Antichrist?"

"I don't think that Jesse, I know it. Now if you would be so kind, please tell me what you remember about him. And please don't leave anything out. I would hate to have to have Brother Lydon help you remember."

Jesse told his story to Father Jordan. When he was done Father Jordan asked him to tell it again. He told it a third time after Brother Lydon came into the room. He felt like he should put up a fight or resist, but he was tired and hungry and just wanted to get out of there. He didn't think Father Jordan would let Brother Lydon do anything to him. Jesse got the impression that more than anything else, Father Jordan wanted him to renounce his version and accept the priest's telling. Jesse suspected that the priest knew on some level that the story Jesse told was the truth. Father Jordan couldn't completely convince himself of his version of the facts as long as Jesse held out. This made Jesse a mission for Father Jordan and not an obstacle. Jesse wondered if that might be all that was keeping him alive at the moment. Brother Lydon seemed like the type of man who didn't spend a lot of time coming up with solutions to problems. He seemed like the type who simply removed the problem. Even though Father Jordan ran the church, the real danger would be Brother Lydon.

Jesse was exhausted when they finally let him go. True to his word Father Jordan had him fed before they sent him out. As much as he wanted to get out of there, there wasn't enough work around for him to refuse a meal out of pride. He headed straight for his small tent and his bed roll. Despite his battered appearance no one hassled him, and he collapsed into a deep and dreamless sleep.

"Do you really think he'll go looking for him?" Brother Lydon asked.

"I believe so," Father Jordan replied from behind his desk. "There is very little keeping him here and since he won't renounce his falsehoods, I think he will go to find the one person whom he believes can vindicate him."

They sat in Father Jordan's office in the church. The room was filled with handcrafted cherry wood furniture and lined with bookshelves. Brother Lydon disliked the opulence of the room and preferred his cell. He believed that books and creature comforts distracted one from one's faith. Brother Lydon was a fanatic. He believed absolutely in the teachings of the bible and that of Father Jordan, whom he viewed as an extension of the book.

"He doesn't seem very motivated. He seems like a weak willed drunkard."

"I know what he seems like, Brother. But I have faith that he has strength in him yet. Despite having no reason to, he has continued to cling to his delusions. I think a weak man would have outwardly renounced his story long ago."

Brother Lydon smirked and began pacing.

"If you say he has the strength to take action then of course I believe you, Father. Him succeeding in finding this minstrel seems doubtful however."

"The minstrel, as you put it, has a plan for Jesse. Once he begins his search this monster will seek him out."

"A plan?"

"Of course. The beast tricked Jesse and his family into believing he saved them from the Changed and then traveled with them to town. Immediately after his plan to Change me was foiled by my faith and God's love he left and took Jesse's mother and brother with him. And yet he left Jesse. He has a plan for him, mark my words. We will track the monster down through Jesse and confront him with the light of the Lord. That is our mission. "

"Of course. I understand now. Thank you for your wisdom, Father."

"Excellent. Now, please leave me. Also please see I am not disturbed. I would like to spend some time in prayer and contemplation."

"I will personally watch your door," Brother Lydon said as he left the room, closing the door behind him.

CHAPTER THREE

"Hey Jesse, wake up. C'mon, wake up!"

Slowly Jesse regained consciousness to find someone half in his tent crouched over him shaking him.

"Leave me alone, Desmond," he mumbled and tried to roll away from the man shaking him.

"Are you alright? Doug said he saw you get jumped and then dragged away. You look like someone gave you the business."

"I'm fine. Someone just wanted to talk to me and didn't know how to ask nicely."

"Was it Father Jordan's people? They were sniffing around asking about you."

Desmond was the closest thing Jesse had to a friend even though he was twenty years his senior. The man had lived in Tent Town for a long time and functioned as its unofficial mayor. He knew everyone that lived there and did his best to keep tabs on them. He tried to foster a sense of community in a place full of refugees and people who had given up hope. He did a good job of it too, in Jesse's estimation. It was rare to see Desmond unhappy or less than cheerful. When people were sick, he would pass the hat for food or medicine. Whenever someone new set up a place in Tent Town, Desmond was the first one to greet them. The only time Jesse had ever seen him lose his happy veneer was when he caught some people roughing up one of 'his people' as he tended to refer to tent town residents.

Desmond stood six foot five with the build of a bodybuilder, and long dreadlocks. He wasn't someone you would want to end up on the bad side of. Jesse was walking back from the bar with him one night a few months back when they came upon three men working over Jeremy, one of the newer residents. Desmond had called out and told them to stop, at which point one of the muggers, without turning around, told him to piss off. He hadn't bothered to reply, he simply ran into the fray at full force. He picked up the man who had spoken by the shoulders and drove his head into the wall they had pinned Jeremy against. Before the other two muggers could react, he punched one of them in the face. The man went down like a sack of wet cement. The third backed away and went into his pocket for something that he never had time to use. Desmond grabbed him by the hair and slammed his head into the wall. In a matter of seconds all three muggers were unconscious or worse. He picked up Jeremy, who had slumped to the ground, like he didn't weigh a thing. He turned to Jesse and said in his most cheerful voice, "Come on Jes, let's get him to the hospital." Jesse always felt safe in his tent after that night.

"Yeah."

"I told you if you kept on telling your story they would eventually give you trouble."

"Well, you were right. Congratulations. Was there something you needed? I'd just as soon go back to sleep."

"Oh yeah. There's someone down here looking for you. "

"It's not a big, tall blonde guy is it?"

"Nope. It's a woman. Pretty too. I told her she should be looking for me instead, but she didn't seem all that amused. Must be my dreads. I've never seen her before."

Jesse sat up and rubbed his eyes. He pulled on a shirt and exited the tent with Desmond.

"Where is she?"

"She said to meet her at Sully's bar. C'mon, I'll go with you."

"Why do you want to go with me?"

"Two reasons. First, so you have someone watching your back. Second, she's gorgeous and I'm curious why a woman that good looking is trying to find your emaciated ass."

"She's probably got me confused with someone else."

"Undoubtedly. And with a little luck I'll be that someone else."

"Let's get this over with."

They found her nursing a beer in Sully's bar. Jesse wasn't much of a morning person, but it seemed to him to be a little early for drinking. She was just as beautiful as Desmond had described. Even though she was sitting down Jesse could tell she was tall, probably about six foot. She had long dark hair and looked to Jesse like she was Greek, or maybe Italian. She was wearing road clothes, walking boots, denim jeans, and a denim shirt. They were stained with dirt and dust. There was no trace of zealot about her. She looked for all the world like a cowgirl.

"She just needs the hat to complete the look," Jesse mused out loud.

"Recognize her?" Desmond asked.

"Not at all. I think I'd remember if I'd ever seen her before."

"Same. Although I'm certain she was in my dreams last night."

"Seems a little too coincidental that someone I've never met comes looking for me after last night."

"What did happen last night?"

"I'll tell you later, let's see what she wants first."

They walked up to the table. The woman looked up from her beer and sized Jesse up. Her eyes lingered on his hands and then again on his face.

"Jesse Chapin?" she said in a voice much deeper than Jesse had expected, with an accent that he didn't recognize.

"Unfortunately. Who's asking?" He took a seat across the table from her. Desmond pulled a chair from another table, spun it around, and sat with his arms crossed over the top of the chair back.

"Thank you for bringing him, Desmond. I appreciate it. If you would excuse us?" She said it in a way that seemed to brook no argument.

"Not a chance, lady," Desmond said back in his most cheerful voice.

"It's been a rough couple of days, lady, and I don't know who you are so Desmond's going to join us. You haven't told me who you are?"

"My name's Julie. I have a message for you."

"A message for me? You sure you have the right person?"

"Yes, although you weren't very easy to find."

"That's surprising, mouth like his, I assumed everyone would know where to look," Desmond said with a chuckle. Jesse glared at him.

"I didn't know you were in Silver City. Finding people out on the plains isn't very easy. Holed up here in this city you can almost forget that we're in the midst of an apocalypse."

"The apocalypse happened, lady," Desmond replied, "we're living on the other side of it. We still get some Changed here in the city, but it's a big enough place that the infrastructure's been rebuilt pretty well. There's not much chance of an outbreak."

Jesse didn't say anything, but he agreed with Julie. Living in Silver City, it was easy to forget that the Changed still ruled most of the world and that humanity had retreated behind the walls. That was why he came to Silver City in the first place. It had the most walls to hide behind. He never had to think about the Changed or farming or his family. The walls didn't keep him from waking up in a cold sweat about once a week after dreaming about that night in the shed, however.

"If you think we're not living in an apocalypse then you must not have left the city recently. Things have gotten worse out there. Worse than when I was a kid. More and more towns are getting overrun. Some people say they've begun to see the Changed during the day recently." Julie looked towards the sun as she spoke. Jesse thought he heard real worry in her voice.

"Well, I don't know how things are out there and I don't want to know. We're safe here in the city. So quit avoiding the subject and tell me why you're here and what you want with me?"

"Fine. I have a message for you, and once you hear it, I hope you will come with me."

"Come with you? Why would I leave?"

Julie glared at him for a moment. She picked up her beer and took a long draught and stared at it. She looked back up at Jesse and took a deep breath.

"Dylan Droge sent me to find you. He asked me to bring you back to him. He told me to say to you 'Free Fallin'. That's all. I don't know if that is enough to convince you to come, but I hope so."

CHAPTER FOUR

Jesse sat and looked at her for almost a full minute before saying anything. He had thought she might be a plant of some sort from Father Jordan, but he had never told anyone the song that Dylan had played the night they met. Only four people would know that, so Julie had to know one of them. He assumed his family was dead so that left him with only one option.

"Why didn't he come himself? Why did he send you?" he asked finally.

"Wait, you think she's on the level, Jesse?" Desmond said.

"Yeah."

"Huh." Desmond was obviously fascinated by this turn of events.

"He couldn't come himself."

"Why not?"

"He runs things where we live. People rely on him "

"He runs what? Where do you live?"

"We live in a town called Malice. Dylan's in charge. He founded the place."

"Malice? What're you? Outlaws?" Desmond said with a chuckle.

"I guess you could say that," Julie replied. Jesse could sense she was angry. He didn't think it was because of Desmond's joking around though. She had seemed annoyed at the start and he was starting to think she didn't want to be here at all.

"What does he want with me?"

Julie took a long sip of beer and leaned across the table to look Jesse directly in the eyes. "Look. I don't know and I don't care. He wanted someone to come find you, so I did. I gave you his message. Frankly, I don't give a shit if you come back with me or stay here in this hole. I'm going to find someplace to sleep tonight and then at first light I'm leaving out of the south gate. If you want to come, be there. I'm done playing twenty questions with a waster like you."

She stood up and gave a sarcastic bow and walked away.

"Oh, I like her," said Desmond.

"That's wonderful, cause she certainly didn't like me. Usually it takes people a little longer than that to hate me. "

"Oh, I don't know. You have your moments."

"Thanks a lot."

"Anytime. So, you going to go with her?"

"I have no idea. I'm not real sure I want to see that guy again. I figured he was as dead as my family. Now that he isn't, I have to wonder why he never came back."

"Welp, only one way to find out."

"I guess." He reached across the table and picked up Julie's half-finished beer. He downed it in one long gulp. "On the other hand, I don't think I really care anymore. The past only seems to get me beaten up lately. I'll see you back home, Des."

Jesse got up and left the bar. He felt the need to be alone for a while. This last twenty-four hours had been more eventful than the last couple years of his life and he wasn't sure that he liked that. It seemed like too much of a coincidence that Father Jordan grabbed him just before he met someone with a message from the exact person Father Jordan was looking for. On the other hand, there was no way for Jordan to know which song Dylan played that night, he thought. It was possible that he'd been drunk one night and had said something but that didn't seem likely. The version of the story he told people in the bar left out a lot of details on purpose.

He dwelled on the coincidence for a long time as he made his way up the main thoroughfare that wound between the various parts of the city. He didn't think he could trust Julie any more than he could figure out why she disliked him so much. He could understand it if she was one of Jordan's stooges. The people in that church didn't like that someone was telling a different version of the parable they had placed their faith in. He didn't think she was one of them though. She might simply be bitter at having to cross the dangerous plains in order to find him. That seemed more likely.

That still left the question of whether he should go with her. He didn't have any desire to leave the city but there wasn't anything keeping him here either. It was dangerous outside the walls. A large part of the reason he had come to Silver City was because it had so many walls between him and the Changed. Leaving the city to travel with a woman he wasn't certain he could trust, to travel a landscape filled with monsters, wasn't enticing. Despite his bluster with Desmond, he wanted to know why Dylan had never come back.

He also wanted to know if Dylan knew what happened to his brother and his mom. He was thinking about them as the sun set. The stress of the last 24 hours finally got to him and he broke down weeping. As much as he denied it, he missed his family terribly. He hated what he had become. No matter how much he drank he couldn't shake the loneliness and the feeling that he had let his mother down. She would have been disgusted with what he'd been reduced to. He wept for a long time. When the tears stopped coming, he had come to a decision. He wasn't going to hide from his past anymore. He was going to see if Dylan Droge had all the answers.

Jesse went back to Tent Town to get a little sleep and to pack up his few possessions. Desmond was waiting for him by his tent.

"Where you been?" Desmond asked.

"Wandered around a bit, doing some soul searching."

"Make a decision?"

"I'm going to go. Not like there's anything keeping me here. Who knows, maybe he knows what happened to my mom and brother."

"You trust this lady? For that matter, you trust this guy you met once fifteen years ago?"

"I don't know to be honest. But what else am I going to do? Stay here hiding from the world and occasionally getting beaten up by lunatics?"

"It ain't so bad here. Least you don't have any Changed trying to eat you."

"I'm tired of it, Des. Life should be more than this. I'm basically a sideshow. I tell my story and sometimes people buy me a beer. Occasionally I go do odd jobs in the city center. Why not go see if maybe there's something more?"

"Ain't nothing out there but monsters and crazies, Jes. Monsters and Crazies."

"Might be that I'm one of the crazies, Des."

Desmond shook his head and walked away. Jesse watched him go for a while and then crawled into his tent and went to sleep.

CHAPTER FIVE

It was still dark when Jesse woke up. He broke down his tent and rolled up his bed roll. He had a backpack that was big enough for both. There wasn't anything else to pack except for a couple of books. He left those in the bin that the community kept for donations. He realized that tent town would be the only thing he would miss. Living in a tent wasn't great but he never felt alone there. He didn't turn around as he left.

As he walked through the city, he realized that he barely knew the place he had been living for the past couple of years. He knew where he was going but now the streets looked strange. It was an ugly city. The buildings were built with an eye toward functionality and not aesthetics. They were large brown square things that brought to mind prisons more than houses. Some of the newer ones in the outer rings were a little better but as he passed through the city center it was just one ugly building after another. He knew the city had sprung up around a military base and that explained some of it. He imagined that the rest of the buildings were built in a hurry to house refugees.

"They could have at least painted them." he said aloud to no one in particular.

He thought about the house he grew up in as he walked the rest of the way. It was a small house but pretty. It had shutters on the windows and a porch that spanned the whole front of the house. It was painted a green that still made Jesse think of springtime. The roof had three gables, one for each bedroom. It was built by someone who knew what the word 'home' meant as opposed to 'housing', Jesse thought.

He was so lost in thought as he approached the south gate that he didn't notice that there were two people waiting there. As he got closer, he saw Julie and was surprised to see Desmond standing next to her. When Desmond saw Jesse, he flashed him a bright pleasant smile. Julie glared at him.

"Come to see me off, Des? Not going to try and talk me out of it again, are you?"

"Nah. In fact..." Desmond reached down and picked up a backpack which he slung over his shoulder, "I'm coming with you."

"Like hell you are!" Jesse couldn't fathom why he would want to come along. He had never displayed the slightest interest in so much as going outside the gates. Jesse had always assumed that Desmond was originally from Silver City. He never talked about how he got there or where he lived before. Jesse realized that he had never heard Desmond speak about his past at all, other than saying he had Jamaican roots. He felt guilty for never asking. He made his living off his own past and that didn't leave much room for anyone else's.

"You think I'm going to leave you all alone with this woman here? Look at her, she'll probably cut your throat and steal your bag your first night out!"

"I can hear you, you realize?" Julie replied sounding not the least bit amused.

"As if I could forget you madam. The way you light up a room!"

"Seriously Des, this is gonna be dangerous, besides tent town needs you. I'll be alright."

"Tent town don't need me, Jes. Ain't like I did much besides smile at people. Look it can't hurt to have a third person out on the road, and in case you haven't noticed, I'm pretty big. "

"Big don't matter when a horde of Changed are surrounding you." Julie snapped.

"She's right, Des. Stay here. I'd feel terrible if anything happened to you because you were out there trying to protect me."

"Jes, I'll be honest with you." Desmond replied, all joviality drained out of his voice, "I ain't doing this for you. I listened to your story a lot. I think your man Dylan might have some answers that other people don't. And like you said, there's nothing keeping us here."

Jesse looked at him for a while as the sun crept over the wall. He had never seen Desmond this serious before. He decided that he certainly didn't have the right to make decisions for anyone else. He smiled at Des and shrugged in a way that said 'Your funeral.'. He turned to Julie and made a motion with his hand towards the gates.

"After you. Take us to this town called Malice and let's see if Dylan has some answers for us."

Julie took a moment to glare at both of them and then picked up her pack. She slung it over her shoulder and fastened the waist strap. Without another word she turned toward the gate and headed out onto the plains. Neither Desmond nor Jesse looked back once they exited the gates.

CHAPTER SIX

The road outside the city was crumbling. It looked more like gravel than pavement that a plane could have once landed on. Silver City and the outlying towns didn't have the resources to repave and didn't see much point to it. Cars were a thing of the past. There wasn't enough surplus gas or oil around to run them and more wasn't on the way. The local farmers used carts to bring their goods to the city that worked as well on gravel as they did on pavement. The only other people who used the road regularly were workers leaving the city during the day to work the nearby farms.

The only reason people in favor of finding a way to repave the road ever gave was aesthetic. The crumbling road gave the impression of a dying world. It looked like every road in every post-apocalyptic movie people had ever seen. Silver City held roughly 10,000 people and was growing. It was taking back territory from the Changed. It was reclaiming the world. To people of that mindset the road was a symbol of failure, a battle lost. It put people in the wrong frame of mind, they would argue.

To everyone else it symbolized a world that was gone and good riddance. Things had changed and it was time to accept that.

Julie, Desmond, and Jesse walked along the broken pavement not giving it much thought at all. They were focused on the journey ahead. They said little to each other as they left the city, each deep in their own thoughts. The silence continued for the better part of two hours before Desmond spoke up.

"So. Are we there yet?"

Jesse laughed out loud.

Julie was less amused.

"Hardly." was her only response.

"Kidding aside, Des brings up a good point. We're jumping off the cliff here with you. Don't you think it's about time you told us where we're going?" Jesse asked.

"Malice." she said curtly.

Jesse wasn't put off, "Right, you said that. But where exactly is Malice?"

"It's in the mountains to the west. About three weeks by foot."

"The mountains?" Desmond spluttered. "How on earth are we going to get to the mountains? We have rations for maybe three days, never mind having to find a place to stay each night."

"You can go back if you want," Julie responded with a slight edge. The questions were beginning to make her angry.

"Hey, look, we're all in this together at this point. You said you came from there, so assuming you know the way, Do you know where we're going to hole up each night?"

"I know the way. Don't know where we're going to sleep each night though."

"Oh, that's just great." Desmond sighed.

"Have a little faith. I got this far, didn't I?"

"That you did. Can you tell us a little bit about Malice? Like, why do you call it Malice?" Desmond question.

"It's called Malice because that's its name."

"This is going to be a fun trip I can just tell." replied Desmond.

"Hope so." Julie said without a hint of a amusment and kept on walking while Desmond and Jesse stopped and watched her go. They looked at each other, shook their heads, and fell in line behind her.

This was how it went for most of the first day. They walked in silence broken up by rounds of questions from Desmond and Jesse followed by enigmatic or evasive answers from Julie.

It was a comfortable early autumn morning and the wind across the plains blew the hazy heat of summer away from them. The sun was warm on their backs but not scorching. If they lived in a different world it would have seemed like a nice hike. As it was, they lived in a world where most of the population had Changed and monsters roamed the night. As the day progressed toward evening they started to look for a farm or town to take shelter in. People were more accommodating of strangers these days, knowing that their fences were all that lay between life and death for travelers. Farms would usually have a shed for people to sleep in or a warm spot in the basement. Most towns would have bunk houses. Most didn't expect payment for a place to sleep, although travelers would offer something in trade if they could. Some would offer a day's labor, if work was needed and then move on. There weren't many places to go so people weren't usually in a hurry to move on.

That first night out on the road they stopped in a town called Harding. A few towns had sprung within a day's walk of Silver City and Harding was the largest of them. They functioned in the same way suburbs had before the Change. People who didn't want to live in the city moved away, but not so far that going back was a hardship. There were farms all along the road into the city as well. This was the hub of civilization on the plains. Most people on the plains considered Silver city the front line in the fight to take the world back. Each year more and more people drifted in. It was unusual for them to drift back out.

When they reached Harding, the sun was just setting. The guards at the gate greeted them affably and gave them directions to the bunk house and a soup kitchen, if they were hungry. Desmond and Jesse had never been to Harding, but Julie said she spent her last night before getting to the City here and knew where the bunkhouse was. There were actually two bunk houses, one for men and one for women. They were long buildings with two rows of bunks going down either side. Desmond remarked that they reminded him of the army as he and Jesse entered.

" Were you in the army?" Jesse asked. He had never once heard Desmond talk about anything prior to the Change or even before he had arrived in Silver City.

"Long time ago, when I was around your age," Desmond replied.

"Huh. Were you in for long?" Jesse questioned.

"Not long." he responded and then said, "Let's go get something to eat." He said it in such a way that told Jesse he was not interested in talking about it. They left their gear on their chosen bunks and went out to the washroom. Once they were washed up, they waited for Julie outside the ladies' bunk. They sttod there for a while but eventually appeared. They walked over to the soup kitchen hoping that the food would at least be edible.

"Food any good here?" Jesse asked as they walked.

"Nope. But it'll fill you up and that's about all you can ask for. I didn't figure you for the picky sort," Julie said with a not inconsiderable amount of snark.

"Hey, I was just asking!" Jesse replied

"Well next time don't ask," Julie snapped.

"I do something to piss you off?"

"Other than forcing me to leave my home to come find your worthless drunken ass? Nope, not that I recall," Julie all but growled.

"Hey now, that was uncalled for." Desmond interjected.

"Yeah, God knows I didn't ask for you to come find me." Jesse replied, a little hurt at her hostility.

Julie glared at him for a moment, "And yet here I am. Look, I didn't want to come. Dylan asked me and I came. I don't know why he wants you and from the looks of you I think he's looking for the wrong person. So you'll have to pardon me if I don't really feel like getting all chummy."

With that she stormed off toward the bunk houses.

"You are just a devil with the ladies Jesse." Desmond chuckled.

"What the hell's her problem?" Jesse responded, exasperated.

"Oh I dunno, seemed like she laid out her problems pretty plainly," Desmond chuckled.

"Ain't none of that my fault! And I'm not a drunk!"

The indignance in his voice did not convinced either one of them.

"Well you do pretty good impression of one."

"Don't you start too."

Desmond slapped him on the back and laughed. "C'mon, let's get some grub. I'm sure she'll warm up to you."

"No one else does. Why would she?" Jesse said glumly.

"That's a good point. You're doomed," Desmond laughed.

"How come you're so damn cheerful?"

"Just needed a change I guess. Plus the dumber you look, the better I look, and that woman there is fine."

Jesse laughed and shook his head. He headed into the soup kitchen. He'd been hungry often enough to not take a free meal for granted. Julie eventually joined them without uttering a word. They ate their fill and then headed back to the bunk houses. Julie said she'd meet them by the gates and sunrise and slammed the door behind her. Desmond and Jesse went to settle in for the night. The bunk house was empty except for one other guy asleep on the far side of the room.

Jesse dreamt about Dylan. In his dream, Dylan was singing him a song and strumming on that beautiful guitar. It was a slow folksy song that Jesse didn't recognize, but it filled him with a feeling of peace. When he woke up the following morning that feeling stayed with him. He wrapped up his bedding, stowed it in his pack and headed out the door with Desmond by his side. It was a good day for a walk he thought to himself as the sun peeked over the horizon.

CHAPTER SEVEN

The first few days on the road were difficult for Desmond and Jesse. Julie set a hard pace and they struggled to keep up. She commented often about them being soft because they lived in the city. She had a point Jesse thought. He was raised working on farms but since he'd arrived in Silver City, the only thing he worked consistently was his drinking elbow. Even the odd jobs he picked up from time to time weren't very intensive. Desmond was in better shape but being twenty years older than Julie took its toll.

They had no trouble finding places to stay those first few days, even though they covered less miles than Julie wanted. Each night they went to sleep in a bed with a stomach full of decent food. They didn't talk much, and the days were uneventful. They hadn't so much as glimpsed a Changed. The towns they stayed in were accommodating and even friendly. For Desmond and Jesse, it almost felt like a vacation. Their normal lives were filled with lonely nights going to bed on bed rolls with empty stomachs. Desmond even took to expounding on why he was never planning on going back to the Silver city and its tent town. The road was clearly the better option in his mind.

The fifth day there was no town for them to stay in. As evening approached, they were forced to look for a farm to hole up in. It was later in the evening than they liked when they finally came across one. The farm they found was small. The fence around it couldn't have contained much more than an acre or two, Jesse estimated. The gate was closed when they walked up. There was no buzzer at the entrance just an antique looking silver bell. Julie pulled the string, ringing the bell a few times. They waited a minute or so and eventually heard a door open and shut from somewhere inside the fence. They couldn't see over it from this close. A viewing port in the gate opened and an older gentleman on the other side peered out at them.

"What do you want?" The older man asked.

"Night's falling and we're stuck out on the road. We need a place to stay for the night." Julie responded.

"Why're you bothering me then? Clearwater is four miles to the west. I'm sure they would love to have you."

"I don't think we have time to get there before night falls, sir. We don't have much to trade for a room or a shed, but we'd be glad to do any work you needed around the farm in exchange for a place to sleep."

"Work you say? I look like I can't take care of my own business to you?"

"Not at all sir."

"That's right. I don't need no punks without the sense to keep from getting caught out on the road at night to tend my farm."

"Sir," Julie said, clearly trying to keep her temper, "We're not thieves or freeloaders. We just need a place for the night and then we'll be out of your hair."

"If you were a thief, it wouldn't make much sense for you to tell me you were. I wasn't born yesterday."

Jesse had about enough of this. He didn't like being outside this close to dark. He was scared of the Changed and the thought of having to potentially sprint four miles to some town they didn't know in full dark terrified him.

"Mister, my names Jesse. We're on the road to see an old friend that we just found out was alive. We're not going to rob you or bother you at all. Hell, we'll sleep outside the house or wherever, we just need to be inside a fence. We're not going to make it all the way to Clearwater tonight."

The man stared at Jesse for a few moments, longer than was comfortable. He then looked at Desmond and Julie in turn. Jesse could see the gears turning in his head, weighing up whether he wanted the lives of these strangers on his hands. After a while he sighed and closed the viewing port. Ten seconds later they heard the gate latch click and it swung open.

"If you're going to stay the night, you might as well stay in the house. I don't want you sleeping outside and attracting a swarm. Rosemary doesn't sleep so well with all the moaning. My names Jack. That's my daughter Lily." He pointed to a woman standing on the front porch of the house pointing a shotgun in their direction. She didn't wave.

"Who are they, Pop?" Lily asked.

"The kind of people who don't have the good sense to stay where they were. Go tell your mother we're having three more for dinner."

The inside of the house hit Jesse with a wave of nostalgia. It had been a long time since he had been in a farmhouse and this one looked very much like the house he grew up in. The furnishings were all functional and handmade. The wood had the smell of homemade stain that filled Jesse with memories of helping his mother treat chairs. Everything he looked at triggered memories of his childhood. It was almost overwhelming.

Jack ushered them into the dining room. Lily followed behind, still holding the shotgun. A woman who looked roughly the same age as Jack was busy setting the table. The smell of beef stew drifted in from the kitchen.

"We really appreciate this." Jesse said.

"Don't think nothing of it, son, but also don't think you're going to rob us or stay for more than the night. We're glad to help folks in need but don't think to take advantage of us. My Lily's pretty strong and can dig a pretty deep hole if you catch my drift." Jack responded in a tone that implied Lily had some practice digging holes.

"Oh Jack, settle down. They look like good folks." replied the woman, presumably his Rosemary, as she finished setting the extra places at the table.

"Looking like good folks and being good folks are two different things Ma." Lily said behind them.

"Enough you two. Welcome to our home. We're glad to have guests, as you can imagine we don't get too many out this way. Folk's usually move on to Clearwater. My name is Rosemary Hart, this is Lily and Jack."

"Pleased to meet you." responded Julie cracking a smile for the first time since Jesse had met her. "We had intended to reach Clearwater this evening, but my companions are out of shape and slow."

"Looks like they haven't eaten in a month of Sundays, no wonder they can't walk very fast!" said Rosemary as she gave Desmond and Jesse the once over.

Desmond took his hat off and gave a little bow to Rosemary, "I'm Desmond Ma'am, this here is Jesse and the mouthy one is Julie. We really do appreciate the hospitality."

"Alright, enough with the introductions. You can drop your gear over by the door. We're just about ready to eat." Jack said as he sat down at the head of the table. The companions walked over to the door and dropped their packs. Lily waited until they had taken seats at the table before sitting down. She kept the shotgun leaning on her chair.

Rosemary came back from the kitchen and ladled a generous portion of thick beef stew into each of their bowls. She went back to the kitchen and returned with a loaf of bread that smelled fresh. Jesse couldn't remember the last time he had fresh bread or even home cooking. Once Rosemary had taken her seat, he picked up his spoon ready to dig in.

"Now hold on, son. This is a Christian household, and we say grace before partaking of the good Lord's bounty. Would any of you folks care to say grace? You look like a prayin' man." Jack said addressing Desmond.

"I'd be honored." Desmond replied before bowing his head and clasping his hands together. He pressed them to his forehead for a moment and then began, "Our father in heaven, we give thanks for the food you have provided for us. We thank you for the hospitality of your good Christian children and we thank you for guiding each of us on our paths as we all walk the road back home to you. Amen."

"Amen." said Julie, Lily, Jack and Rosemary in unison. Jesse found himself dumbfounded and staring at Desmond. He had never figured Desmond for a praying man. He was learning quite a bit about this man he had called friend for several years now. He wondered what the fact that he knew next to nothing about Desmond said about the value of Jesse's friendship. During the prayer he noticed that everyone else had bowed their heads except him and Julie. She clasped her hands but rather than bowing she had looked at each of the people in the room for a moment. Their eyes and met when she looked at him and he didn't need to be psychic to see the disapproval. He had no idea what he had done to upset her so much, but he had a hunch he wouldn't be kept in the dark for much longer.

The food tasted sublime after a hard day on the road. No one made much conversation during the meal. Once the last morsel of stew had been sopped up with the last hunk of bread, Jack leaned back and looked at his guests.

"So where are ya'll headed, Silver City?"

"We're actually coming from there." Desmond responded.

"Ain't too many places to go besides the city." Lily said, her voice suspicious.

"We're heading to a town called Malice." Jesse said. Julie flashed him a look as he said it. He had no idea what he had done now.

"Malice? Never heard of it. Doesn't sound like a nice place." Rosemary replied.

"Visiting an old friend. Haven't seen him since the change, figured he hadn't made it till I got word a couple of weeks ago. The young ones are long to see a patch of the world." Desmond replied.

"Ain't much to see these days unless you like overgrown foliage and monsters." Lily replied.

"That's true, that's true." Desmond replied, "But we're slowly taking the land back, a little bit more each day."

Jack barked out a laugh. "That ain't quite the case. Sure, around here it seems like that, but the truth is we're losing ground. There's more of them each day. We're even hearing more reports of people Changing in towns, never mind out on the road." He shook his head and went on, "It seems like we're taking land back but the truth of it is we're only building in big circles around the City. The further out we push the more we lose settlements. Sure there's a few other cities around what's left of this great country but they're too far apart. There just aren't enough people left to bridge the gap."

"Now, now, Jack, there's no need to be so gloomy" chided Rosemary, "After all, the Reverend Jordan Changed back, so could others. This plague may end yet."

"That Reverend Jordan is a snake oil salesman if I ever heard one. I doubt he ever actually Changed. Just a trick to get followers. Ain't no coming back from the Change. We ain't getting our world back and there's no sense hoping we will. All we can do is our best to get by."

"I agree with you." Julie said, "About the Reverend Jordan that is. He is as full of it as a person could be without exploding, but I don't think you're right about the other stuff. Yeah, we lose some settlements here and there, but we're building more than we lose. Heck, Malice is the furthest out into the wilds and she's doing fine apparently."

"Well I certainly hope you're right young lady. I'd like to believe the world will be a better place when Lily here manages to find a husband. You looking for a woman Jesse? She's a bit hot headed but she cooks like the dickens!"

"Pop!"

"Oh, Jack, hush. Don't embarrass her. "

Jesse blushed and smiled at Lily before addressing Jack, "I'm not really looking to settle down just yet sir."

"Ah well, can't blame a guy for trying. Anyone up for a spot of whiskey?" he asked with a laugh as he got up and headed towards the kitchen.

"Here let me clear the table." said Jesse stacking up the empty dishes and carrying them into the kitchen.

Jesse walked into the kitchen and placed the dishes by the sink. Jack was opening a bottle of what appeared to be homemade whiskey.

"I make it in the shed out back. It don't taste great, but it gets the job done and I ain't gone blind yet." he said with a grin. He pulled two glasses down from a cabinet and poured a finger of whiskey in each. He handed one to Jesse and asked him out to the porch. Jesse glanced into the dining room and saw that Desmond and Julie were chatting comfortably with Rosemary and Lily. He followed Jack out onto the porch.

The moon had risen outside and cast a pale glow across the yard and the fence. The crickets had begun their nightly concert and a slight breeze rustled the leaves on the apple tree that stood next to the house. It was the peaceful kind of night that almost made you forget the horrors waiting on the other side of the gate. There were three chairs on the porch around a small table. Jack was sitting comfortably in one of them and Jesse sat down across the table from him.

"Nice night. Quiet. Peaceful like." Jack said after a few moments.

"I forgot how quiet it can be at night."

"Noisy in the city at night?"

"Most nights, yeah. I live in a tent community so there's never much in the way of peace. You get used to it though."

"I reckon people we can get used to anything. Heck, that's half the problem."

"How do you mean?"

"You don't seem particularly naïve, Jesse, but maybe living in the city as you do, you ain't aware of things as much." He leaned over and picked up his whiskey and took a slug. His face scrunched up as he swallowed, and he coughed a couple of times afterwards. "People have gotten used to the zombies." he said with a rasp. He gave another cough, cleared his throat and grinned at Jesse, "Smooth whiskey."

"Changed."

"See, there you go. Changed, zombies, what's the difference? They're basically dead people who aren't good for much aside from killing the living. We call em Changed because it makes us feel better, like they're gonna change back and everything is gonna be hunkey dorey. But they aren't. So we might as well use the perfectly good word we had for em back before they were real."

He gestured towards Jesse's whiskey. Jesse looked at it a little apprehensively. He was practically a professional drinker but after seeing Jack drink he was worried about what it would do to him. He picked it up and gave it a sniff. The vapors made his eyes water. He wondered briefly if the old man was trying to poison him. Not being able to see any way around it, he took a sip. Immediately his mouth felt like it was on fire. He swallowed and the burning feeling followed all the way to his stomach.

He gasped and then sucked in air in hopes of getting rid of the fire in his stomach. His eyes began to water, and his sinuses began to itch. Unable to figure out which sensation he should address first, he sneezed and then burped.

"Don't worry. The second sip is nowhere near as bad as the first." Jack said with a grin.

"Anyways Jesse, all I'm saying is it's all well and good that your friend Julie thinks things are going to get better, but don't you believe it. That's just people getting used to things. There's more of them every year and less of us. I'm afraid there won't be anything left for Lily soon. So, you should enjoy what you got while you can. Ain't safe heading out to the rim. Better to just go back to the city and live it up."

"That may be, sir. I've had my head in the sand for a while, so I don't really know what's going on with the outer settlements. Folks I live with are basically refugees from over run towns and homesteads though and it's true, the number of people in the camp just goes up, never down. But I don't think that's any reason to give up."

"Oh, I don't think people should give up. I'm just saying that you have to be realistic about our chances as a species."

"Well if you start giving out this whiskey, I'd say our chances are pretty much nil." Jesse said with a wry grin

"Hah!" Jack smiled out into the night and took another sip. His face scrunched up again, but he didn't cough this time. "Maybe some of these fool preachers I hear are right. Maybe this is our flood."

"Noah survived the flood."

"That's true he did. So, tell me Jesse, you think you're God's chosen? You live in the city so you must have heard this Reverend Jordan fella. He seems to think he's been chosen to lead us out of the wilderness with all his rubbish about changing back. You ask me he's starting to look like he's going to be leading people down the same foolish road that all those preachers did right after the Change"

"Well, I don't know about being God's chosen but I wouldn't bet on it. And you're right about Jordan being a snake oil salesman. But I will tell you truly, he did Change and he did indeed Change back. I was there."

Jack laughed and shook his head, "Young man, I've met about a dozen people who were 'there'. Every time I go to market I meet a few more."

"Yeah, but unlike them I really was. I was seven years old..." and he proceeded to tell Jack the story. After he finished, he took a swallow of his whiskey. It was better the second sip but that didn't keep him from breaking into a coughing fit. He did feel less like he was going to die, so he had to give Jack that.

"Way I usually hear it told, they don't mention a fella with a guitar and a bunch of people singing." Jack said after ruminating on Jesse's tale for a while.

"That's cause most of the people telling it weren't there and Father Jordan would rather people didn't remember Dylan."

"I guess I can see why. He doesn't come off very well in your version."

"He doesn't come off well because he's a liar and might very well be out of his mind."

"No wonder he was called to preach." Jack grinned. Jesse couldn't help but laugh. He went on, "I remember a singer back before the Change that went by the name of Dylan. He sang songs about the world changing. Maybe this Dylan of yours can do more than just sing songs," he paused for a moment, lost in a memory, "Well, we should head back in. Rosemary will start to wonder where we are."

He got up put his hands on his hips and stretched out his back. He turned to go back into the house and started to whistle. Jesse recognized the song as one his mother used to sing about the times a' changing. He picked up his glass and tossed the remaining whiskey out on the lawn before heading back in. He hoped it wouldn't kill the grass.

When they got back to the table, Rosemary was slicing into an apple pie. Jesse hadn't had pie in so long he had begun to think such things were more of a myth rather than reality.

"Where did you two run off to? We were starting to think that you'd up and left for the city." Rosemary said with a smile in her voice.

"Had to have some man talk, woman. Don't be sticking your nose in it." Jack replied in a practiced mock stern voice.

"Oh well, don't let silly old me butt in on your manly business. Would you both like pie?"

"More than just about anything, Ma'am!" Jesse said, not bothering to hide the enthusiasm in his voice. He was quite certain he could eat that whole pie by himself if given half a chance.

"I wouldn't let it bother you too much, Rosemary," Desmond said, "In my experience, man talk usually means grunting at each other and farting out the Battle Hymn of the Republic."

"Ah, the classics." Lily interjected. They all laughed happily while the pie was served. Jesse tore into his piece like it was a dream and he wanted to finish before he woke up. Julie inquired at the whiskey offered earlier and Jack beamed at her. Jesse would have tried to warn her, but he was too intent on his pie. Jack returned with a glass for her. She took it in one gulp and slammed the glass down loudly. Her eyes bulged and she made a noise like she was trying to keep from screaming. After a moment she let out a small cough and tried to speak but all that came out was a low groan. Jack winked at her and assured her it took some getting used to.

Desmond and Jesse both had seconds and thirds on pie and then helped clear the table. Once dinner was done Jack led Jesse and Desmond to the den where they would be sleeping. Lily took Julie up to her room. Rosemary wouldn't allow the men to sleep in the same room as Julie saying that it wasn't proper, and she wouldn't have it in her house. After the pleasant evening no one was in the mood to argue.

Laying on a rough, but cozy enough, cot, Julie was glad to be away from Jesse and Desmond. She liked Desmond well enough, but she didn't like Jesse and she was still bitter at having to travel all this way to find him. She had warmed up to Lily over the course of the evening. Life for a young woman wasn't easy before the Change and Julie sometimes thought that the Change had set women back a hundred years.

"Thank you again for the hospitality." Julie said to Lily as they settled in for the night. The room was small, just barely enough room for Lily's bed and the cot they had set up for Julie. It was sparse, with only a couple of other small pieces of furniture and a couple of quilts hanging on the walls. Despite the spartan nature of it, it was warm and Julie was thankful for a roof over her head.

"We don't get too many visitors out this way. At least not the kind you'd be willing to break bread with. It's nice to just chat with some new people. So, thank you too."

"Must get pretty lonely."

"It does. The town isn't too far but there's always so much work and my folks are getting up there. It isn't so bad though. There's just not much time to dwell on it, I guess. Your man Jesse seems nice."

Julie laughed.

"He's not my man by any stretch. I only met him a few days ago. He does seem nice though, you're right. I just don't know how much backbone he's got."

"Hopefully, he's got some. Soft people don't last too long out here."

"Ain't that the truth."

"He looks like he's got some steel in him. If nothing else, that Desmond has enough steel in him for both of them. Just meet him too?"

"Yeah, he insisted on coming. I don't know what his story is, but I reckon you're right. He covers it with all the laughter and jokes but there's a hardness behind it."

"Well, looks like you could do worse for traveling companions. He may turn out to be a marshmallow, but that Jesse is certainly easy on the eyes."

"That he is. That he is." They both laughed.

"Well, morning comes early on the farm. Good night, Julie."

"Good night, Lily."

Julie drifted off into a peaceful sleep. She dreamt of the road and of getting back to Malice.

In the next room Jack and Rosemary dreamt of things they missed from before the change. Jack dreamt of bowling alleys and good Irish whiskey. Rosemary dreamt of her family. Downstairs Jesse dreamt of a beautiful guitar and the music it might make.

Desmond lay awake lying on his back and staring up at the ceiling listening to the night sounds and Jesse's heavy breathing. He was thinking of things from before the Change as well. After a while, the tears that were his usual nighttime companion came and he cried himself to sleep. He didn't dream.

CHAPTER EIGHT

"You folks be careful out on the road now. If you don't dawdle you should be able to make it all the way to Smallville before sundown. " Jack said as they gathered at the gate.

The morning had been a pleasant one for everyone. Jesse and Desmond had woken to the smell of food being cooked in the kitchen. Once they had packed up their gear and cleaned up, they joined Julie and the family for breakfast. Rosemary had cooked enough eggs and bacon and pancakes to feed everyone. Not wanting to be rude Jesse and Desmond ate till they felt like they were going to explode.

"I'm starting to reconsider your offer of your Daughter's hand if means eating like this regular!" Jesse exclaimed. Desmond smacked him in the back of the head and made him apologize but there was no need as the family had been more amused than offended.

Once breakfast was done it was time for them to be on their way. Rosemary was kind enough to give them some food for the road, bread and dried meat. "Go on and take it. It would just go to waste otherwise." she had responded to their protests.

"After that breakfast we'll be lucky to make Clearwater!" Julie said warmly.

"You'll do fine, just don't let these two slack on you." Lily responded.

Jack shook all of their hands and smiled at them. "I'm glad we could do you a kindness. Your journey is going to be a long one I'm afraid. Be careful and don't do anything foolish and you'll be fine. Jesse, thanks for giving me something to think about. I'll be praying that you're right."

"You're a good man, Jack. There's not that many left these days but

I'm glad to have met one. You as well ladies. I won't soon forget your kindness."

Rather than a handshake Lily and Rosemary hugged the trio and shooed them on their way.

They heard the gate close and lock behind them as they walked away. It was just about the saddest sound Jesse had ever heard. They walked in silence for a while. Eventually Julie, who was walking ahead of them, said without turning around, "You don't find that measure of kindness too much out here." He couldn't be sure, but Jesse thought it sounded like she was crying.

They made it to Smallville an hour before sunset that night. The walk had been pleasant for Jesse. He was starting to get his legs back under him and the quick pace didn't bother him as much. He wasn't as stiff and sore that night in the bunkhouse either. He hadn't spent a lot of time moving around much in the city and was enjoying the exertion. Jesse imagined that wouldn't last very long. He figured the long days of marching between towns and sleeping in uncomfortable beds would get old quickly but for now he felt happy.

The previous night with the Heart family had instilled him with a sense of peace that he hadn't felt in a long time. Tent Town back in Silver City had been a community but he spent most of his time on the periphery. He hadn't wanted to know the people that lived there. He had felt like a refugee, adrift without a home. If Desmond hadn't been the pushy sort, he probably wouldn't have even bothered to learn anyone's name there. He spent his days trying to forget the people he did know, drowning names and faces in a sea of booze. After a while he felt like he had lost all connection with his childhood. He told and retold his story so many times that it eventually lost any meaning to him. It didn't feel personal anymore. It felt like describing the plot of a book. The Heart's had reminded him of what family life was like. It felt good and warm. He kept thinking throughout the day that he should be feeling melancholic or bitter about his own lost family but those feelings never came. Happiness wasn't a companion that Jesse traveled with often and he relished every minute of it.

Desmond was glad to see Jesse looking contented. He had known the young man for a while now and had started to wonder if Jesse was capable of being happy. Being out on the road felt good to Desmond. He had been longing for a change of scenery. As much as he cared for the people of Tent Town he had never intended to stay as long as he did. He didn't like being in one place for very long if he could help it but had been drawn to the refugee camp. He was a natural nurturer and Tent Town was filled with lost souls who needed someone to care for them. He had let himself get stuck. After a while he stopped thinking about the road and the inertia of routine took hold. Things there were better now than when he got there. People shared food and fostered a sense of community and that was largely due to his efforts. The night after he found out the woman wanted Jesse to go with him, he had wandered the tents talking to the people. At the time, he hadn't meant for his rounds to be farewells but as the night moved towards dawn, he had decided that it was time for him to be going.

He told Janie Jones that he was leaving. She seemed the most likely to him to keep the place together. She hadn't been happy about it but said that she understood. She thanked him for everything and assured him that she would do her best to see that his good work wasn't undone. As he was leaving, she said one last thing to him. He had been dwelling on it since they left. She had said "You got a sadness in you, Des. You can keep trying to outrun it or hide it behind your cheerfulness but someday you're going to have to face it." He had smiled and tipped his hat to her and simply said "Good luck," and went to meet Jesse and Julie at the gates.

The following night was spent in a town called Holly. The night after that they slept in Coventry. The days were spent walking mostly in silence. The three companions found themselves lost entirely in their own thoughts. They spoke a little when they broke for meals. Mostly they talked about the weather or the state of the countryside they were passing.

They were now traveling through territory that was less populated. As they moved away from the city the roads became less well trod. The rusted husks of cars, abandoned years ago, were more numerous. Farms were fewer and farther between. Jesse had never been this far out before. Wellersville where he grew up was closer to the city and surrounded by more settlements.

The difference was remarkable to to him. People had spent a great deal of time and effort removing the remnants of the way civilization used to be. Some of the cleanup had been practical. In order to have working roads, the cars and buses had to be removed. The vehicles also provided good day nests for the Changed, so it wasn't really safe to have them around. Jesse wasn't sure where they went, but he had always imagined a huge graveyard of old cars and trucks somewhere just beyond the horizon.

As they moved through the fringes of reclaimed territories Jesse began to understand the other reason people got rid of the cars. It was depressing and more than a little frightening. He thought back to what Jack Hart had told him about it being easy to forget that they were living in the middle of an apocalypse. Out here it was impossible to not be reminded. Not for the first time he wondered what the great cities of the past must have been like. Places like New York and Chicago. Both cities had fallen in the first days of the Change. Too many people in too confined a place. Jesse imagined they would be a nightmarish shell of what they had once been.

Nature had come storming back challenging humanity's dominance out here. The rusted cars were surrounded by huge fields of untended wheat and weeds. This had been farm country before the Change and in the absence of farmers the country had become completely overgrown.

Jesse couldn't help but dwell on the fact that they were only a few days out from the city. Humanity had not reclaimed as much land as he had imagined. It was a sobering thought.

"It's creepy out here." he said to no one in particular.

"It gets worse. Pretty soon the roads will disappear." Julie replied.

An involuntary shiver went down Jesse's spine.

It was an hour before sunset when they arrived at a settlement called Coltrane. Jesse was never more glad to see a wall and a gate in his life.

CHAPTER NINE

Coltrane was smaller than most of the settlements they had passed through. There were a handful of buildings that had seen better days. Most of the town was constructed of aluminum shacks lined up in rows near the northern portion of the wall. A bunk house and a soup kitchen were built near the main gate. Both were spartan affairs that had few amenities. There was only a single bunkhouse to house both men and women, unlike the separate ones in most of the towns they had come across. When they dropped off their gear, they noticed that no one else was staying the night and it looked like it had been a while since anyone had used any of the beds. They picked out three bunks close to the central heater. Nights had been getting a bit cooler as they got closer to the mountains. Once they settled in, they set off for the soup kitchen for dinner.

The soup kitchen appeared to be as little used as the bunk house. When they entered there was only a woman in the kitchen that looked like she was preparing the soup. When she heard them come in, she turned to them, smiled, and waved.

"Good evening! Welcome to Coltrane!" she said with genuine enthusiasm.

"Good evening Ma'am." Desmond responded. He had taken to speaking for the group most of the time. Jesse was quiet by nature and Julie had seemed to become more sullen as the days went on. He was gregarious by nature and despite the bleak landscape was still enjoying the newfound movement in his life. "The soup smells delicious! Although it looks like we might be your only customers." he went on, "My name is Desmond, this is Jesse and Julie."

"Please to meet you all! You can call me Louise. We don't get many travelers out this way, so no one had thought to have some soup on. My grandson came and got me when he saw you come through the gate. It'll be ready in a bit. It's not much but it'll fill you up."

"Well, we certainly do appreciate it. We don't have much to offer in trade, but we'd be glad to help out if there's anything needs doing around town." Desmond responded. They always made the offer even though most of the towns didn't ask anything of them. He wondered if that would change as they got into more sparsely populated country where the travelers were rare.

"Thank you for your kind offer but we're just glad to be able to offer a night's rest and a full belly to anyone who comes by. Y'all heading to Silver City?"

"Heading the other way actually." Julie said, cutting off Desmond, "Making our way out to Nature Springs."

Desmond looked at her questioningly. She hadn't had a problem letting people know they were headed to Malice before. He wondered why she was lying.

"Still a ways to go then. You ask me you should be heading the other way. There's not much out here anymore. If you're looking for work, there are more farms in towards the city."

"I have a brother out there that I haven't seen in a long time. Desmond and Jesse were keeping me company and watching out for me. Woman all alone on the road isn't always so safe."

"Well, they seem like fine men. You folks sit down and shake the dust from your shoes. I'll have some soup and bread over to you soon as it's ready."

They sat down at one of the few tables in the room. Desmond was glad for the rest. After the gloominess of the walk that day the hospitality was nice. He wondered why Julie hadn't seemed to want him to mention Malice. Once they saw that Louise was back at work cooking he leaned in close and in a quiet voice asked why she had lied.

In a voice just above a whisper, she replied, "Malice has a bit of a reputation for weirdness the closer you get. Most of the bigger towns near the city wouldn't know it but we're getting farther out."

"What kind of weirdness?"

"There's lots of rumors but the central theme usually revolves around the people of Malice being a cult."

"A cult?" Jesse, who was leaning in to hear their conversation, said a bit too loud. Julie made a gesture for him to lower his voice.

"It's nothing that bad, but it can make some people nervous. When I first left to find you a lot of people gave me weird looks or walked away when I told them I was from Malice."

"Are you a cult?" Desmond asked.

"Of course not! But Malice is a tight knit community, in every sense of the word. The farmers don't come to town to sell their goods, they come to share them. Farmers who come looking to sell are turned away. That sort of thing gets rumors started." Julie responded, slightly indignantly.

"So Malice is a commune?" Jesse asked.

"I guess you could say so. Although I would say more of a congregation."

"A congregation?" Jesse sounded concerned to Desmond.

"Like in a Church?" Julie responded sarcastically.

"I know what a congregation is. Are you sure you aren't a cult?" Jesse replied, matching her sarcasm.

"Absolutely. But I will let you make your up own minds once we get there."

Louise called over from the kitchen to let them know supper was ready. Julie popped up and went over to get her soup and some bread. Desmond and Jesse simply looked at each other and wondered what they had gotten themselves into.

The soup was delicious. Each of them went back for seconds, lavishing praise on Louise's cooking talents. As they finished up their meal, a man came into the kitchen and waved to Louise. They talked for a moment before he came over to the companions. He was short but powerfully built. He had a farmer's build and the dark tan of someone who spent time working in the fields. His face had a young look to it, but his receding hairline and white beard placed him firmly in his 50's. He didn't seem quite as happy to see them as Louise had been.

"Good evening and welcome to Coltrane. My name is Stephen Marr, I guess you could say I'm the mayor." He offered his hand out.

All three stood up and shook his hand in turn introducing themselves, then sat back down. Stephen sat with them.

"We appreciate the fine meal." Julie said.

"You're quite welcome, however I have to ask how long you are planning to stay?"

"Just the night." Julie responded.

"Fair enough. Our stock is a bit low and we have a good number of locals in town. I'm afraid we simply don't have much to spare. We lost two farms in the last two weeks."

"Lost farms?" Desmond asked with some surprise.

"Overrun by Changed. They've been getting worse lately it seems. More aggressive."

"How can they be more aggressive?" Desmond asked. To his mind the Changed were nothing but hunger and aggression. He didn't see how there was any room for them to get worse.

"They're not retreating as quickly at dawn. I don't know that that's true, have you heard anything like that?"

"We haven't heard anything like that." Julie responded.

"Louise tells me you're heading towards Nature Springs?"

"Yup." Julie said, a little too quickly. Stephen gave her brief look but then continued on.

"We haven't had word from there in a couple of weeks. That's not all that unusual I guess but with losing two farms everyone here is a bit on edge. You ask me you're better off heading the other way, towards the city."

"Thank you for the concern and the food. We do appreciate it. We'll be out of your hair first thing in the morning." Julie, unable to keep all of the concern out of her voice.

"I'm sorry we can't extend you much more hospitality but there's going to be a lot of belt cinching here soon and we can't afford any more mouths. If you leave early enough you should be able to reach Nature Springs by early evening tomorrow."

"That's the plan." Julie said. Stephen got up and bid them a good night. They thanked him once again for the hospitality. He went back over to Louise and she turned to wave at them and then left the room with Stephen.

"Doesn't make much sense for Changed to ignore the fires," Desmond mused.

"I've never heard of them doing that. Usually they'll break off whatever they're doing at the first hint of sunlight and go hide until night. Ignoring the flames and continuing to go after people speaks of intelligence or at least malevolence." Julie responded.

"That's all we need. For those things to get smarter." Desmond said. He shivered at the thought and stood up, "Well, I for one am ready to get some sleep. I'll see you kids at the bunkhouse." He got up and headed out of the building.

Julie and Jesse said in silence for a moment watching Desmond leave. Julie went to get up and follow him but Jesse put a hand on her arm. "Tell me more about Malice" he said. She looked at him for a while and then shrugged his arm off.

"You'll see soon enough. Dylan asked me to not tell you too much before we get there and I won't. "

"He happen to say why he wanted me kept in the dark? I'm starting to lose a little bit of trust here."

"All he said was that he wanted you to see things for yourself before you made any judgments. At any rate, I'm going to bed. I suggest you do the same. We have a longer walk than usual tomorrow and we need to leave at dawn if we're going to make it."

She left the room leaving Jesse there by himself.

CHAPTER TEN

A hot wind blew across the plains when they set out at dawn. The temperature had dropped overnight and was now ramping itself back up. The night in Coltrane hadn't been a pleasant one for Desmond. It had taken him a long time to fall asleep and when he eventually drifted off his dreams were full disturbing images of being chased by the Changed.

"You look like hell." Desmond said matter-of-factly when he saw Jesse in the morning. Jesse only smiled wanly and shrugged, "Didn't sleep well. I'll be fine." He clapped Desmond on the shoulder and walked past him on the way to meet Julie at the gate. "Seriously, I'm fine. You can stop giving me your mother hen look."

"If you say so." Desmond replied, the expression on his face not changing. Together they walked to the gate to meet Julie. She was already gone before either of them woke up. As they approached the gate, they saw her leaning on the wall with her arms crossed glaring at them impatiently.

"Hurry it up. I don't really want to get caught out in the middle of nowhere at dusk because you two like to sleep in."

"Back off. We're coming." Desmond said angrily. He was getting a little tired of being treated like a child by Julie. He had hoped she would warm up to both him and Jesse a little over the course of the trip. but it seemed to him that the opposite was happening. This was the first time he had spoken angrily to her however and he saw a change in her expression when he did so. For a brief moment surprise and then what he read as regret flashed across her face. Before he could say anything else her annoyed expression returned. She turned and headed out the gate without another word. Desmond followed with Jesse at his side. He glanced at Jesse and it appeared that he was lost in his own world and had missed the exchange.

The country they were moving through now was the kind of wasteland they showed in the science fiction movies Desmond had watched as a kid. Overgrown fields, rusted out husks of cars, dilapidated houses, and other detritus of a world that no longer existed. The highway they walked along was choked with cars strewn across four lanes. Some had been heading east the way they had come, others had been going west toward the mountains.

"Why would they be fleeing in both directions?" Jesse asked shattering the silence among them. Julie looked up at him, startled as if she had just woken from a dream.

"Panic probably," she said without much conviction. She had never really thought about it before. She was about the same age as Jesse and had grown up post-Change. She never thought much about the world before the Change or even during. She was a practical person and those questions would only serve to clutter the mind in her estimation. She believed in taking things as they were and dealing with them straight on. She wasn't very interested in asking 'why'. 'Why' didn't put food on the table. She was certain this tendency is why Dylan had asked her to fetch Jesse. There had been some protest when the decision was announced but those protests were mostly out of concern for a woman traveling alone. No one thought she wasn't capable. Knowing Dylan as she did, she imagined he had other ulterior motives in sending her, but she couldn't guess at what those might be. She trusted Dylan and that was all that mattered to her.

"Panic isn't quite right."

Julie and Jesse both stopped walking and turned to Desmond when he said that. The tone of his voice was very different than normal. He was looking down the road with a faraway look in his eyes.

"Des?" Jesse questioned.

"The early days were filled with panic. Panic and fear. Lots of people died. No one knew what was happening. Everyone had seen so many zombie movies that the immediate reaction was that the dead were rising."

"How much do you remember from before Des?"

"How old you think I am, Jes?"

"I dunno. Forty?"

Desmond laughed.

Jesse had never thought to ask Desmond his age before. He had never once heard Desmond talk about his past. All he would say was that he came to Silver City from further East than where Jesse was from. He had never said where exactly or why. Jesse wasn't one to pry. He always figured people usually tell you what they want you to know without prodding. He had gotten so used to telling his own story that he never bothered to ask anyone else theirs.

"I'm fifty-three."

"No way!" Julie blurted out, eliciting a chuckle from Desmond. She coughed and looked embarrassed.

"I've always looked young." he said with a smile. He watched Jesse do the math and his smile faded.

"So, you were 22 when it happened?" Jesse asked.

"Yup. 22 and married. My son had just turned one."

That sentence hit Jesse like a punch to the gut. He could almost feel the wind knocked out of him. He knew for sure that Desmond had no family. People with family didn't usually end up in Tent Town. He stood there stunned for a few moments.

Julie also kept quiet. She knew less about Desmond than Jesse did but was surprised to see that he didn't know about Desmond having a family.

She didn't think that could be a good sign. In the silence, she thought she could hear the herd of deer she could see in the distance. The the sound of flies buzzing was impossibly loud. Looking at the sun she realized they had been standing there for a while and coughed to break the silence.

"We need to get moving again guys," she said with more gentleness than either of the men would have thought her capable of. Desmond, who had been looking into the distance nodded and said, "Of course." and started to walk. Julie and Jesse fell in on either side of him. The highway here was clear enough that they didn't have to walk single file as long as they stuck to the shoulder.

"So, what happened Des?" Jesse asked eventually.

"Things Changed." Desmond said with a deep sigh.

CHAPTER ELEVEN

I remember she was wearing a green checkered dress that I bought her on a whim one day at Macys. It was a long sundress that had a little sash that looked like silk. She was even more beautiful than usual in it, I had thought. Despite that, she was still yelling at me. It was a few weeks after the Change had started. People knew that something was going on and there were rumors and weird news reports, but it wasn't to the point where people had started to panic. Everyone thinks of the Change as something that happened quickly. That wasn't really the case. It started slow. It was probably a month and a half after the first incidents that things got bad.

That was after the government had started making announcements about travel restrictions. They hadn't imposed martial law yet though, so you could still move freely. They just asked that you didn't. We lived in Boston and I had a gig in New York that I intended to make. She thought I was crazy for wanting to go. I probably was but we needed the money.

I was a horn player in those days. Mostly a session guy for Ska bands and Jazz groups although, I had a few people I played regular with. This particular gig was with a Ska outfit that had jumped on the third wave and never got off. It was fun music, and I enjoyed the guys in the band. The gig was opening for some band who had a couple of songs playing on the radio. They weren't big yet, but they were on their way and opening for them would be pretty good money.

My wife had recently been laid off and our son had just turned one, so I didn't see what choice I really had. The word on everyone's lips was that there was a plague. Our landlady kept referring to it as an airborne toxic event. I don't even know what that means, but I remember her saying it over and over when I went down to tell her our rent was going to be late. She told me that that was ok and to just get it to her whenever we could. The news hadn't frightened me up until that point, but when our landlady told us it was ok to be late with the rent, I knew we were all in trouble.

So, Frances, that's my wife's name, was yelling at me for wanting to go to New York. She was scared of all this talk about zombies and she didn't understand how I could leave and not be there to protect her and our son, Stuart. As a compromise I said 'Why don't you come along?' and suggested we could go to her Mother's in Maryland afterwards. I was guessing that being close to her mother would help. She lived near Washington D.C. and it made sense to me that if things were getting bad then D.C. would be the best protected place around. She wasn't thrilled with the idea of doing a lot of traveling with the restrictions on but was ok with it as long as we were all together. "Besides," I said, "The travel restrictions are only for driving at night." It's almost funny to look back now and realize how little of an idea we had.

We packed enough for a two-week trip. We didn't have much really. We were getting by but only just. We lived on love and spaghetti O's, too young to have a clue, too young to be parents, and way too young to care. Once the car was loaded, I stopped in to see the landlady again and let her know we were going to New York and then Maryland and would pay her this month's and next month's rent together. I felt bad about that but there wasn't really any choice. I had enough money to get us to New York and not much more. After we got paid for the gig I'd be alright though. My landlady told me that it was ok and when I turned to leave, she grabbed my hand. I turned around and she took my other hand and looked into my eyes. I will never forget the fear in her eyes or what she said.

"This is going to be bad, Desmond. I've been watching the news and I think this might be the big one. You take that wife and kid of yours and you go hole up somewhere safe. I'll pray for you."

I tried to reassure her that things weren't as bad as all that and this would blow over like swine-flu or any of the other diseases they tried to scare you with on the evening news. I told her we would be back in a couple of weeks and we'd laugh about all of this. She smiled and said she hoped so, but the smile never reached her eyes.

I never saw her again.

We had a little Honda hatchback at the time. Filled up with all the stuff for Stu and our own bags, it looked like we were going away for months. We had taken our time getting ready since I didn't need to be in New York until the next day. Driving out of Boston was a hassle at the best of times. On that particular day it graduated from annoying to nightmarish. It took hours to get away from the city. All the time I was thinking about our landlady's eyes.

Some of it was normal city traffic but I think most of it were people like us. At that point no one had seen an actual Changed. Everyone had heard rumors but that's all it was. The travel restrictions actually spooked people. You can't really blame them. Anytime someone goes on TV asking you to do something it's a little frightening. It makes it harder to dismiss the crazy stories as crazy. Outwardly you put on a big show saying its nothing and it'll blow over. Inwardly though, in that place where you have a harder time lying to yourself, you start to wonder things like 'If it's nothing, why are they asking us to not leave town?' I was putting on a brave face for Frances but she knew me well enough to know I had doubts. She wasn't stupid either, she knew something was wrong. We were both relieved to have a plan and to be moving rather than sitting still waiting for the government to come knocking. Even though it turned out to be the sort of thing you can't outrun, moving feels better than sitting still.

Because of the traffic we weren't going to make it through Connecticut before dark. We were barely going to make it to Connecticut that night. The travel restrictions had said to avoid driving after dark but they hadn't implied there would be checkpoints or that it was illegal so we pressed on. It didn't take that long to drive through Connecticut on the busy days and I figured that there wouldn't be many people on the road so we could fly through.

We were making good time driving down I-95. That was a major road up and down the east coast in those days. I had been right about there being no cars. We'd see one or two but mostly had the highway to ourselves. I was pushing it too, driving about 90. Frances kept telling me to slow down. She hated when I drove fast. Especially with Stuart in the car. She was probably right too. I had a lot of accidents in my day, mostly my fault. That night we just missed another. We were coming around a curve past the exit for a town called New London and I had to slam on the brakes. We actually spun out to the point where the car almost flipped. Luckily, we stopped in time. In front of us was what had to be a twelve-car pileup. There were cars everywhere. Some were flipped over; some were halfway on top of the cars in front of them. It was a mess and it looked like it had just happened. Most of the cars still had their lights on and I could see people starting to get out of their cars, staggering around.

I threw the Honda in reverse and backed out of the middle of the road over to the shoulder. I was afraid of someone coming around the corner and slamming into us. Once we were safely out of the way I got out to help. I told Frances to stay in the car with the baby and to call 911. The washed-out light from the streetlights overhead made the scene look like a horror movie. People were staggering about and groaning loudly. I called out to see who might need help and a few of the people turned toward me and began to lurch in my direction.

As they started toward me, I became aware of two things. The first was that the wind had picked up considerably and that second was that there was light coming from behind me. I turned in time to see a couple of large trucks come around the same bend. The trucks stopped in front of the accident without having to slam on their brakes like I had. That made me think they were the cops or the ambulances although I couldn't tell because I was looking into their headlights. I started to walk towards the trucks when the first spotlight passed over me and I realized the wind was from a helicopter. It trained back on me for a moment and I shielded my eyes. That was when Frances started yelling at me to get back in the car. The Honda was parked behind the arc of the lights so she could clearly see that the trucks were military. I was practically blind, so I stumbled towards the sound of her voice, shielding my eyes. I sometimes wonder if shielding my eyes is what saved my life. A Changed wouldn't have shielded its eyes. When I got back to the car, Frances was nearly hysterical. She kept asking me why there was an army truck at an accident. I was just as baffled as she was.

As we stood there, soldiers began to climb out of the back of one of the trucks. Two of them came over to us and one shined a flashlight right in our faces. He held the light on us for what felt like an eternity. Now, I was a law-abiding citizen, but back in those days a black guy in a car at night had a lot of worry about when he got pulled over by the police, never mind by the army. I was so scared I nearly pissed myself. After a few moments he lowered his flashlight and told us to double back to the exit we just passed and to find a hotel. I remember he looked pretty spooked himself. As we got back in our car, we saw that soldiers had piled out of the trucks and were moving toward the accident in a line. We didn't need to be told twice, we headed out of there as fast as that little hatchback could go.

We doubled back to the New London exit and took it. Once we were off the highway I pulled over and got out. I was shaking and needed a few moments to calm down. Frances got out after checking that little Stu was asleep. We hugged each other for a while and then leaned on the car talking it through. Neither of us had any idea why the military would be dealing with an accident. I mentioned the weird way people had been staggering around and she mentioned something that hadn't really registered for me. None of them were talking. They weren't asking for help or screaming or making much noise at all outside of a low moaning. That thought alone was almost more frightening than the soldiers.

We decided that we wanted no part of sticking around here. She surmised that our best bet would be to find the Merritt Parkway and take that rest of the way. That seemed like a good idea to me. Once we figured out where we were in our outdated road atlas, we plotted a course and set off. We would have to find our way through some Connecticut back roads, but it wouldn't be a long trip to the other highway.

At least I thought it wouldn't be.

I think all the roads in Connecticut were built in 1800 and designed for people to ride on with a horse and buggy. Every road we got on was more twisty and narrower than the last. After a while we were lost. I wasn't too proud to ask for directions, but nothing was open. Every little town we passed through felt like a ghost town. It wasn't all that late, but the travel restrictions seemed to have taken hold with the people of Connecticut.

It had been a stressful evening already and being lost and apparently alone really started to get to us. Frances had gone quiet and my shakes were coming back. I was starting to understand how people in horror movies felt. Darkness and loneliness are queer things when you're used to being in places where there isn't much of either. I was Boston born and raised and like all cities it was never really dark there. When I was on the road with my various bands, we played in places with more darkness, but I never felt alone. This was different. You start to feel like you're on an island and everything that's not on the island wants to get at you. It feels even more primal when you have your wife and son with you. You are their protector, the thing they can hide behind. Now my wife wasn't the kind of woman who would hide behind anyone, but I was clear in my head that it was my job to keep them safe.

My mind started to play tricks on me. Or so I thought. I kept thinking I saw people on the side of the road, just outside the edge of our headlights. I kept telling myself that I was imagining things but didn't stop me from glimpsing them. In retrospect, I realize that I was seeing people, or rather I was seeing the Changed. After a while we saw a sign for the Merritt and let me tell you that feeling of relief was better than sex. It lasted about as long too because it was only a minute later than I saw the guy walking down the middle of the road. Staggering would probably be a better word than walking. The man was staggering down the road. There were no streetlights, so the only real light was from my headlights and the ambient light from the stars overhead. He saw my headlights and began to move toward us. I couldn't tell if he was hurt or not, so I stopped the car. I was about to get out when something thudded against my window.

I looked out just as there was another thud and screamed. This was the first time I saw a Changed up close. You've all seen enough to know what they look with the deep hollowed out eyes and the drawn tight dry looking skin. It had both hands on the window and had its face up close. Frances screamed next to me and that woke the baby in the backseat. We may have never seen a Changed before, but we had seen plenty of zombie movies. The thing pounded on the glass again. I tried to retreat away from it. There was another thud, this time from the front of the car. I got a good look at the thing that had been staggering down the road. It had bumped into the hood and now appeared to be trying to climb up the hood of the car. This being a hatchback that wasn't a long trip.

I watched as they tried to get into the car. I was frozen and only gradually became aware of Frances talking to me or yelling at me rather. She was asking what the hell they were over and over again. I turned to face her and saw another three of the things were coming up to the car on her side. She hadn't seen them yet and I shouted out a warming just before they started pounding on the window. One of them began banging on the back window and this brought me out of my stupor.

I reached down with my left hand and dropped the seat back. I then pivoted and was able to unlock the baby seat straps and pick up Stu. I handed him to Frances so that she could cover him up. If any of the glass broke, I didn't want it to shatter on him. I put my seat back up and tried to start the car. It stalled. I distinctly remember taking the Lord's name in vain and pounding on the wheel and yelling something about not being in an actual horror movie. I tried the key again and this time it started. Before I got it into gear lights flooded into my eyes from somewhere up ahead. Then we heard the first gunshot. The thing next to my window flew away like a balloon in a strong breeze. There were two more gunshots and two of the Changed on her side of the car flew away. Frances ducked down in her seat covering up Stu. Not wanting to miss a chance I started to drive forward. This knocked the one clamoring on the hood off and he went under the car. Running it over felt like driving over a pitted dirt road. We heard a few more shots as we drifted towards the car in front of us. When we got closer the top lights began to shine and we realized it was a police car. I stopped the car and waited for the shooting to stop.

It felt like we were sitting in that car with bullets whizzing by us for a year. People talk about time slowing down in moments of fear or stress and it is most certainly true. After a while, the shooting stopped and there was a knock at the window. It made me flinch until I realized it wasn't the thud like Changed made but a simple knock. It was followed by a voice.

"You folks alright in there?" it said. I decided it was ok to start breathing again and rolled down the window. He shined a flashlight into the car as I told him we were ok. I asked him what those things were, and he told me his best guess was zombies and that he knew how ridiculous that sounded. I remember what he said next pretty clearly because at the time it struck me as hilarious or at least it did in the state of mild shock that I was in. In retrospect it doesn't sound funny but at the time I almost wet myself laughing. He said, "Some of the boys down at the station are calling them meth heads but I'm not one for denying what's right in front of me. If it staggers like a zombie, moans like a zombie, and attacks people like a zombie, it probably ain't some kid whacked out on meth." He laughed a bit too. The sheer absurdity of the thought of being attacked by zombies while driving around in Connecticut made it hard to not laugh. It was that or scream.

Once the laughing died down the other officer called out to the one I was talking to, who's named turned out to be Benmont Campbell, and shined his light down the road. I glanced in the rearview mirror and saw that another dozen of the things were walking down the road towards us. Benmont cursed and told us to follow them. They would take us back to the station to stay the night. He said it was the safest place around and that none of the roads would be safe till morning. He got back in his cruiser and drove off. I'm not sure I ever let the car get more than ten feet away from them on the ride to the station.

I had another good laugh on the way over. Frances eventually asked me why I was laughing. I answered that I was laughing at the idea of a young black couple getting pulled over in rural Connecticut driving a new car and happily following a cop back to the station. That whole evening still seems utterly absurd to me all these years later.

We went back to the station without incident. When we got there

Benmont told us that they had received three or four more calls about the things so he and his partner would have to head back out. Before he did, he took us into the station and introduced us to the late night dispatch officer. Her name was Nancy Ritchie and she was more spooked than we were. After we were introduced, she asked Benmont what was going on. He just took his hat off and shook his head. He told her he had no idea, but to keep the doors locked.

It was a small station, so Nancy set us up in one of the cells. It wasn't very comfortable, but it did seem safe. There was no one in any of the other cells. Nancy said it was a pretty sleepy town and they never had much more than the occasional drunk or teenager in need of being scared straight. That was how we spent the night. Frances slept on a cot with Stu held close and I slept on the other in fits and starts. I got up a few times to check on my family and to see if they had any news on the situation or what the things were. Each time she told me they didn't. She did tell me that there seemed to be more of them now. They had been coming across them for the past few weeks. No one they contacted had any help for them. Benmont, who had arrived back at the station at some point, had gone so far as calling the FBI but they wouldn't answer any of his questions. They would only say that there had been similar reports and that an investigation was underway. Nancy suspected there was a government cover-up although Benmont apparently thought it was much simpler. He thought that no one actually knew what they were. If it had seemed like a transmutable disease, he would have suspected the government but the medical exams of dead ones they had brought in didn't reveal any kind of pathogen.

It was a long night. Jail cells aren't comfortable in the best of times. When you're worrying about your wife and child and wondering if you are about to face a zombie apocalypse then sleep is mostly out of the question. The one consolation was that the things went away during the day. He wasn't sure what happened to them, but they had no reported incidents when the sun was up.

I won't soon forget him. His matter-of-factness and honesty about it all made it seem less grave. We talked a bit about what we were going to do once day broke. I told him I had a gig in New York and then we were moving on to Maryland, near D.C.. He wished me luck and as dawn broke, he left. He said he was going home to his family. I like to think he lived through those horrible days ahead. Once the sun was fully up, I gathered Frances and Stu and we headed on to New York.

The first thing we did when we got to the city was book a hotel room. Our original plan had been to head down to her mother's right after the show but after the previous night we weren't in a hurry to travel at night again. My show wasn't until seven that evening so we took turns getting some sleep. I went down to the newsstand while she was asleep to get a few papers and see if there was any news on what was going on.

The papers were full of stories that looked like they had actually been written by the FBI. Everything had an air of 'Don't panic, it's nothing but hysteria' type stories. All except the Post that is. Its front page had one huge word over a blurry photo that could have been one of the things we saw the previous night. The headline screamed 'ZOMBIES!'. It made sense that all the more respected papers had the government approved stories and the Post didn't. People looked at the Post as a bastard child that would do anything to take attention away from the other papers. The Enquirer was another paper with a dodgy reputation that had a headline about zombies. I bought both of those and headed back up to the room. Frances and Stu were still asleep so I put on the news quietly and read the articles in the paper. They were written with so much hysteria I would have had trouble taking them seriously if I hadn't seen the things with my own eyes.

The TV news wasn't much better. Most of the stations were reporting that there was nothing wrong. Almost across the spectrum the story seemed to be that there was a particularly nasty strain of the flu that was keeping people in their homes and that's why so many towns and cities seemed to have fewer people in them. I remember thinking that would have to be one hell of a flu bug to make a noticeable dent in the number of people on the street. One local station was doing a report on a decrease in homeless people in shelters and on the streets. They didn't put forth any theories as to why, but I could see in the reporter's eyes that they had a theory. Another station, mostly known for its right-wing spin on everything, was blaming the rumors of zombies and the flu outbreak on the current President who leaned to the left. I'm still struck by the stupidity of blaming what I was starting to think was the end of the world on the political leanings of a President. I guess that's neither here nor there really. If you looked closely the signs were all there in the media. Whomever was pushing the 'everything's fine' stories was serious about it, most stations had a consistent message although a few of the newscasters seemed nervous. One guy who had a bit of a reputation as a loose cannon kept looking off to the side during his show, like someone was standing there feeding him lines. I suppose someone was. The story was there though if you were willing to piece the disparate facts that were spread across all the news channels. The cover up wouldn't last much longer but for that day people were still able to tell themselves everything was fine.

Frances woke up after a while and I took a turn sleeping. She was badly shaken from the night before but seemed better after some sleep. I slept until an hour before sound check and headed down to the club. She stayed at the hotel with Stu since we didn't like to bring him to clubs. It was too loud and she had seen me play plenty of times before. We met at a show when I was still with my first band. She was at the bar after the set and I had left the dressing room for a drink. She said my playing was great and that I was the only standout in the band. I told her she should listen more closely to the baselines if she really believed that. She looked at me funny and said 'Aren't you the bassist?'. Eight months later we were married.

Tonight's show was a one off gig with a group called Bealzabeat. I had played with them a few times but I wasn't their regular horn player. He was off sick somewhere and that's why they asked me to come play. Looking back, he had probably Changed already. Not to cast aspersions on the dead but he was a real dirt bag. Most of the band stayed clear of drugs and most of the seedier aspects of showbiz life but not this guy. I don't even remember his name now. He was a boozer and an asshole.

The sound check ended up being the highlight of the evening for me. I got there a little early and we ended up jamming on a lot of old Ska tunes. It turned out they hadn't heard word one from the other blower and were starting to get worried. They were glad that I had showed up since they had had to cancel the previous show without the guy.

The show that night was ok. They had some good songs, and I had some room for a solo or two, one of which was pretty good. It was hard to really get into it since the club was half filled and most of the people that did show up were listless and barely even dancing. It seemed like the crowd's mind was collectively elsewhere. We ended up cutting the show short and skipping the encore. No one really seemed to mind. Afterwards I said goodbye to all the guys and told them to keep me in mind if they needed a more permanent replacement since I was looking for work. They had a good sound and with a few tweaks could do alright for themselves.

I headed back to the hotel after the show. Outside the club the streets seemed empty for New York. I had to walk back since there wasn't a cab in sight. For a Friday night at 11:00 PM the city felt more like Peoria than New York. Once I was back at the hotel Frances jumped into my arms as I came through the door. She had been nervous for me to be out at night. Before I could really get settled, she put the news on and told me to watch. It seemed like every station was now running the same story. Some of those things had gotten lose in Citi field during a Mets game and over a hundred people had died. Some from the Changed but most from the panic that had gripped the crowd. It had been a nationally broadcast game. The cat was out of the bag now. The news said to tune in during the morning for a statement from the President. Frances kept repeating that this couldn't be happening. I went to bed a little while after that, figuring there wasn't anything I could have done about it that night. I'm not sure if Frances slept at all.

We decided to stay in the hotel again the next day rather than pressing on to her mother's. We figured the roads would be jammed solid. I was also convinced that the President was going to declare martial law and completely restrict travel, not just at night, and I didn't want us to get stuck somewhere halfway to her mother's. I couldn't think of anything worse than having to try and survive a zombie apocalypse in Delaware. We were also not in a hurry to get stuck out on the roads at night again either.

It turned out to be a good decision. She called her mother who informed her they were already on their way to stay on her Uncle's farm in Missouri. She said the roads weren't too bad and that we should head out there as well. Frances and I argued over that. Missouri was a long drive and it still seemed like Washington would be our safest bet. She just wanted to be with her family. We went back and forth on it until the President came on. It turned out he was broadcasting live from Colorado and not the White House. Whether that meant he was on the road or if he was holding up in NORAD I never found out. The latter was what my paranoia insisted on and it freaked me out good. It certainly won the argument for Frances. If the President wasn't in D.C., then we weren't going to be either.

His speech was designed to reassure people, but it had the opposite effect. He talked about how the Flu appeared to have psychosomatic effects on some people, making them more violent and disoriented. He went on for a while about how people who were suffering these issues should be restrained and authorities should be notified at once. He stressed that they were not zombies and shooting them would be considered a capital crime. I would guess a lot of people died because of that section of the speech. You always think that the government is omniscient when it comes to things like this, but I know now that they had no idea either. He didn't declare martial law during this speech, but he did expound at length about how the travel restrictions were being enforced and that anyone on the roads at night would be subject to imprisonment.

The news station went back to a round table discussion of the epidemic and the ramifications on the economy. One of the pundits went on a long rant about how a situation like this would never have happened if the other party had been in power. I muted it after that. I wasn't much for politics, but I knew stupid when I saw it. They'd made politics a game and it seemed like all that mattered was winning rather than actually governing. I liked the President, had voted for him, but you could have the rest of the politicians in Washington. They were spoiled children whose only connection to the people they governed was campaign photo ops.

We stared at the muted television for a while. With the TV off, we could hear Stu's quiet breathing. It was a peaceful sound like a light breeze over a mountain meadow. I listened to it until Frances broke my revelry with a question.

"If this is a flu epidemic, how come no one is sick?"

She pointed out that during a normal flu season you can't go five feet without hearing someone sniffling or sneezing. Where were all the sick people? She had gone out early that morning to get some food and to stretch her legs and hadn't run across anyone who had so much as coughed. I thought back and realized that no one at the show seemed unhealthy either. I thought that this was probably just coincidence, but I don't think either of us believed that. None of the things we saw the previous night looked like people made delirious with the flu.

I went out and bought some supplies for the drive to Missouri. The stores were starting to look empty. People had probably started hoarding before the first travel restriction. I got what groceries I could, and on a whim picked up some camping gear. On the walk back from the camping store I passed a pawn shop and made a decision. I went in and bought a gun. It made me sad to do it and I knew Frances would blow up at me but if things went down the way they were starting to look, then maybe it wasn't such a bad idea. The guy who sold it to me didn't ask for ID or say anything about a waiting period. He had been pretty distracted and hadn't even batted an eyelash when I asked if he had any firearms.

There was a small crowd gathered outside the electronic store next door to the pawn shop when I walked out. It was a scene straight out of a movie. People were looking in at the array of TV's in the window. The eyes of the people in the crowd were much too wide. Some were crying. One man was nodding his head and had a frightening grin. Whatever had happened that scared most of the people there made him happy. Looking at him made me uncomfortably aware of the gun in my jacket pocket. I didn't wait to find out what had happened. As I hurried back to the hotel room, I said a small prayer that whatever this was that was happening would be over soon. I guess in a way my prayer was answered. Things began to happen very fast.

When I got back to the hotel room Frances was staring at the TV with the same wide-eyed horror that the people at the electronics store had. I asked her what had happened, and she looked up at me and burst into tears. I dropped everything in my arms and rushed over to her. The sound of her crying woke up Stu and he began wailing. I looked at the TV and that was the first I saw of those terrible images.

There was a so-called church that was on the news a lot back then. They got on TV by showing up and picketing soldiers funerals. They had a message that our soldiers were dying because we as a country tolerated homosexuals. In their twisted logic, everything bad that happened to the US was because of God's wrath over our wicked ways. I remember images of people with wild eyes holding up signs that said 'God Hates Fags' and other such awfulness. They were a despicable group of people whose notions of Christianity and God and Jesus were about as far away from the faith I was raised in as the moon is from Neptune. Well they had apparently decided that the epidemic was a sign from God that the time for protesting was over and the time for action had arrived.

They had kidnapped the entire staff of an abortion clinic as well as a bunch of men and women who had been leaving a nightclub that catered mostly to homosexuals and crucified them. I'll never forget the images they were showing on the news. There were several rows of crosses with those poor people up on them with signs hung around their necks. I've seen plenty of awful things since then but nothing quite as terrible as that sight.

The reverend who was in charge of the church had been waiting for the police at the site as brazen as you could be. He had made a statement to the officers that they read on the news that declared that they were no longer trying to get people to change their evil ways. They were claiming to be God's justice and no longer would abominations be tolerated. He was the only member of the church they found. The rest had simply vanished and that a manhunt was on.

By that evening things had started to get worse. Another video had been shown that afternoon of a large group of Changed in Florida attacking a gas station. It was taken with an actual video camera, so it was much clearer that the video from the baseball game. You could see the gaunt skin, pallor, and the sunken darkened eyes. They looked like monsters. Or demons. I think the situation might have not gotten so out of control if the images of the Changed and those poor people up on the crosses hadn't been so close together. Even so I place the blame squarely on those preachers that got interviewed that day.

Interviewing prominent religious leaders in the face of the atrocities committed in God's name made sense. The mostly secular reporters who did the interviews weren't prepared for the response. The interview I saw was done live. If it hadn't been, I wonder if they would have showed it. The pastor they talked to, I don't recall his name, but he led a huge church in Texas with 25,000 people showing up every Sunday, was quiet for a while after the reporter asked for his reaction. He sat there holding the cross that hung from his neck in his fingers and looking at it. I figured he was overwhelmed by the horror of it all but that wasn't the case. I remember it took me a few seconds to realize what he had said, it was so unexpected. He said that he agreed with the actions of that little church. The reporter was completely gob smacked by his answer and tried to stutter out a question but he just sort of waved her off. He thought for a few moments and then began to expound about God testing his chosen people and how he would punish them if they failed. He spoke of floods and exiles. He talked about how we should love what God loves and hate what God hates. After a few minutes of impromptu sermon, he said he believed there was no flu but that God was turning his eyes from the United States because of our tolerance of sin and the monsters we had seen were the result of his anger. He then removed his microphone and walked out of the interview room. The channel cut to a commercial. I felt sick to my stomach.

Over the course of that day there were several more interviews that followed a similar track. A majority of the country's most influential preachers had endorsed the murder of two dozen people. There were some dissenting voices, but they were drowned out in the noise that followed. After a while I turned the television off. I was raised Christian and I believe in the words of Jesus and it seemed to me that Jesus was getting put off to one side in favor of some older thinking. Frances and I both prayed that night for a long time before we went to bed. We hoped people would come to their senses while we slept and that the situation would not get worse. Unfortunately, our prayers weren't answered.

We left at dawn the next morning, everything we had piled in the car along with a week's worth of food and a bunch of camping gear. I told Frances about the gun as we packed the car. She said she was glad to have it just in case. We put it in the glove compartment. I had expected an argument, but I suspect after the nightmares of the previous day she was ready to concede that a gun might not be a bad thing to have.

The roads weren't terrible as we made our way out of the city and onto the highways heading west. We listened to the news as we went, and each story was worse than the last. I imagine you already know what we heard. Riots had broken out everywhere. Angry mobs had taken the word of the preachers and decided they were right. San Francisco was in flames and so was a lot of Florida. Anywhere that had a reputation for being home to gay folks had become a target. Later it would be more than just gays. The fear and violence spread to Muslims, Hindu's, and eventually to everyone else. A church full of people was burned to the ground in retaliation. Every story on the news was worse than the one before. Through it all there were also more and more reports of the Changed running amok. The president gave a speech imploring people to stop the violence and declared martial law, but it was too late. Fear, paranoia, zealotry, and simple opportunism won the day.

We drove for two days as the country descended into chaos. At night we just pulled off the road and camped. The roads had gotten worse as we went along. By the third day the going was very slow. People had fled the cities and were all trying to go somewhere safe. It still amazes me how fast it all happened. It makes me wonder how firm our foundation was to begin with.

Our third day out of New York was when we really got stuck. We were in Illinois and got caught in the crush of people leaving Chicago. The highway seemed to have reached its capacity and traffic was stopped. There was a red pickup truck in front of us. A Ford with Pennsylvania plates. We looked at that truck for hours that day. There wasn't a lot of noise in that jam. People weren't honking or screaming at each other. Whether they realized there wasn't any point, or they were simply too shell-shocked from watching the country fall apart to care how fast they moved I don't know. I do know that truck probably saved my life although I have no way of really knowing for sure.

As the sun began to fall, we had given up on getting to Missouri that day. Traffic hadn't moved at all for an hour. Frances and I had talked about potentially abandoning the car and walking the rest of the way. We decided to just hunker down in the car that night, sleep in shifts, and decide in the morning. It was full dark by then and we were arguing about who would sleep first when we started to hear the screams. I got out of the car to see what was happening.

I couldn't tell where the noise was coming from, but I did see people gathered on the side of the road looking out into the fields. I couldn't see over them, so I climbed into the bed of the truck in front of us and looked out. The area was lit by streetlamps and headlights which gave it an unhealthy yellowish glow. On either side of the highway something was moving towards us. You could see the writhing movement as it came at us in a wave through the corn. It wasn't long before the first of them stepped into the light.

We were surrounded on either side by two swarms of the Changed. There was nowhere to go. Dread settled into the pit of my stomach like I'd swallowed a bowling bowl. I remember hearing gunshots. I saw muzzle flashes lighting up like firecrackers. The screaming was everywhere now. I decided to grab Frances and Stu and make a run for it. I started to climb down from the truck bed when the world ceased to exist for me. Once second, I was climbing, the next everything had gone black.

I woke up the next day lying on my back in the bed of the truck. Everything was quiet and my head hurt like hell. I touched my forehead and felt dried blood and the gash the bullet had left. That's how I got this scar. A bullet had hit me and skipped off my skull. It was enough to knock me out, but it didn't kill me. I tried to stand and a wave of dizziness passed over me. I fell back down and threw up. I tried to get up again after the world stopped spinning and had a bit more success. I stumbled to the back of the truck and saw my car behind us. The windows were broken. I climbed out of the truck and lurched over to my car. Frances and Stu were gone. There was blood on the seats but no sign of them. The glove compartment was open, and the gun was gone.

Frantically, I began to scream her name. That was when I became aware of other people yelling around me. I couldn't tell you what they were yelling, only that none of them were Frances responding to me. I began to run around as best I could looking for her. After ten minutes I found her. She had apparently taken off running with Stu down the median of the highway. There were a number of other bodies around her. Most in similar states of distress. The Changed had caught her and all but torn her to pieces. I found no sign of Stu, not even a shred of his clothing.

My gun was lying in the grass a few feet from her body. I went over to it, picked it up, put the muzzle in my mouth and pulled the trigger. Nothing happened. It was empty. She had emptied the clip. My attempt to avoid the pain failed, I sat next to her body and cried. I cried until the tears would no longer come.

I buried her on that median using a shovel I found in the truck that had saved my life. There weren't many other people around. Most of them were wandering around as shell shocked as I was. One young man came and stood beside me after I had filled in the dirt over Frances. He put his arm around me and said, 'God Help Us'. Then he walked away. I stood over the grave for a long time.

I went back to the truck and found a rifle in the cab and a bunch of bullets. I packed those into a backpack I had purchased at the camp store along with a few changes of clothes and whatever food I could carry. Then I set off down the road to see if I could find Stu. My guess is that she gave him to someone to take and then tried to hold off the swarm along with the other people who had died on that spot. I never found a trace of him.

They walked in silence for a while. The shadows around them were getting long as they got closer to Nature Springs. Jesse wasn't sure what, if anything, he should say. He had spent most of his life closed off from people because of his own losses. He had no idea how to comfort someone else in the same situation. It had been a long time since the events Desmond had told them about, but Jesse knew that those wounds never really healed. They might scab over but if you picked at them, they would just start to bleed again.

"How come you never told me?" he asked finally.

Desmond smiled at him in the way that a father might smile at a son and said, "Don't much like talking about it Jes. Besides, you had your own pains, you didn't need to add mine to your collection."

"What did you do after that?" Julie asked.

"Well if you know your history you know how fast things went downhill then. The government collapsed. Most of the large cities began to fall. It wasn't more than a few days after that that America as a unified country ceased to be. Can't really organize the troops if the guy next to you on the firing line turns into a monster."

He paused for a moment looking into the distance at the sun getting redder in the sky.

"As for me, I followed that highway for a few days looking for any kind of trace of Stu. There were other people moving along the road as well. Some were in families, most solo. Everyone had a shell-shocked look to them. I asked anyone coming from the other way if they had seen anything, but no one had. Eventually I followed a group of people to a car factory that was off the highway. It had a big fence all around it. I holed up there for a while. The nearby town had mostly emptied out so me and a few others would go out during the day and gather supplies. The Changed would try to get in at night with little luck. The fence held and none of them seemed to have the wherewithal to climb. Places like that are where the towns began to spring up again once the struggle to survive got a little less desperate seeming."

"How did you avoid the Changed on the highway before you got to the factory?" Julie inquired.

"Car trunks. I'd climb in at night and go to sleep. In the morning I'd kick my way out through the seats. The Changed are dumb. They can't work things like latches or keys. They're not all that smart about finding someone hiding either. Their main advantage is numbers. The crush of a swarm is usually enough to take down a wall. They don't feel pain and they're pretty much made of violence. They just keep coming and coming until the sun comes back. I guess they're sorta like vampires in stories."

"Most of the Vampires I've read about seemed pretty harmless to me. Sparkly annoying teenagers." Jesse opined.

"Hah, yeah, people's ideas about Vampires Changed a few years before the Change. Before then they used to be pretty scary."

"Hard to imagine scary Vampires." Julie said with a chuckle.

"You should both read more."

They crested a small rise and saw Nature Springs on the other side. No more than a mile's walk from where they were. There was a large column of smoke coming from one of the central buildings. Julie commented that they must be burning trash. After the long walk and hearing Desmond's story they were all ready for a hot meal and a comfortable bunk.

Desmond felt good despite bringing up memories that he did his best to keep buried. He hadn't told anyone that story in a long time. He had worked hard to close off any memory of his pre-Change life. That Desmond had been weak and had failed to protect his family, in his mind. Better to just let that Desmond die and get on with life. For the first few years after the Change he shut off all feeling. He became a survivor. People knew him as being big, quiet, and quick to fight if the situation called for it. He had become a hard man. After a while that stopped working for him. His better nature won out before he completely lost himself.

When he got to Silver City, he gravitated toward the tent city. He saw that everyone else there had been through similar things and he became their caretaker. In his mind he had failed his family, but he wouldn't fail those people who found themselves in that little community. He stayed there as Silver City grew and Tent Town became a more permanent place for people to live. Life was never easy, but it could have been much worse in his estimation.

All the walking and now telling his tale had left him feeling like a young man again. He felt as if he was undergoing a cleansing process. He didn't know if Jesse would find what he was looking for but for Desmond the trip had been exactly what he needed. He felt like he was finally able to leave a heavy weight behind him and he was ready to move on. He was glad he could be here to help Jesse do the same.

"They must have a lot of garbage to burn." remarked Jesse as they got closer to the town.

"Maybe they're burning something else." Julie ventured. She had been thinking the same thing. The column of smoke seemed to be billowing up more than a normal garbage fire would.

"Seems awfully close to the center of town to be burning garbage." Desmond said after a few moments.

They started to get more nervous as they got closer to the town. There didn't seem to be any other lights other than the glow from whatever was burning. They had yet to see a town that didn't have a light over the gate but here there was nothing lit.

Their nerves turned to fear the closer they got. Eventually they broke into a sprint as full dark started to descend.

"Oh. Shit." Jesse said speaking for them all as they got to the gates.

The gates were broken open. They passed through them and saw that the fire was actually one of the buildings. Several of the other structures appeared to have already burned down. There were bodies in the streets and everywhere they looked was destruction.

Nature Springs had been overrun.

They stood there in silence looking at the chaos and destruction. Jesse had never seen a town that had been overrun before. It was worse than he ever imagined. Broken doors, broken windows, and debris filled his vision.

"What do we do now?" Jesse asked.

""I....I don't know." Julie responded quietly.

Julie had stopped here on her way out to find Jesse. It had been a small and tight-knit community. They hadn't been happy to have a visitor but they fed her well and sent news with her to pass to other towns. Now they were all gone.

As they watched the fire slowly burn itself out in the center of town the sun slipped down behind the mountains and darkness descended on them.

The quiet of the town was shattered when a low moan drifted to them on the wind. Followed by another. And another. The town was dead, the gates were broken, and the Changed were waking up.

CHAPTER TWELVE

Sidney Lydon was in a terrible mood. They had lost a whole day of traveling because Jesse and his friends had not stayed the night in Clearwater. It was only a few hours from evening, and he had no idea where to go next.

He had arrived in Clearwater the previous evening with fifteen other men from the Church of the Risen. As they had the previous night they spread out and asked the locals about Jesse. Unlike the previous night no one seemed to have any idea who they were talking about. Eventually they gave up asking. Brother MacGowan had suggested that they ask at the local farms within a five or six mile radius and even though he knew it was a good idea it made him angry. He did not want to be out here searching for the blasphemer. He believed his place was in Silver City helping Father Jordan running the day to day business of the church. He didn't like the outdoors, never had growing up. That was why he left his family's farm and went to Silver City. Father Jordan had sent him because it was essential and important work but nonetheless the long days on the road made him more grumpy than usual.

He had accepted Brother MacGowan's plan to question people at local farms and divided his men up into three teams to cover more ground. They would leave early in the morning and then return to Clearwater late in the afternoon. He spent the rest of the evening proselytizing to the locals and then turned in. He had hoped more of the men would join him in spreading the word, but it was only MacGowan that came along. It didn't surprise him. The men that Father Jordan had sent with him seemed to have been picked more for their physical prowess than their faith.

Now it was nearing evening and he hoped the other groups had had better luck. Everyone he had talked to looked blankly at him when he asked about the companions. The farm they were coming up to now was the last on his list. It was owned by a man named Jack Hart according to people in Clearwater. As they were walking toward the farm he was reflecting on how if they had to do this again, he was going to bring Brother MacGowan with him on his team. The three men that he had taken weren't much for conversation or thinking at all. They were hulking specimens who looked mere moments from breaking into violence at their most peaceful. After an increasingly unsuccessful day wandering the countryside they looked positively menacing. He thought briefly about having them wait a ways back from the gate so as to not frighten the local but thought better of it. The people out here seemed to be made of a sturdy stock and wouldn't be easily intimidated.

They arrived at the farm and he rang the bell that hung by the door. He waited a while and then rang it again. Eventually he heard someone calling out for him to 'hold his horses' from the other side of the gate. After a few more moments the hatch opened up. An older man looked out at him with obvious agitation.

"Who the hell are you?" he demanded.

"Hello, I'm sorry to trouble you, my name is Brother Lydon of the Church of the Risen..."

The man snorted at that. The absolute contempt in the snort surprised Brother Lydon and caused him to falter for a moment. The man took the opportunity to interject.

"I ain't buying anything you're selling. I got no interest in your silly club and your jumped-up lunatic boss."

He had more to say but Brother Lydon cut him off. He felt his fury rising at this man's impudence and derision.

"Sir, I'll ask you to speak respectfully of Father Jordan who has been restored. And while I wish I had time to help you understand the good works done by the church, unfortunately we have to be on our way soon. We are only here to ask if you have had visitors recently, specifically a young man named Jesse Chapin. He would be traveling with two companions."

"The hell do you want with Jesse?"

Brother Lydon smiled when the man asked this.

"We simply need to know if he told you where they would be heading after they left here?"

"What for?"

"The Church has business with him."

"Yeah, I'll bet you do. From the looks of your friends I can't imagine its good business. Tell you what. How about you and your Father Jordan go fuck yourselves."

"How dare you?" Lydon nearly shrieked. His companions began to advance on the door.

He was trying to compose himself when he heard a voice call out from behind him.

"What's going on Dad?"

The man in the door's eyes went wide and Lydon spun around to see two women coming towards the gate down the same path they had. One was about the same age as the man and the other was much younger. They were carrying several bags with them. The younger had a rifle slung over her shoulder. Lydon guessed they were the man's wife and daughter. He turned back to the man in the door and said in a voice loud enough for his companions to hear, "Get them."

"Lily, Rosemary, RUN!" Jack shouted and started to open the gate.

Lydon's companions reacted instantly to the order. They bolted towards the two women. Rosemary looked wide eyed at the advancing men and couldn't react to what was happening. Lily dropped the bags she was holding and shrugged the rifle off her shoulder. She brought it up and aimed at the advancing men but neither of them stopped. She aimed at the ground in front of them and pulled the trigger. Nothing happened. She looked at the gun and realized the safety on. She flicked it off and brought the rifle to bear again only to have it knocked out of her hands with a vicious slap from one of the men. The man then backhanded her across the jaw and stars exploded in front of her eyes. The other man grabbed Rosemary by her wrists, bending her arms behind her. The third man pulled a pistol from a shoulder holster and trained it on them.

Jack grabbed the shotgun he kept by the door as the gate opened and he slipped outside pointing the gun directly at Lydon. Lydon was just standing there smiling serenely at the scene.

"You let them go, you son of a bitch, or you're going to be breathing out of your chest."

"Now, now, now, Mr. Hart, let's not let things get out of hand here."

"What do you people want?" Rosemary said, nearly growling.

"All we want ma'am, and please forgive us the unpleasantness, is to know where Jesse Chapin went when he left your farm. Your husband decided to insult me rather than answer a simple question and look where that has gotten us."

Lydon found that he was rather enjoying this. He didn't believe that Hart would shoot him, not as long as he had his wife and daughter covered. He didn't relish violence, but he did love being in control. Prior to joining the church, he had rarely had any control over his life. Now the church had given him power and he would certainly not let either the church or Father Jordan down. Not even if it cost these heathen farmers their lives. For the first time it occurred to him that he was perfectly willing to kill people, or have others kill people, for the church. He pictured himself with wings and a flaming sword briefly and his smile grew.

"Jeh.....Jesse?" stammered Lily, blood dripping from her mouth and nose.

"Yes, young lady. Jesse Chapin. He is a liar and a blasphemer. He is skilled at tricking people into believing his words but make no mistake his tongue is a tool of the devil. We are seeking him to bring him back before Father Jordan so that we might save his soul and perhaps save the world in the process."

"You're insane!" cried Rosemary.

"Ma'am please understand that we do the Lord's work. Father Jordan is the vessel that Jesus speaks to the world through and I am the implement that Father Jordan has decided to use to remove a great evil from the world. I will not fail in this task. Though violence is a last resort we are not afraid to do the Lord's bidding."

"Smallville. They went on to Smallville. Now let them go."

"There, was that so difficult? Gentlemen, let the ladies go."

The men let them go. The one who had been holding Lily stayed between her and the rifle. The one holding the pistol kept it on them as they walked over to Jack.

"Get your mother inside, Lily."

She did so. Jack kept his gun on Lydon.

"Please understand Mr. Hart that if you are not telling the truth we will be back. I will not fail in my mission because some nothing farmer allowed himself to be sweet talked by a child's lies."

"I see you anywhere near my farm again and I won't hesitate to shoot you and everyone you're with. You and your Father Jordan are parasites who haven't learned the lessons of the Change. I hope you don't get back to Clearwater before dark, you pathetic son of a bitch." He backed through the gate keeping his shotgun level with Lydon's head.

Lydon smiled at him the whole time, using it to hold the fury that was rising in him in check. He stood staring at the gate for a long time. His companions waited patiently for him to give them an order. They knew their place and they knew their jobs. He believed that Hart was telling the truth about Smallville. It made sense and confirmed the westerly path they were taking.

As they walked back to Clearwater, he reflected on what had happened. He had never considered himself a violent man. When he had been mugged or beaten prior to joining the church he had never fought back, usually crawling into the fetal position in order to minimize the pain. Though he hadn't actually done the violence at the farm he knew with cold certainty that had Hart refused to answer him again he would have ordered the execution of one or both of the women until he answered. Control, he thought. Violence and control. He ruminated on those concepts all the way back to Clearwater.

Later that evening, as Lydon lay in his bed a troubling thought crossed his mind. Those people, the Hart's, couldn't have known Jesse for more than an evening. No more than shelter for the night and possibly a meal. Why had they been so ready to defend him? He knew this Dylan

Droge was the ultimate target but he wondered if Jesse might not be just as dangerous. With those thoughts he drifted off to a very troubled sleep.

CHAPTER THIRTEEN

The sound of moaning filled the air. It washed over them like the sound of a nightmarish orchestra playing in some long dead music hall. The town was small compared to others they had stayed in. It was little more than seven buildings surrounded by a large wooden wall. Only five of the buildings remained. The gate they had used seemed to be the only way through the ten-foot-high wall.

They stood there stunned with the shock of their discovery. Julie could barely wrap her mind around the town simply being gone. She had heard of towns and farms being overrun but had never seen the damage firsthand. It looked like a hurricane had rolled through. Windows were smashed, doors were ripped from their hinges, debris was strewn in the streets. She tried to picture it as it was when she came through before and couldn't. The destruction was too complete. It had erased her few memories of the town and surely as it had erased the town itself. The moaning seemed to be getting louder.

"If they broke in, then there must be a sizable swarm out there." Desmond said, breaking their silence.

"Well, we can't just stand around here waiting to greet them, we've got to get out of here." Jesse responded.

"And go where? The next town is a day's walk from here." Julie retorted.

"Would you rather stay here and die?" Jesse nearly shouted back. He could feel the hair on the back of his neck rise and his arms were breaking out in goosebumps despite the warm night. He was terrified and that fear was threatening to overwhelm him. He kept flashing back to that night on their farm growing up when Dylan had saved them. He wondered if

Dylan was out there tonight waiting to swoop in again.

A crash to their left snapped them out of their stupor. Something had come stumbling out of one of the buildings that was still standing. The structure looked like some sort of bar to Jesse. As the thing stumbled out into the light given off by the still smoldering building, they saw that it was a Changed.

Desmond was the first of them to move. A broken door was lying on the ground next to the building opposite the one where the Changed had exited. He rushed over to it and picked it up. He smashed it back down to the ground splintering it. He grabbed one of the longer pieces of shattered wood and charged the Changed. The thing had taken notice of them and began advancing on Julie who was the closest. Desmond ran past her and slammed into it leading with the board. They toppled over in a heap with Desmond landing on top. The wooden board he had stabbed it with was sticking out of its chest as he straddled the monster, pinning its arms to the ground with his knees. He pulled the board out with both hands, raised it over his head, and brought it down with a yell into the creature's face. The board went clear through its mouth and pinned it to the ground. It stopped struggling, let out one more gurgled moan and then was still.

Desmond stood up and wiped his hands on his pants, "Well, that's one down."

"We shouldn't kill them." Julie said, her eyes never leaving the dead Changed.

"Doesn't look like we have much of a choice, little lady." Desmond responded matter-of-factly.

Julie glared at him, "They used to be people and as far as you know, they might be once again." She shook her head and sighed. "You're right though, if we want to get out of this then we're probably going to have to fight our way out. May God forgive us."

"We can debate morality later, those moans are getting louder. Des, help me see if we can get the gate closed or at least barricaded." Jesse yelled. He could feel panic threatening to overwhelm him.

"Good idea. I'll see if there are any guns lying around." Julie said and darted toward the building with the missing door.

"Be careful! There could be more in those buildings!" Desmond called out after her before going over to help Jesse.

The gate had been on a track and normally would have slid into place. It was currently lying flat on the ground. There was a large beam that dropped into place to reinforce it. The hinges that held the beam had snapped off completely and the beam was fractured in the middle.

Jesse and Desmond were able to get the gate upright with a herculean effort. They couldn't quite lift it up enough to get it back on the track. Jesse called out for Julie to come help them and got no response.

"Shit." he said. "Let's at least slide it over some so it's blocking the entrance. It won't stop anything, but it might slow them down. With another huge effort they were able to slide it over in front of the opening. Jesse started to run towards the house Julie had entered. Before he got five feet, there was a blast and a Changed came flying out of the second story window backwards, followed by the remaining shards of glass. Julie stuck her head out of the window and looked down at them.

"I found some guns!" she shouted.

"That's great! Come help us with the gate." Jesse called up.

She ducked her head back in the window and after a moment came back out the door on the first floor. She was carrying two shotguns and what looked like three belts with holsters. Once she reached the gate, she put them down carefully and helped them with the gate. Together the three of them were able to get it back on its track, slamming it into place with a loud thud. It will hold for a little while, Desmond thought, but not if there was a full swarm. Since the hinges and the beam were broken, they took the two halves and braced them against the gate. After they finished getting the beams in place, they heard a muffled thud on the other side of the gate followed by a loud moan.

"That's not going to hold very long." Jesse said out loud but mostly to himself.

"Let's see what else we can brace it with," Julie said. She then bent over and picked up the gun belts. She handed one to both Desmond and Jesse before strapping the last one on herself. She grabbed the shotguns and tossed one to Desmond, "I only saw two of these," and handed him an extra box of shells.

"Not a lot of bullets if it's a swarm." He said looking at the box of shells doubtfully.

"If it's a swarm we're going to have to try and outrun it or find a better place to hold up until dawn. One of these buildings must have a cellar or something."

"No way am I spending the night in a cellar trying to hold off a swarm. I'd rather take my chances running." Jesse said, sounding shaken.

"First things first, let's get more stuff to brace the gate. Maybe there's a tractor or something around." Desmond said while loading the shotgun, "Let's stick together."

Jesse took the pistol Julie handed him and looked at it doubtfully. He had never fired a gun in his life and couldn't imagine he would be able to hit the broadside of a barn. He looked in the chamber and saw that it was loaded with six bullets. He fervently hoped he wouldn't have to fire any of them.

They moved together through the town. The moaning was loud, but it seemed to be entirely outside the walls. They all hoped it would take a while before the monsters piled onto the gate. The Changed had the advantage of numbers but they weren't smart and that was what they were counting on it order to stay alive. Jesse shivered and thought that the town's previous residents had probably counted on the same thing.

They circled around the perimeter of the town square hoping to find a cart or a tractor. As they went past one of the intact buildings, they heard banging coming from a closed door. It was slow and rhythmic. The sound something mindless might make trying to get out. Julie waived Desmond over to the door, "I'll open, you shoot" she said. He nodded in assent and backed up a few steps noting that the door would swing outward. He raised the shotgun as she grabbed the door handle. He took a deep breath and she nodded at him. She turned the handle and yanked the door open while simultaneously diving to one side to avoid the shotgun blast. There wasn't just one Changed behind the door but two. At point black range Desmond's shotgun blast ripped them both in half sending body parts flying backwards into the house.

Desmond ducked his head into the house and immediately leapt backwards with a yelp. A third Changed emerged from a side room. It swiped at Desmond and opened a jagged cut on his cheek. He stumbled backwards and landed on his backside, dropping the shotgun as he landed. The Changed stumbled out of the house towards him before a loud crack sounded and it crumpled to the ground.

Desmond turned and saw that Jesse had fired his pistol. He put it back in the holster and was shaking his hand in pain.

"Jesus, that hurts!" he yelped.

"Never fired a gun before, Jes?" Desmond asked.

Jesse shook his head and shrugged, "I'm not really the gun type."

Julie had moved into the house, shotgun trained on the Changed Jesse had shot, ready to finish the job. It didn't move at all, "Nice shot" she said from inside before progressing further in. It was a small two-story house with a kitchen, living room, and pantry on the first floor. She reconnoitered the first floor in a matter of moments. She noticed a rug covering the middle of the kitchen floor and swept it aside. There was a trap door underneath. She yelled for them to come inside.

They joined her and looked at the door for a few moments. Desmond finally pulled it open while Julie aimed her shotgun down. It was pitch black. Jesse shivered knowing what the other two were thinking. He did not relish the idea of holding up in a basement while Changed ran wild over their heads.

Desmond rummaged around the kitchen for a few moments before coming up with a wind-up flashlight. He shone it into the basement and they saw that it was a typical root cellar. There was no one down there and more importantly no Changed.

"There's enough room for all three of us. It wouldn't be easy to defend, but as a last resort we can give it a shot." Desmond remarked.

"If we slip down there now, they may not find us." Julie said in a tone that suggested she wasn't convinced.

"You might be right but I'm not willing to chance it. We only have a few bullets and I think we can agree that this is a full-fledged swarm bearing down on us. Besides, if it's so safe, why didn't the residents hide down there?" said Desmond.

"That's a good point. I haven't seen any bodies." Jesse interjected.

"Not yet."

They closed the trap door but didn't replace the rug. Jesse had a bad feeling that they would be back.

CHAPTER FOURTEEN

The moaning outside the walls was getting louder. It was no longer possible to discern the direction it was coming from. It blanketed the town in its awful drone.

Jesse and Desmond proceeded slowly past the houses looking for something to brace the gate with. Julie brought up the rear keeping an eye on their flank. They circled the entire town and found nothing large enough or heavy enough to be of any use until they got to a shed behind the last house.

The doors had a latch but was not locked. Carefully, Jesse opened it from one side while Desmond brought his shotgun up. It was empty except for several large barrels. Desmond lowered the shotgun and looked closer at the barrels. They had one word written on them: 'Petrol'.

"Anything in there we can use?" Jesse asked.

"These barrels are marked 'petrol'. Gas."

"Gas? what would they need gas for? Heck, where would they have gotten it?"

"No idea on either front but we may be able to use them."

"How? They heavy enough to use to barricade the door?"

"Nope, but..." Desmond started to respond but Julie cut him off.

"We could blow them up." she said.

"That's not a bad idea." Desmond conceded, "If we got them over by the gate and blew them, it would take out half the swarm."

"What about the other half?" Jesse asked.

"Worth a try as a last resort. Help me move them over by the gate. How good a shot are you, Julie?"

"Good enough to hit one of those from a ways away."

Jesse and Desmond moved the barrels over by the gate. There were three in all. The gate creaked under the strain put on it by the Changed trying to force their way in. Once the barrels were in place Desmond and Jesse went back to the town square where Julie was standing.

"We should keep searching the buildings, there might be something useful yet. Julie, stay here and keep an eye on the gate. If they come through, yell for us."

She nodded and handed Jesse her shotgun. He took it but felt uncomfortable with it. He didn't like guns and certainly didn't want to carry two of them. He didn't relish the idea of killing the Changed either. He couldn't put his finger on why, but it made him uneasy. He imagined it was because he knew they had once been human beings. He understood the necessity of it in their current situation and saw that Julie did too. Desmond didn't seem to have any problems with killing them. Jesse guessed he wouldn't hesitate either if he had seen his wife ripped to pieces by them.

Desmond and Jesse entered the house next to the one with the trap door. It was in shambles like the rest of them. Furniture had been overturned, glassware broken, holes had been punched in the walls. It looked to Jesse, as if a tornado had run through it. In a sense, he thought, that was exactly what happened. Something about it bothered him although he couldn't put his finger on why. They poked around some more but didn't find anything of use and moved on.

The next building wasn't a house. It was the largest of the remaining buildings. Desmond guessed it was the de-facto town hall. They entered through a large room with chairs and tables scattered around and overturned. A podium was on one side with a hole punched through it. It was just as chaotic as the other houses had been. A door on the far side of the room stood ajar. They went through it, Desmond in the lead.

The door led to a long hallway with two doors on either side. The end of the hall ended in a third door that was also ajar. It led outside. They paused to listen for a few moments but all they heard was the drone of the moans filtering in from outside. They heard no sounds that they could place as coming from inside the building.

They reached the first door on the right-hand side of the hall and Desmond motioned for Jesse to stand to one side and open it. Jesse did so as Desmond raised his shotgun ready to fire. Nothing moved inside the room. Desmond stepped inside turning the shotgun from one side to the other as he did. The room appeared to be an office and aside from windows which had been broken inwards it looked untouched. There was a large desk in the middle with several chairs arrayed around it. One wall was dominated by bookshelves and the other filing cabinets. There was a glass case that was standing open next to the filing cabinets. Desmond went over to look and turned to Jesse.

"This was a gun case. Empty now though. Key is still in the lock. Looks like someone cleared it out in a hurry."

"You notice anything weird about all this?" Jesse responded.

"How do you mean?"

"Not sure. Can't put my finger on it."

"Well if it comes to you, don't keep it a secret. Come on, let's keep looking."

They proceeded down the hall in the same fashion with the other doors. Behind one was a storage closet. They found nothing of real use as it looked like mostly municipal supplies. Another door led them to a smaller meeting room. Like the office and the closet before it, it was completely untouched. Behind the last door they checked was a set of stairs leading downward. Neither Jesse nor Desmond relished the idea of going down into the dark basement.

"I don't really need to know what's down there. Do you?" Jesse said hopefully.

Desmond was about to respond when they heard something move in the dark. Desmond pulled out a flashlight he had picked up in the closet and shone it down in the basement. "Anyone down there?" He called. There was no response. He sighed deeply.

"We should check it out. This may be a better place to hole up than that root cellar if it comes down to it."

"Not if there's already Changed down there." Jesse replied fearfully.

"Only one way to find out."

They sighed deeply and then began to descend the stairs.

Julie stared at the gate and barely took notice of the drop of sweat that slid off her forehead and down her cheek. She had spent a lot of time on the wrong side of the gates in her life. Growing up she would always be the last of her siblings to return to the farm at night, worrying her mother terribly. She loved the huge empty world that they lived in. There were so many places to discover and new treasures to bring home to her family. She would never forget the look on her father's face when she brought home a huge box of records she found in the trunk of an abandoned car or the night her whole family spent singing along as they played them on the turntable she had found earlier. It was the single happiest memory of her childhood.

She had never been afraid of the outside world. She had also never been afraid of the Changed. They were too slow and to brittle to scare her. There had been occasions where she slipped out past the gate at night and ran through the darkness. On some such occasions she had come upon a Changed or two and was always able to outrun them. When she got older and met Dylan, she began to fear them even less. She had never seen a swarm before.

Tonight, when faced with the swarm waiting outside the flimsy gate, she was afraid. They were trapped in the town with no way out. The moaning had taken on a steady ear-shattering pitch. She was no longer able to estimate how many were outside surrounding them but she imagined it was in the hundreds, or perhaps thousands. It was only a matter of time before the gate gave way again as it had before. Once the gate broke the Changed would sweep through like waves crashing on a beach. They would not be able to fight them. The numbers would simply be too overwhelming. Blowing up the gas barrels would take care of the first wave or two, but it wouldn't be enough. Their only chance she thought was the root cellar and that was a slim chance at best.

She thought about Jesse and Desmond. Her regard for both was increasing. When she first met them, she thought Desmond was ok, but that Jesse was a waste. He looked to have given up and she couldn't abide that kind of weakness. She had doubted if he would make it through the arduous journey ahead of them. He seemed to have taken to the road, however. She had noticed that every day he looked a little less miserable and a little more engaged with the world around him. She knew he had had it rough losing his family at a young age, but things were rough in this world. You had to move on and get busy living she thought. She had started to hope that he might actually be the person Dylan thought he was. Now she wasn't sure if they would live through the night.

The gate creaked ominously as she watched, sweat dripping out of her every pore.

CHAPTER FIFTEEN

They descended into the basement, the small flashlight their only light. The stairs didn't creak on their way down, much to Jesse's surprise. The basement was silent and cold. The clammy air made Jesse's arms erupt in goose bumps. He hadn't realized how warm and sweaty he was until they got to the bottom of the stairs.

Desmond moved a little of the way in. It looked like the basement was a large storage area stretching under most of the building. The small flashlight wasn't bright enough to pierce the farthest depths.

Jesse stepped off the bottom step and onto the floor and found no purchase for his foot. He slipped in something and came crashing down the rest of the way. He landed hard on his shoulder sending a flash of pain down his arm. The shotgun he had been carrying flew from his grip and skittered across the floor into the darkness. He swore loudly. Desmond was immediately by his side helping him up.

"What happened?" Desmond asked failing to mask the fear in his voice.

"Slipped on something, the floor is wet."

As feeling returned to arm he noticed it felt wet too. He asked Desmond to shine the light on his arm. He did so. It was hard to tell in the yellow light, but it looked like he had slipped in, "Blood." Jesse said.

Both men stood stock still listening as intently as they could for any sound. After what seemed like an eternity Desmond forced himself to start moving again.

"Let's see if we can find a light switch. This place might be on generator."

Jesse forced himself to start moving again. He took every step very carefully not wanting to slip again. They looked around in the meager light afforded them by Desmond's flashlight but found no evidence of a light switch.

"Must be at the top of the stairs and we just didn't notice it." Jesse said looking longingly at the faint sliver of light near the top of the stairs where they had left the door open. "I could go check." he offered.

"Ok."

They hadn't strayed too far from the stairs and went back over to them together. Jesse sprinted up the stairs and found a switch outside in the hall. Desmond remained at the bottom of the stairs. Jesse flipped it but nothing happened. He flipped it up and down several more times with similar effect.

"Where would the generator be?"

Before Desmond could answer the door, which had opened outward, slammed into Jesse knocking him away from the cellar entrance and onto the ground, closing on his ankle painfully. He looked up and saw a Changed standing over him. It had come in the open door at the end of the hall. Jesse's blood ran cold, and he began to struggle to get the pistol he was carrying out of the holster. He tried to get his ankle out from between the door and the wall, but the monster was leaning on the door as it came closer. Jesse fumbled with the strap that held the pistol in place. His fingers were slick with sweat and he couldn't grip the strap.

The Changed advanced slowly and began to moan.

It was nearly past the door and on top of Jesse when the door crashed into it sending it flying into the opposite wall. Desmond had come barreling out of the basement and had shouldered the door into The Changed. It stumbled and fell sliding down the wall. Desmond pressed the barrels of the shotgun into the monster's head and pulled the trigger. The report in the small hallway nearly deafened them.

Julie flinched at the sound of the shotgun being fired. She turned away from the gate and surveyed the town. The gunshot sounded like it came from the general direction of the town hall. An image of the town being overrun by Changed passed through her mind and she shivered. When she had been in the town last it had been a quiet place. The people had been nice, if not overly so. The population was made up of mostly younger families. People who had grown up in the Changed world like she had. She had also noticed a few older folks. She guessed the settlement had been founded by a few large families that had been close. There were a lot of settlements like that around. People who didn't want to go to one of the bigger towns or Silver City. Dylan had once referred to it as the old-time pioneer spirit. He had also used the phrase 'manifest destiny' which she liked but wasn't totally sure what it meant. She had wanted to look it up but hadn't gotten around to it. She sighed deeply and wondered if she would ever see her home again. As if in answer, her attention was snapped back to the gate by a loud crack.

A large fissure had appeared in the gate. Time was running out. The gate wasn't going to hold much longer. She turned to see if she could spot Jesse and Desmond to warn them and was relieved to see two people walking towards her from the direction of the town hall. Her relief was short lived. Before she could call out to them one of them tripped and got back up jerkily. Her blood ran cold when she realized that the two figures were not her companions.

Shooting guns had been a hobby for her. She enjoyed the challenge of hitting targets and had to admit to herself she liked the feeling of power, however imagined, that guns gave her. Watching the two Changed advance on her, she realized just how false that feeling of power was. Fumbling with the holster, she removed the pistol. Checking the barrel, she saw what she had seen the dozen or so times she checked it - Six bullets. She knew she needed to save at least one for the cannister. More if she could help it. In order to save ammunition, she would have to get close.

She swallowed and began to advance on them at the same pace they were coming towards her. Despite her fear she had steel in her. She would not let her feet conqueror her and keep her from doing what needed to be done. In her mind, this streak was why Dylan had chosen her to go and find Jesse. He knew that she would not back down from anything, and she would never be overwhelmed by the challenges.

Once the distance between her and the Changed had closed, she dropped to one knee and aimed her pistol at the head of the Changed closest to her. She had decided to fire from one knee in case the kick from the gun sent her flying. Once the first Changed got into a comfortable range, she fired, aiming for the head. A gun of this caliber should take the head clean off. She missed. The Changed kept advancing and had not so much as flinched. She waited until it was roughly four feet from her before she fired again. This time its head disintegrated as the bullet crashed into its face and then weakly out the back. She waited for the approach of the second Changed before firing again. This time it only took one shot.

The bodies had barely stopped moving when she heard another large crack behind her. She spun and saw a large chunk of the gate break off and a Changed was getting through. More were filling into the space that had been created.

"Shit."

After a quick prayer Julie was ready. She emptied all of her remaining bullets at the closest gas canister.

They doubled back to the storage closet and found a crank lantern in one corner. Thanking God that it still worked, they lit it and went back down into the basement. With the brighter light, they saw that there it was indeed blood at the bottom of the stairs. It led away in a trail that ended at a door on the far side of the room.

They stared at the door for what seemed like an eternity, not really wanting to open it. Jesse finally moved to pick up the shotgun he had dropped. He opened it the way Desmond had showed him earlier in order to make sure it was loaded. He closed it again with a loud clack.

"I think I figured out what was bothering me about the town."

"What's that?"

"There's no bodies."

They let that sink in for a moment.

"You're right. The Changed certainly don't drag people away."

"Maybe they escaped?" Jesse said with more hope in his voice than he thought he still had left.

"Or Changed." Desmond replied grimly.

"Yeah, or Changed."

"Or..." he sighed resignedly, "They're behind that door."

"Safe to say someone is behind that door or least went there to die."

"One way to..."

He stopped abruptly the sound of three explosions in very quick succession rocked the room, showering them in dust and plaster from the ceiling.

"Oh shit." Desmond said and was instantly moving. He flew up the stairs taking them two at a time. Jesse was right behind him. At the top of the steps, Desmond turned and tore down the hallway to the door they had come in. Jesse caught his foot on the top step and crashed into the wall, landing on the corpse of the Changed, dropping his shotgun again. It hit the ground and fired once. The shell ripped a hole in the wall and launched the gun backwards directly into Jesse's stomach knocking the wind out of him. Desperately, he scrambled to his feet and off the corpse. Desmond stopped and turned when he heard the gunshot. Jesse waved him off.

Desmond crashed through the front door and out into the street. The scene was one of pure Chaos. The gate was gone as was a large portion of the wall that surrounded it. The wall around it that was still standing had caught fire and was burning with a devilish fury. Several of the buildings nearest the gate had also caught fire as they had been showered with smoldering chunks of debris. The rubble at the heart of the explosion was on fire, and to Desmond's horror was crawling with Changed. They were pouring into the town through the blaze, oblivious to being ignited themselves. There were a number of dead Changed in front of the destruction. They hadn't made it far in before the fire had killed them. In the middle of the town square laid Julie, sprawled on her back and not moving.

He ran to her side and checked her pulse. She was still alive. He thanked God and scooped her up into his arms. Behind him Jesse came running out of the town hall. Jesse surveyed the scene and screamed at Desmond, "Des, look out!" and started running again. Holding Julie, Desmond turned and saw a Changed was nearly on top of him. It had come out of one of the buildings they hadn't searched yet. He took a step back and stumbled, falling painfully on his backside, made even more painful by the weight of the unconscious Julie in his arms. The hard charging Jesse reached the monster before it got to Desmond and Julie. He fired the other barrel of the shotgun and nothing happened. A dud round. Not wasting any time, he swung the gun like a club and connected solidly with the Changed's head. It went down backwards. Jesse raised the gun over his head and brought it down again. Its head cracked like an ancient cantaloupe.

Desmond got back to his feet. The Changed were still pouring in and slowly putting the fire in the rubble out with the sheer crush of bodies. There wasn't much time before they would be entering the town without obstruction.

"Looks like we're out of options. We need to get to that root cellar." Desmond shouted over the sound of the fire and the moaning of the Changed.

"That's not an option anymore, look!" Jesse shouted back pointing to the house with the cellar. It had caught fire in the explosion and was starting to burn furiously.

"Shit. We're going to have to go to the town hall basement and try to hold out till morning."

They ran with the same thought in mind, "What's behind that door?"

CHAPTER SIXTEEN

Julie came to as they crashed into the town hall. Desmond laid her down on the floor and ran to close the back door. Jesse began pushing tables and chairs up against the front door. She stood up, shaking her head trying to clear out the cobwebs and remember what had happened. She looked blearily at Jesse and had trouble focusing.

"James?"

Jesse stopped pushing the table he was pushing and looked over at her.

"You really must have hit your head. Are you ok?"

She looked at him blankly for a moment and then shook her head again. It took a moment, but she remembered what had happened; the force of the explosion flinging her like a ragdoll across the town square.

"I'm ok, Jesse, just a little dizzy."

"Try to get undizzy, we're about to have a lot of company."

Desmond appeared behind them and saw Julie standing. He breathed a sigh of relief.

"Glad you're ok. Lend me a hand?"

She followed him back down the hall and into one of the offices. He waved her over and together they pushed a bookshelf out into the hall and in front of the back door. They went back and moved another one in front of the door. After they were done, they both looked at it doubtfully.

"This won't hold them for more than a few seconds." Julie said.

"Well, that's a few more seconds we get to live. We're not going to be able to barricade the basement door."

"There's a basement?"

"Yeah, a big one that has at least one room off it. Something bad happened down there but I don't know what. That's where we're going to make our stand unless you have a better idea."

She cast her eyes on the bookshelves blocking the back door again and shrugged. She had no better ideas. Together, they went back to the front room and helped Jesse pile tables and chairs in front of the door. Through the windows, Julie watched the Changed wash into town without catching fire. They didn't have much time.

"We should get down there and see what we can do to fortify it."

They quickly ransacked the offices and the storage closet, finding another lantern. When they heard the first scratches on the front door, they headed down to the basement. Jesse went down last and pulled the door closed behind him. As he locked it, he wondered if he would ever leave the basement again.

The door opened outward so there wasn't much they could do to blockade it. There wasn't much to use even if they could. A few folding tables and chairs. One corner held a large number of boxes. There were no windows.

"We need to see where that door goes." Desmond declared. "It may be our only hope."

"Well, let's do it." Jesse responded.

The door opened inward. Jesse checked the handle, unlocked. He kicked the door open, ducking down as he did so. Desmond stood behind him aiming a shotgun into the room. Julie held the lantern behind him.

The scene in the room was something out of a nightmare. Blood and viscera covered every wall with gore. Dozens of corpses lay in neat rows throughout the room. It looked like the bodies of every man, woman, and child that lived in the town were in there.

"Oh, God." whispered Desmond.

Jesse turned and sprinted to another corner of the basement and threw up. Julie stared at the horror before her.

"Those look like gunshot wounds." She said flatly.

Desmond moved forward into the room. It was half the size of the main basement and had no windows. The bodies were lined up neatly on one side of the room except for two. One was lying to the left of the door at the end of the trail of blood. It was lying half on the body of an older man who was leaning on the opposite wall as the rest of the corpses. It looked like he had died facing them. He still had the gun he had used to shoot himself in his hand. Desmond noticed he was wearing the white collar of a minister. On the eastern wall of the room, away from the corpses, were stacks and stacks of wooden crates. They covered the entire wall of the rectangular room.

"They killed themselves, didn't they?"

Desmond jumped at the sound of her voice. He hadn't heard her come into the room behind him. He turned and met her eyes. They looked at each other for a moment, each trying to steel the other to the tragedy before them. He realized just how strong a person she was in that fleeting moment. He knew she would not falter in the face of what lay ahead. He wondered if he could say the same about himself.

"Looks like."

"Why would they do that?"

"I don't know. I guess they gave up hope when they got swarmed."

"That doesn't make any sense." Jesse said in response. He had thrown up everything he had in his stomach and followed them into the room.

"Why not?" Julie asked.

"Look around. The basement is basically untouched. The whole building doesn't look like it ever had a Changed in it. If they had done this out of desperation or fear of getting overwhelmed, why do it before they're even in the building?"

Desmond nodded and looked around. Jesse was right. There was no sign of struggle or fighting in this room or in the rest of the building. Some of the houses looked like there had been some fighting in them but he was no forensics expert and could be mistaken. He noticed the corpse that looked like a minister had a book next to him. He bent down to pick it up. It was a bible.

"They seemed like normal people when I was here before. A bit standoffish maybe but nothing out of the ordinary."

Desmond watch as Jesse went over to the corpse of a young girl. She couldn't have been more than seven. The same age he was when he lost his family. It was clear that her father had shot her before killing himself. Jesse closed her eyes. Desmond noticed she was wearing a cross. Looking around he noticed they were all wearing similar crosses. He pointed that out to the others.

"Must have been some sort of church." Desmond said after a few moments.

"More like a cult" Julie bitterly shot back.

"Same thing." Desmond responded surprised at Julie's tone.

"No, it goddamn isn't."

"Whoa, ok, ok, I wasn't trying to pick a fight. It's not something I'm an expert on."

"It's ok, sorry, I overreacted but there is a huge difference."

"Could we debate this elsewhere? I don't think I want to be in here anymore." Jesse said as he stood up and turned away from the body of the young girl.

They heard a crash from above.

"I don't think we have much choice." Desmond said as he dropped the bible. A small piece of paper fell out. He knelt down to pick it up and saw it was a handwritten note. He stuffed it in his pocket.

Jesse could feel panic seeping in from the edges of his consciousness. He asked Desmond what he meant. Desmond was moving towards the wall with the crates when he answered.

"We can't defend the main basement. Once they break through the door up there, we've got nowhere to go. No, this room is where we make our stand. Help me with these crates. We need to get them in front of the door. The wall looks like its concrete so it should hold."

Panic settled over Jesse like a new snow covering a field. The idea of trying to wait out the night in a room full of people who had killed themselves, presumably in the face of the same horror they now faced was too much. He dropped his shotgun and bolted from the room.

"Shit."

"I'll get him." Julie said and took off after Jesse. She found him huddled in the far corner of the basement. His knees were drawn up to his face and he was weeping when she knelt beside him.

"Jesse." she said softly.

He didn't acknowledge her.

"What the hell is wrong with people? Whyd they do that?"

"I don't know. But I know that I'm not ready to give up like they did, and I don't think you are either."

"That kid was maybe seven years old. That's all she gets, seven years. Probably didn't even understand what was happening. " He paused for a moment. "I was seven when I lost my mom and brother."

"I know. C'mon Jesse. We don't have much time."

There was another crash from upstairs.

"Please, Jesse."

"Why did you call me James?"

"What?"

"Upstairs. You called me James."

"I was still fuzzy from hitting my head. I have a," she took a deep breath and let it go, "friend. Named James."

"It was my brother's name."

She sighed deeply and rubbed her eyes. Her fingers came away damp.

"I know."

They heard a thump above them that sounded like it came from the door.

"We're out of time. Let's go."

They both got up and went back to the room. Once again as Jesse closed the door behind him, he wondered if he would ever see the other side.

CHAPTER SEVENTEEN

Desmond had hauled a few crates over when they got back in the room. Once the door was closed, they pushed them in from of it. They helped Desmond haul more over. They stacked them from floor to ceiling in front of the door. At Desmond's suggestion, they decided to make a line of them across the room to the back wall so it would act as a brace.

"We're going to have to move some of these bodies in order to do that. Jes, you keep hauling crates. Julie, help me with the corpses."

She put the crate she was carrying down and went to help Desmond. They began to move the stiffening bodies to one side as gently as they could. The blood was still relatively fresh, which made the bodies slippery. More than once they dropped one. Desmond tried to think of them as sacks of rice rather than bodies. It helped a bit. As they moved the last one, Jesse cursed loudly from the far wall.

"There's a goddamn door back here!" he shouted.

Desmond came over with one of the lanterns to get a better look. It was a small door, the kind that would lead to a crawl space. Julie kept moving the crates over to set up the brace.

Jesse took the pistol from his holster and opened the door. It swung outward. Desmond shined a light into it as Jesse pointed the gun into the darkness on the other side. Nothing moved. It was a concrete tunnel big enough for a fairly large person to crawl through.

"Crawl space?" Jesse asked.

"A crawl space wouldn't go straight out like that I don't think. It's some sort of tunnel."

"Why would someone have a concrete tunnel in from their basement? It kinda looks like it angles upwards a bit."

"I wonder if it's an escape tunnel?"

There was a crash from outside the barricaded door that startled all of them.

"Sounds like they're through the basement door." Julie called over to them.

A few moments later they heard a thud from the main basement. A low moan followed. Abandoning the tunnel door Jesse and Desmond helped Julie move the rest of the crates to block the door. A moment later there was another thud, this time right outside. At the very same instant, one of the lamps began to flicker. Another thud. Another flicker.

"How long till morning?" Jesse asked, breaking the silence.

"Six hours give or take." Julie replied, her voice held an edge of fear

The banging on the door started to come faster.

The door was still holding strong after an hour. One of the lamps wasn't so lucky. It had gone out a half an hour earlier. Julie and Desmond sat on either side of the crate barricade. Jesse was over by the small door to the tunnel. It was cracked so they could hear if anything came down it. So far, they had heard nothing. After some discussion they decided it was most likely an escape tunnel. It wasn't that unusual a feature for newer settlements to build, Julie said. The opened one and found it was full of canned goods. They had thought about opening more in the hope of finding another lamp but they were fearful of moving anything away from the barricade. They could tell from the banging and moaning that the other room was filling up with Changed.

Each minute felt like a thousand years to Jesse. He found himself staring at the lamp. He was almost more frightened of the lamp going out than he was of the Changed outside. The notion of spending the night

in a room full of murdered children and their dead-by-their-own-hands parents frightened him into near incapacity. He kept trying to push the thought away, but it kept pushing its way back in. His heart skipped a beat every time he blinked thinking it was a flicker of the lamp.

Desmond couldn't help but stare at the dead bodies. He just could not wrap his brain around the idea that these people killed themselves in a panic. This room was clearly built for just this occasion. If it was in fact an escape tunnel and Julie was right about the crates being full of supplies, then why had they killed themselves, he wondered. His mind went back to the note that had fallen out of the bible. He had a feeling that it would explain what happened, but he had no desire to read it while still in a room with the bodies. For the first time in years he wished he had his horn. It had always been the thing that comforted him when he needed it and he needed comfort now more than ever. As he stared at the bodies, he began to see the faces of his wife and son in them and almost wished the lamp would die so he wouldn't have to look anymore.

Julie spent the time trying to push away the thought that the basement had no windows. Come daybreak the Changed wouldn't need to retreat. The sun wouldn't filter in. She was afraid that morning arrival wouldn't save them. The more that thought seeped in the more she dwelt on the idea that the tunnel, if that's what it was, was their only hope. That thought was even worse. Ever since she had gotten stuck in an abandoned refrigerator as a little girl she was terrified of small spaces. She wasn't sure which would be worse, facing a room full of Changed with nowhere near enough ammunition or crawling on her hands and knees in a tunnel the size of a coffin that may not lead anywhere.

Outside the door, the banging and moaning grew louder.

Another hour passed and the second lantern began flickering. The barricaded door began to creak under the pressure of the bodies arrayed against it. Desmond had begun pacing in the limited room.

Julie found herself nearing panic. Despite trying to deny it, she had realized they were going to have no choice but to go through the tunnel. The door was holding for now, but it would not hold forever. She figured they had another hour before it cracked, even with the brace of crates against it. There were just too many of the monsters relentlessly pushing against it.

It was Jesse who broke the silence.

"We're going to have to try the tunnel. The light is going to give out before the door does, but the door isn't going to last much longer. I'd rather go while we still have something between us and them."

Before anyone could say anything else, there was a loud creak from the ceiling. The creak was followed by a crack and then a crash outside the room.

"Jesus Christ!" Desmond shouted. "I think the ceiling just collapsed out there."

They all looked up simultaneously. There was dust coming down from above them but there wasn't any structural damage they could see. Whatever had happened outside the room had not halted the pounding or the moaning.

"If the ceiling collapsed that might have killed a bunch of them." Julie said hopefully.

"Yeah, but it also means it might collapse on us." Jesse said.

"I think we need to take the tunnel now. I don't know where it goes but anywhere has to be safer than here. Even if it doesn't go anywhere it puts another door between us and them." Desmond responded.

As he said that the lamp flickered for the last time and went out, plunging into absolute darkness.

Julie screamed and felt the world shrink in the darkness. She could feel the four walls close in and imagined she could sense each of the dead bodies in the room. For a moment she imagined them rising up in the darkness and immediately pushed the thought away. For the first time in her life, she thought she understood what madness felt like.

"Ok everybody. Calm down and listen to my voice." It was Desmond speaking in a way that Jesse had never heard him talk before. He thought it was the way a father speaks to a son who has had a bad dream. "Julie, I'm going to come over to you and take your arm. We're going to go over to Jesse and we're going to get in the tunnel. I will go first. You will go second and then Jesse will bring up the rear. You are going to hold on to my ankle at all times and Jesse will hold on to yours. We are going to come out the tunnel on the other side and we will make it through to the day. Which town are we staying in tomorrow?"

"Tull."

The fear in her voice shook Jesse to the core.

Her voice sounded to Desmond almost like she had gone into shock. He didn't think that was the case, but she obviously did not want to go into the tunnel. He guessed she was claustrophobic. Frances had been the same way. He had found out when he tried to get her to visit Howe caverns with him one summer early in their courtship. He had been fascinated by big underground places back then. The tunnel did not frighten him but the idea of her losing it while they were in there did.

"Ok, I'm coming over to you now. Tell me about Tull."

And she did. She flinched when he grabbed her arm but almost as quickly relaxed. She grabbed him and hugged him, and he hugged her back. He broke the embrace and took her hand.

"Talk to me, Jesse."

"What do you want to talk about?"

"Anything you want."

Jesse told him about his mother's troubles with trying to teach him to read. Guided by Jesse's voice Desmond led Julie over to the tunnel. He nearly tripped once when he stepped on something soft that rolled under his foot. He regained his balance and did his best to not think about what he had just stepped one.

There was another sharp crack behind them just as Desmond clasped Jesse's hand. They all flinched. Desmond guessed that was the start of the door giving way. They didn't have much time. He got down on his knees, took a deep breath, and crawled into the tunnel. Julie followed behind him with one hand on his ankle as he had instructed. She had given the shotgun back to Jesse who had it strapped on his back with the barrel facing behind him. He followed them into the tunnel with his hand on Julie's ankle. There was enough room for him to reach back and close the door behind them. This time he hoped that he would never see that room again.

"Julie?" Desmond said questioningly.

"Yeah?" She responded in a voice that was much higher pitched that normal. Desmond could feel her hand shaking on his ankle.

"Where did you grow up?"

"What?"

"Tell me about the place you grew up."

"Now?" The high-pitched quality subsided a little, replaced with the tone of annoyance they were more used to.

"Sure, we've got some time to kill."

She told them about her life while behind them the moaning and banging receded.

CHAPTER EIGHTEEN

My father was a tough guy. Not the kind that goes to bars and picks fights, but the kind that didn't need to talk to get his point across. He had a look that could stop, or start, trouble on a dime. My mother ran off when I was two and my brother Paul was one. We lived in a town outside New Babylon way down south.

New Babylon is about the same size as Silver City. Probably has about the same number of people. We went there pretty rarely, and I don't remember all that much about it. I know compared to the town we lived in it seemed huge. Our town, Bowie, was mostly dirt and wooden buildings. It was the place to go for farmers looking to blow off some steam. It had a few bars, a trading post, a distillery, and a whore house. It wasn't really the best place for kids, but my brother and I had happy childhoods. It was the kind of community without many kids so everyone took on the role of parent.

My father was the sheriff. The town wasn't that big, so it wasn't that big a job. At least during the week. Most weekends people would roll in for a good time. People would get rowdy or out of hand and my father would take care of things. You couldn't really kick people out of town so he would just lock them up in a makeshift jail and then kick them out of town at dawn the next day. The rest of the week he had most of his time to himself and he spent it with us.

In private, he talked a lot about how he was glad for the Change. He said he never really fit in the world the way it was. He had been an accountant before things went all to hell. He loved westerns though. He talked a lot about how his heroes were always guys like Clint Eastwood and John Wayne, actors in cowboy movies. After the Change there was no need for accountants but there was a need for tough guys who were willing to do hard work, he'd say. I think he always saw himself as a cowboy who was born in the wrong time. I don't think he would have chosen the way it happened but things rolling back to a cowboy kind of lifestyle was wish fulfillment for him.

As kids, it was pretty great. There was no school, so people in town took turns teaching us what they knew. Most of the whores didn't have kids or much to do during the day, so we never really missed out on much by our mom skipping town. When they weren't watching us, a lot of the women would go scrounging during the day and would bring us back books and toys.

I don't mean to make it sound too idyllic. The women weren't happy and most of the men in town were drunks. You see the towns we've been through and they're mostly hard-working people who are trying to make the best of a bad situation. Bowie was full of people who had given up in the face of the Change and spent a lot of time just waiting for the Changed to overrun the town. My dad was living out his wild west fantasies for sure, but most were miserable.

I didn't really see that side of things until I got older. All I know is that it was a great way to grow up and my childhood was filled with happy times.

We left when I was thirteen and my brother was twelve. Things were a little less happy by that point. Most of the people we had grown up with had moved on. A lot had died, usually from drinking, some from suicide. Manyof the women that now worked at the whore house were younger and more desperate. The spirit of survival that had brought a lot of towns together in the early days had completely been lost by then. A world with Changed in it had become normal. "The new frontier spirit has passed on to new frontiers" Dad used to say. Still we stayed on because the town needed someone to keep order on Saturday nights.

What finally drove us out was some drunks seeing me on the street and deciding I was an easy mark. Three of them jumped me when I was on my way back from the town store. I had been picking up the food the store set aside as my father's pay for being sheriff. They grabbed me and dragged me into an alley. One of them grabbed the bag of food, the other held me down while the third went through my pockets.

I was big for my age. What they didn't realize was, I was also strong for my age. My father had made sure that we exercised every day and that we knew how to defend ourselves. He wasn't the kind of guy that looked at his daughter as a doll and placed all his energy into his son. He raised us equally. If my brother could lift a weight, then I had to as well. I loved my dad.

When one of the drunks went for my pants, I kneed him in the chest and when he fell back, I wrapped my legs around his neck and jerked hard to the right. It sent him sprawling. The one who was holding my arms jerked back in surprised and let me go. Drunks aren't the smartest people or have the quickest reactions. I was able to pop up, I spin and punch him in the throat as hard as I could. He fell over backward gasping. The third dropped the bag and charged me. I ran at him and on the way, I stepped on the balls of the one I had sent sprawling, pushing off him, I dove into a roll under the hands of the third. I almost got away cleanly, but he grabbed hold of my shirt and tore off a strip of it. I ran into the street and over to the bar across the road called Suffragette City, a nod to the name of the town, I think. My father usually started his evenings there and tonight was no different. I barged in and called out for him. I told him what had happened. I saw something in his eyes in that moment that I had never seen before. I told you he was a hard man but that was when I knew he was perfectly capable of killing a man and that's what he had in mind.

He walked out into the street. It was nighttime and there was nowhere for the drunks to go so he didn't need to hurry. I followed him out. We saw the three men immediately coming out of the alley. They were carrying the limp form of the man I'd punched in the throat between them. There was a moment when they saw him there and realized with full clarity what was about to happen. I won't forget how they looked as it dawned on them that they had fucked with the absolute wrong person.

Dad asked me with controlled rage in his voice "Those them?"

I nodded.

He drew the pistol from the holster on his belt. Very deliberately, he checked to make sure it was loaded. The men had started to talk at this point. I don't know what they said other than to beg for their lives. I was transfixed watching my father. His eyes lingered on the gun in his hand for a moment or two after he was sure it was loaded and the safety was off. He then raised it and shot each of the men carrying the third in the chest. They both went over backward in a spray of blood. He walked over and shot each of them in the head as they lay on the ground. He pointed the gun at the one they had been carrying and held it there for a moment. Then he holstered it and walked back to where I was standing. He ruffled my hair and said, "Looks like you already took care of the third." He told me to go find my brother, get home and pack up. We were leaving, he said.

He came home later that night and sat down in the big chair we had in our small house. My brother and I had packed up what we could. We didn't have much in the way of luggage. He smiled at us both and I noticed the creases across his face for the first time. He looked older than he had ever looked to me before. My brother asked him where we were going to go. All he said was north. After a few moments he fell asleep. The next morning, we left Bowie and never went back.

Those men were the first my father and I killed. They were also my last.

We headed north as he had said we would. The first few places we stayed in were just as rough and tumble as Bowie. We never stayed in one place for more than a day for over a month. I don't think my father had any real idea what he was looking for at the time, just that he would know it when he found it. We were leaving his dreams behind and looking for a place where he could start a new dream.

My brother and I were very close. He was a gregarious kid. I tended to be a bit shy and thoughtful, so he generally spoke for us. We really were best friends growing up. After that night, I think our relationship changed a bit. Both he and my father grew more protective of me but there was an edge of guilt for my brother. He spent a lot of time thinking he had let me down and he couldn't forgive himself for it. We were still best friends, but he spent a lot more time trying to please me and he wouldn't fight back as hard when we roughhoused.

For my part, I hated it. I didn't want to be treated like someone who had to be protected. I get why they reacted that way, but it drove me nuts. Somehow my crushing a man's windpipe with a punch at the age of thirteen made them see me as more delicate than they used to. To this day he still tries to protect me as much as he can. He really didn't want me to go to try and find Jesse.

We were on the road for a while until we got to a town called Pink Houses. The reception we got there was very different from any of the other towns. We were greeted by a young couple who offered to put us up. The town had no bunkhouse for travelers. Instead they took turns taking care of people. They introduced themselves as Jack and Diane Cougar and told us it was their turn. We were too tired and dusty from the road to argue and went off with them.

They had a nice little house that they had worked hard to make comfortable. Pink Houses had a lot of places like that. It was a much larger town than Bowie was. There were four streets lined with houses and other buildings. There was even a bandstand in the town square. We saw other kids running around as we walked to their place. Once there they put on some stew for us and showed us to their water pump out back so we could get cleaned up. After getting rid of several days worth of grime we sat down to dinner with them.

Jack earned his keep as a teacher for the town's children. Diane served as the town librarian. They told us we had arrived just in time for market day. All of these concepts were completely foreign to my brother and I, but they made my father smile. They talked late into the night about the town and how they were trying to forge a lifestyle there that was more than just survival. They did a pretty good job of it.

There was a mayor but most of the major decisions were made at town meetings. There was a small elected council that served six month terms whose primary function was to keep everything organized. They created an agenda for a monthly town meeting.

The mayor was an older professor of sociology who had gathered like-minded individuals in the chaos that had followed the Change and set up shop here. Once the wall was up, they had set about getting farms going around the town. Eventually things grew and all the houses they had put behind the wall had been refurbished. It was as pretty a place as Bowie was ugly.

After the meal, the mayor himself stopped by to see the travelers. He offered my father a pipe and took him for a walk. My brother and I helped wash the dishes. I remember feeling very much like I had stepped into one of the storybooks the women had scrounged for us in Bowie. The Cougars thought our dad would be a while and put us to bed in a second floor bedroom. They had an actual bed with a mattress and a box spring and sheets on it. It was the most comfortable bed I had ever slept in.

Our father woke us up the next morning by telling us we were going to stay for a while. The mayor had offered him a job to help manage the towns communal stores. The next day was a town meeting on top of being market day. The town voted on giving my father the job. They also voted to let us stay in one of the unoccupied houses. After a few days of getting settled in, my brother and I started going to school with Mr. Cougar. When we weren't in school, we did odd jobs for people around town. All the kids who were over the age of ten did the same. Once we were done we would come home, and my father would work us out just as he did in Bowie. He didn't want us to get complacent. Eventually, it became apparent that he had no intention of leaving.

My father was happy there. It wasn't the same kind of happy that he was in Bowie. It was the kind of happy that a man gets when he knows his family is provided for. He had had a chance to live out his cowboy fantasies and was glad for it but was ready for a sense of normalcy.

He died when I was eighteen. He fell off a ladder while working on our roof and broke his neck. I like to think he died at peace with the world. I wasn't in town when it happened. I had joined one of the scavenger teams when I was sixteen and spent most of my time exploring the world around us, digging up whatever pre-Change treasure I could. My brother had signed up with the guard and had been on duty.

A month after the funeral I met Dylan.

CHAPTER NINETEEN

They fell silent after she was done telling her story. The only sounds filling the tunnel was the shuffling of their pants against the concrete floor and the faint sound of moaning and banging behind them. They had no idea how long they had been crawling. The impenetrable darkness all around them destroyed their sense of time and distance. The faint sounds seemed to come from everywhere and nowhere at the same time. The sense of displacement had become almost as overwhelming as fear of the Changed behind them.

With each passing minute, Jesse understood a little better how it was that people went insane trapped underground. He had been able to focus on Julie's story while she was talking, but now that she was done, he felt his mind slipping away from him. His hand was still firmly on Julie's ankle and he was terrified to let go for even a second for fear that somehow he would become un-tethered and slip away into the dark never to see the light again.

Desmond's voice floated back to him asking how they were doing. All he could manage was a breathless 'ok so far'. The sound of his own voice in the blackness seemed strange. He was very close to panicking.

Julie responded that she was ok as well. Her voice sounded as on edge as Jesse's.

They continued to crawl as the sounds of the Changed grew fainter and fainter behind them.

167

The realization that he could faintly see shapes around him dawned on Desmond so slowly that he thought his mind was playing tricks on him. After a while he could no longer deny that he could see the outline of his hands. He looked ahead and squinted and while it was still very black the darkness had lost its pitch quality.

"I think we're almost out." he said. It was the first time any of them had spoken in a while and he felt Julie's hand flinch on his ankle and then immediately tighten again.

"How can you tell?" Jesse asked.

"There's some light filtering in. I can see my hands."

"Must be starlight."

Sensing the end of the ordeal they redoubled their efforts. Another five minutes passed, and Desmond could see the end of the tunnel up ahead.

"We need to be quiet now. It's still night and we don't know where this empties out."

Slowly they crawled the last twenty yards to the mouth of the tunnel. Julie and Jesse stayed back at the very end as Desmond peered outside.

Julie could feel her skin nearly crawling with anticipation of being out of this nightmare. She had no idea how long they had been in the tiny tunnel but now that the end was in sight she did not care if there was a swarm waiting for them, she simply wanted out.

After a few moments Desmond turned and said "It looks clear, let's get the hell out of here. Quietly though."

One by one they exited the tunnel. It ended on a platform made out of what looked like a combination of brick and concrete. Standing on the platform they marveled at what they saw. The platform was built onto a ledge that was situated halfway down a giant pit. Looking down they saw a large pool of water at the bottom and looking up there was steep rock wall for another forty feet. A metal ladder fastened to the sheer rock wall went to the top of the pit. The other side of the pit was a hundred yards away. They could barely make it out in the starlight.

"I think we're in a quarry or something." Desmond guessed.

Jesse looked around and said, "I wonder why they ended their escape tunnel here?"

"I would guess it was a sewer tunnel or something already in place and all they did was build this platform." Julie responded.

"It's a good spot if you think about it," Desmond said, "Changed can't climb down a ladder or up a bunch of rocks. I wouldn't swear by it, but I would imagine they can't swim either. There's some overhang above us so even if they just walked off up there, they wouldn't land on the ledge. Great place to hole up until morning."

"It would be even better if there was a grate or something we could use to block the tunnel." said Jesse.

"Well, I vote we stay here till dawn. We can try and get some sleep in shifts. Someone should stay up and keep watch, especially down the tunnel." said Julie.

"You two get some shut eye. I'll take first watch." Desmond then turned to Jesse, "I'll wake you in an hour or so and so forth."

Jesse nodded and sat down on the platform with his back to the limestone wall behind him. He was asleep almost immediately. Julie fell asleep moments after he did.

Desmond sat next to the tunnel holding the shotgun and said several prayers of thanks for them surviving the day's ordeals. When he finished praying, he did his best to listen to the sounds around him. The breeze blowing through the quarry and the occasional splash of some small animal down in the water were the only noises he heard. At any moment he expected to hear moans coming from above them or from inside the tunnel but they never came. Presently his mind drifted back to the note that had fallen from the bible back in the basement. He pulled it out and was glad to see the starlight was bright enough for him to read. He smiled at that. Thirty years ago the pollution would have made that impossible. He missed the old world, but the new world did have a few advantages.

The note was written in a beautiful longhand. The handwriting had such flourish that it almost looked illuminated to Desmond. He had been expected a note scrawled in the handwriting of a madman and the finery of it shocked him. It made him more fearful of reading the note. The ravings of a lunatic cult leader he could handle. This handwriting was that of someone sane, Desmond thought, and that made what he read in the note a thousand times worse.

The note read:

Praise the Lord. In His infinite wisdom the Lord has sent us the sign letting us know our time of tribulation is over. He is now ready to open His arms and accept us into Heaven. We have been diligent in our faith in these times of testing and finally we have passed. Praise Jesus for today we walk with the Lord!

For any who come across our miracle, this message is for you. The Lord has sent the Changed to destroy those who have been unfaithful and have ignored the Lord's word. They are here to cleanse the planet of homosexuals, abortionists, liberals, communists, atheists, and others who have forsaken the path of righteousness. Know that you are living in the end times, the time of tribulation, and the only way to find Salvation is to repent your sins and place your faith in the word as laid down in the good book.

Rejoice! The Lord will love you if you love him!

Amen.

Reverend Frank Mathers

Desmond crumpled the note up and threw it over the edge of the platform and into the lake below. He thought back to stories about some of the large churches opening their doors to let swarms of the Changed in assuming the righteous would be saved or some damn thing. He would never understand people who killed themselves presuming to know the mind of God. He was a Christian and believed in God and Jesus, but he never could quite connect how the faith he was brought up into had anything to do with 'those fools' as his mother called them.

He leaned back and looked up at the stars. He watched the sky as the stars melted into the dawn. When the sunlight crested the edge of the quarry, he woke up Julie and Jesse.

Groggily, Jesse sat up and saw that it was light out. Never in his life had he been so grateful to see sunlight.

"Why didn't you wake me up and get some rest yourself?" he asked Desmond.

"Wouldn't have slept. Besides, you kids needed it more than me. So, Julie, where to today?"

She stared at him for a few moments completely unable to process the question. She had slept as deeply as she ever had in her life. Her joy at waking up and seeing the sun was only matched by her surprise and it took a moment before she could compose herself enough to speak.

"I guess it depends on where we are. I don't know how far or in what direction we crawled but assuming I can get my bearings we should be able to reach Tull today without much trouble. Day after that we'll reach Malice."

"Thank goodness!" Jesse proclaimed. The previous night had broken his enthusiasm for the road. He missed Silver City and his tent. He missed Wellersville and the home he grew up in. Most of all he missed his Mom and his brother. The trip had shaken the dust off feelings he had long since thought he had put on the shelf, never to be taken down again. He wished he had kept them buried. Some feelings were just too painful.

"Well, no time like the present. Ladies first!" Desmond said with the enthusiasm of someone who had passed through the fire and came out the other side with a better understanding of how precious life was.

Julie began to climb the ladder, followed by Jesse. Before Desmond started climbing he looked down the tunnel one last time. He said a small prayer and began to climb.

The sunshine that day felt glorious to them and despite the lack of sleep and the previous days exertions they made record time to Tull. As they walked, they talked more freely than they had on the entire trip. Jesse and Desmond both quizzed Julie about her growing up and her time in Pink Houses. Desmond also asked her about her husband. Jesse noticed she dodged most of those questions. Once or twice, she had glanced at Jesse as she did so.

Jesse had a question that he wanted to ask. He could feel it form deep in his gut and there it sat unasked. He realized over the course of the day that he was afraid to ask. He was afraid of what the answer would be. As long as he did not ask, she would not have to answer and the hope that he felt burning deep within him would remain. That night in Tull he slept fitfully.

Desmond spent the night examining a new feeling as well. He could not explain it and he did not even understand it. He felt almost as if some part of him was missing, like he had dropped some part of himself. The feeling persisted the next day on the walk to Malice. It was only when they saw the town for the first time on the horizon that he realized what it was. Somewhere in that tunnel he had let the guilt of what had happened to his wife and son go. He felt redeemed. He stopped suddenly once the realization hit him. Both Jesse and Julie asked if he was ok. He smiled a broad smile, put his arms around both of them and said, "Yes, yes I really think I am."

Together they walked toward the end of their journey smiling and laughing in the way that only people who had escaped certain death can.

CHAPTER TWENTY

Brother Lydon kicked at the ashes of the house and tried to keep his rage from boiling over.

He knew they had a problem as soon as he saw the smoke on the horizon. He felt his anger starting to rise the closer they got to Nature Springs and now that they had arrived, he was afraid he was going to lose control. Each day he felt like they were losing ground and since the fugitives had apparently told no one their ultimate destination he still did not know where they were going.

And now they may have actually died.

He surveyed the damage to the town and could not imagine how anyone had lived through it. The town's wall was three quarters ash and rubble. Every one of the buildings had at least some fire damage and most had burned to the ground.

The largest building, which he guessed was some sort of meeting house, was still smoldering. His men were searching the town for any sign of their quarry or any of the residents. There were very few bodies lying around and the ones they had found appeared to have been Changed. His guess was that there was a basement under one of the houses, most likely the meeting hall, where people had made a last stand. He was sure a swarm had descended here and that left very little chance that anyone was still alive.

"You. Mr. Sumner. Check that building over there. See if there is a basement."

Paul Sumner, who towered over Lydon, nodded his head and went immediately to the building. They had been on the road for a while and Brother Lydon had no intention of upsetting him. He was convinced that the man was insane. Every time he looked at his boss Lydon's eyes were twitching, and his mouth was curled into a sneer. And that scared him. He had been around a few hard men in his time and knew that look. He also knew that people who had that look all the time were not thinking on the same level as most of humanity. They were the eyes of a killer.

Sumner had no delusions about who and what he was. He had been a thug his whole life. Lydon was something different. Something had changed in him the day he had that girl beaten back in Silver City. It was like some mental block had been lifted. He went from high strung church functionary to a wildcard overnight. In Sumner's estimation, there was nothing more dangerous than a wildcard.

Lydon watched Sumner enter the remains of the town hall and begin searching for a basement. One would be found, and it would be full of Changed, he mused. Like shooting fish in a barrel. An evil grin crossed his face. He loved killing Changed. According to Father Jordan they were the empty vessels of those who God had deemed worthy of ascending and that killing them was not a sin. The thought of killing Changed did not lessen his irritation at the state of their mission. If they were dead, then he would have to double back along the route they had come and start asking people where Chapin had been heading in ways that would convince people to answer. He was doing God's work rooting out the anti-Christ and God would understand if he had to resort to torture. He did hope it would not come to that, however. Not because he was loath to torture people but because of the time he would lose. He knew he was only a day or two behind them now, assuming they had escaped this conflagration.

He called another one of his companions over. He could never remember the man's last name, only that his first name was Angus.

"Yes, Sir?"

Lydon smiled at being called sir. He enjoyed that these men had now accepted his authority. Early on they laughed and kidded around and felt ok making jokes at his expense. They were all hired muscle with only a tenuous connection to Father Jordan's cause. Because they were not directly involved in the church, they did not seem to realize the importance of this mission. Lydon had to make an example of Angus a few nights after the incident at the Hart farm in order to establish once and for all who was in charge. There had been discipline after that night.

"You mentioned there were two possible destinations for them after they left here. What were they again?"

"I'm not too sure that's going to matter. If they came here, I doubt they survived."

"That's not what I asked."

Angus gulped.

Lydon enjoyed seeing the fear in his eyes. Fear created discipline.

"Tull to the southwest and Black Horse to the northwest."

"And which does your gut tell you they went to?" he paused and then added, "Assuming they are not still here?"

"I would guess Black Horse. It's closer. There aren't many towns this far out, but Black Horse is the first town in the Rockies town chain. If they were to go to Tull then the only place they would have to go after that would be Malice and Malice is pretty much the end of the line."

"Thank you for your assessment. Please continue to search this mess. How much longer do we have till we need to move on to Black Horse?"

"About two hours if we want to cut it close."

Lydon nodded and waved Angus off. Lydon heard the man sigh in relief and enjoyed it. Ever since that night at the farm with that horrible family he had felt good. He realized that he had been sent there so God could deliver him a message and once he understood what the message was, he had wept tears of joy. He was to be God's flaming sword on earth. His true avenging angel. These men he was traveling with would be his army once the battle came. Once they found this Dylan Droge monster, he would do his best to capture him and bring him to Father Jordan but if that was not possible, he would not hesitate to end the abomination. He loved Father Jordan and would respect his wishes, but he was taking his orders directly from God now, and if they contradicted it would be Father Jordan who would lose.

Lydon was ruminating on how Father Jordan would react if Droge should be struck down when Sumner called out to him.

"We found a nest!"

Lydon grinned and walked over to where Sumner was. He took his pistol out of its holster and checked that it was loaded.

Clearing the nest took less than twenty minutes. The Changed were crammed into a large basement room and were sluggish during the day. Lydon had enjoyed it, nonetheless.

Once they waded through the now dead Changed, they found a door that had been smashed in. On the other side was a room full of corpses. There were also some Changed in the room but they made short work of them. It was clear that people had barricaded themselves into the room, then killed themselves. Lydon went through all the corpses to see if Jesse was among them and was heartened to find that he was not.

"There's a tunnel over here." called Sumner.

Lydon went over and inspected the tunnel.

"They must have escaped through here. From the lack of bodies, I surmise that when the swarm came, the town retreated down here. This was probably at the suggestion of Chapin. I would not be surprised to learn that he convinced these people to kill themselves. "

He thought for a few moments before going on.

"I think we are done here. Sumner gather up the men. We are going to move on to Black Horse."

"You think they are going to pass through the Rockies?" Sumner asked before he could stop himself.

"It is certainly possible. If they do, we will follow them. We will follow them to the coast if we have to. My father always said that the coast was a modern day Sodom and Gomorrah so it would make sense that they head there."

Sumner just nodded and went out to gather up the rest of the men. If it came to crossing the Rockies, he may have to re-evaluate how willing he was to continue following a man who he now believed was a psychopath caught up in a religious fantasy.

Lydon stayed in the room with the corpses for a while. He prayed over the bodies asking the Lord to forgive them. Suicide was a sin of course but if they were tricked by Chapin then it was as if the Devil himself had spoken to them. Once he was done praying, he went upstairs and led his men out of town.

The flames slowly consumed what was left of Nature Springs.

CHAPTER TWENTY-ONE

Malice was built in the foothills of the Rockies. Low hills surrounded the town with scattered copses of pine trees dotting them. In the distance the hills grew into full-fledged mountains that loomed over the land like protective sentinels. The town itself had a quaint look from this distance. The houses appeared to be mostly wooden cabins with a few made of brick and mortar. There were about two dozen buildings in all, as well as some smaller structures. A large watchtower stood next to the gate. It was tall enough to see the entire town and probably for miles around. It could certainly see the top of the hill Jesse, Julie, and Desmond were standing on. To the north and south, large fields of grain and corn were visible. People could be seen moving among the crops. The main gates to the town were wide open.

It was as inviting looking a place as Jesse had ever seen. It instantly drew him back to childhood memories of Wellersville. Though up close that town had looked run down rather than charming. From a distance, it always looked warm and friendly. Jesse wondered if the appearances here would be deceiving as well.

They were no more than two miles away from their destination with hours of daylight left. Jesse could tell Julie was excited to be home and that Desmond was glad for their journey to be at an end. He was not sure how he felt. He would be glad to get off his feet for a while and was looking forward to the comfortable beds that Julie had promised. He still couldn't shake the cold lump of fear and anger that had taken up residence in his stomach. He had lived with questions his whole life and was now facing the prospect of getting some of those questions answered. He was afraid that it would open old wounds that he had long since cauterized with booze and solitude. Most of all he was scared that if Julie's husband James really was his brother, as he suspected, what would his brother think of the man he had become. He did not think he could stand to see the inevitable disappointment in his brother's eyes.

These thoughts and feelings mixed in with his other big question on his mind. Why had James never come back for him? They had not been close as children, but family is family. If he had thought there was a chance his mother and brother had been alive, then he would have scoured the earth for them. Jesse had grown up alone and miserable. The closest he had ever come to being happy was this trip with Desmond and Julie.

He noticed that Desmond was looking at him oddly as they all stood looking down at Malice.

"You ok, Jes?" he asked.

"Just nervous I guess."

Julie smiled at him, "There's nothing to be nervous about. This is a good place. I promise."

"I believe you Julie. I guess I just...I don't know." He sighed deeply. "Well, no sense wasting any more daylight. I'm looking forward to meeting," he paused briefly as his throat caught unexpectedly, "your husband. And I'm looking forward to sleeping in one of those comfortable beds you've promised."

She looked at him thoughtfully and then smiled brightly, "Well then. Let's go!"

Together they covered the last miles to reach their destination.

The first thing Jesse noticed as they got close to Malice was the bell in the guard tower. There had been no one in the tower as they covered the last mile toward town. As they got close, someone climbed up and began ringing the bell and shouting something they could not quite make out.

"That a warning bell?" Desmond asked.

"It can be, although in this case I imagine he's ringing it because we're coming." Julie responded.

"Think they recognize that it's you?"

Before she could respond a man came running out of the gates and shouted, "Julie!"

"James!" she shouted back and took off running towards him.

"I think that's a safe bet." Desmond said with a laugh and clapped Jesse on the back.

Jesse barely felt it. He had gone rigid. A cold sweat broke out all over his body. He watched as James and Julie practically jumped into each other's embrace and kissed each other deeply for a very long time.

Desmond saw Jesse's reaction and with some concern in his voice said, "You ok, Jes?"

Jesse did not respond. He just watched. Eventually they broke their embrace and turned to face Desmond and Jesse.

"Desmond, Jesse, this is James." Julie said with a smile. When she saw Jesse staring at James the smile slowly left her face. She turned to her husband and saw that he had the same look on his face as he stared at Jesse. She had been worried about what would happen when they saw each other and held her breath.

As Desmond looked at James, he began to realize what was going on and just who James was. His eyes met Julie's and she nodded slightly to him confirming what had just dawned on him. He found that he too was holding his breath.

James was the first to break the silence when he simply said "Jabber?"

Jesse could not tear his eyes away from James. He was older, with a face that showed the years he had spent on the road. It was full of hard lines earned by being out in the sun. He was taller but not much thicker. His hair was long and a bit shaggy and not the close crop of his youth. Through all this he could clearly see the echo of the twelve-year-old boy he was the last time he had seen him.

"James?" he said. His voice cracked as he said it. His vision blurred as his eyes filled with tears. For years he had believed his brother was dead and now here he was standing in front of him. A million thoughts went through Jesse's mind at light speed. His emotions exploded in every direction at once.

James walked toward Jesse with his arms raised to embrace his long lost brother. Jesse began to walk toward him too. As they got close James's face lit up in a smile that nearly went from ear to ear and that was when Jesse reared back and punched him in the jaw. James reeled and fell back on his backside. Julie shouted and broke towards him. Desmond stepped into her way and grabbed her. He whispered in her ear, "No. Let them get this out of the way now."

James shook his head and rubbed his jaw. Jesse looked down on him, breathing heavily with tears streaming from his eyes. Eventually Jesse dropped to his knees in front of him, all of his anger spent.

"Why didn't you come back for me?" He said through the tears and could not say anything more.

James got up and scrambled over to Jesse, dropped to his knees and wrapped him in a hug. After a moment Jesse wrapped his arms around his brother and hugged him back. They remained in each other's embrace crying for a long time.

When he could finally manage it, James simply said, "I'm sorry."

When their tears were spent, they broke the embrace and looked at each other.

"I missed you."

"I missed you too."

"Mom?"

James shook his head. Jesse nodded. One miracle would have to be enough, he thought.

"Your wife is hot."

"You hit harder than I remember."

They looked each other in the eye again and broke out laughing. They hugged again and stood up. They walked over to Desmond and Julie who had both resumed breathing but were still watching with concern.

"Jesse, this is my wife Julie Hewson-Chapin."

Julie smiled and hugged Jesse. She whispered in his ear, "I'm sorry I didn't tell you. I promised not to." He gave her a squeeze and whispered back, "I understand, Sis." She laughed and gave him a little shove.

"James, this is my friend Desmond. Des, this is James, my brother."

They shook hands and Desmond said, "Very pleased to meet you. I've heard a lot about you. I do have one question though. Jabber?"

James laughed and Jesse shook his head. It was Jesse who answered, "That's what he used to call me. Jabber. Apparently, I was a pretty talkative kid."

"You used to be talkative?" Desmond said with genuine surprise.

"Compared to him I was."

"Well, I imagine you are all tired. Why don't we go back to the house? You can all get freshened up while I make dinner. Stories can wait until after. I'll tell Langhorne to let folks know that we'll do introductions tomorrow."

"That sounds wonderful." Julie said taking James's hand.

"Where's Dylan?" Jesse asked.

"Yeah, I'm looking forward to meeting this guy." Desmond said.

"He went out on a walkabout last night. I'm not sure where he's going but he said he would be back in two days."

Jesse could barely believe it, "All this and he's not here?" He was stunned.

"He'll be back. The timing's bad but he always has a good reason for doing things when he does them."

"Well, coming back would be a good start." Jesse said with a bitterness that surprised even him.

"All I can do is ask you to trust him, Jesse. When he comes back, we'll explain everything."

Jesse nodded, "That would be good."

"Alright, enough chit chat. I heard something about food and getting cleaned up. Your wife told us that you had actual showers with running water. Please tell me she was not embellishing. "

"We do indeed have showers with running water. We even have hot water. C'mon, let's get you folks home." James said. He turned and walked into town with Julie's hand in his.

Jesse and Desmond looked at each other and smiled. They followed after them through the gate into Malice.

CHAPTER TWENTY-TWO

The house that Julie and James shared was a two-story log cabin. It was not fancy, but it felt very comfortable to Jesse. The walls were varnished in a light tone that gave the main room a cheerful look. A darker varnish had been used in the bedrooms which actually seemed to make them feel cozier. The main room covered most of the first floor and had a high ceiling that led to a skylight flooding everything with natural light. There was a kitchen and an indoor bathroom on the first floor along with the main bedroom and a small dining room. The second floor was a loft that was split into two smaller bedrooms.

Desmond and Jesse took turns taking showers while James prepared chicken, potatoes, and corn on the cob for their dinner. When they went to their rooms after their showers, they each found a fresh set of clothing waiting for them. It was simple fair, jeans and work shirts, but there was also clean underwear and socks. After the time spent on the road, clean clothes seemed even more luxurious than the shower. Neither of them could remember the last time they felt clean. Even before they left Silver City, showers were something of a myth. Mostly they sponge bathed themselves or went to the public bathhouses. Neither had ever left them feeling clean.

Once Jesse had changed into the new clothes, he laid down on the bed. It was a soft mattress covered with quilts and sheets. The pillows were stuffed with a soft goose down. Half an hour later he was surprised to find Desmond standing over him shaking him mildly.

"C'mon, Jes. Plenty of time to sleep later. Let's get some food and see what your brother has to say for himself."

"Wow, I guess I fell asleep. I can't believe all this. Beds, running water, clean clothes."

"Yeah, I know what you mean. Seems almost too good to be true."

"Well, if it ain't true then I think I might be alright if people just keep on lying."

"I'm with you on that. I do have one question though. How did they have clothes for us?"

"Huh?"

"The clothes. They didn't just run out and get this stuff. It was here waiting for us. I don't know about yours but mine fit perfectly."

"I don't...boy, that does seem a bit odd doesn't it?"

"A bit. Especially since they couldn't have known I was with you. They only sent Julie to look for you. I'm a tag-a-long."

"We'll just have to add that to the long list of questions we already have. C'mon, let's go eat."

Smells from the kitchen drifted up to them as they went down the stairs. Their mouths started watering and any questions they had went right out of their heads. They had not eaten anything but thin soups and stews since they had visited the Hart family. Jesse's stomach rumbled at the thought of real food.

When they got to the bottom of the stairs Julie was waiting for them. Jesse and Desmond's jaws both dropped. She had showered and put on a simple floral sundress. She looked stunning. They had seen her in nothing but baggy road cloths, and by the end she had been as dirty and grungy as they were. The dress highlighted how chiseled the muscles in her arms were. He could very easily believe that this woman had killed a man with her bare hands when she was thirteen. He had absolutely no delusions about who would win if she picked a fight with him.

"Nice to be in fresh clothes isn't it?" She asked and they nodded in agreement. "James is just about done cooking. Come to dinner."

She led them to a small table set for four people. The place setting was simple but pretty like the rest of the house. There was a jug of water along with another jug of darker liquid on the table.

"Is that beer?" Desmond asked.

"Yeah. The guys over in Pink Houses taught a few people here how to make it and we started to grow the ingredients. Last year was the first crop where we were able to brew a few different kinds. That's a lager."

They sat down around the table as James called out that dinner would be ready in about two minutes. Desmond poured himself a mug of beer, took a long sip, and barked out a laugh. "That's about the best I've ever tasted. That makes the stuff in Silver City taste like cold mud. If you folks can brew stuff this good, I may never leave."

"That's the hope." Julie said casually.

Desmond looked at her appraisingly. Before he could ask what she meant, James appeared wearing an apron and carrying a huge tray of food. He laid it out on the table, and it looked as good as it smelled. He went back to the kitchen and returned without the apron and took his seat. He smiled at them all.

"I hope you fellas don't mind if I say grace?"

"Be my guest." Desmond responded.

He bowed his head and said, "Lord, we thank you for the blessings you have given us. Thank you for returning Julie home safe. Thank you for helping her find Jesse and Desmond. Thank you for reuniting my brother and I. Thank you for this meal we are about to receive and thank you for allowing me to not overcook the chicken. Please be with those who have forgotten your words. Amen."

Desmond and Julie had bowed their heads along with James. Jesse stared at his brother while his brother prayed. He could not wrap his brain around his brother being alive and here in Malice. He certainly could not fathom how the shy and quiet kid he grew up with had turned into this weathered and handsome man before him. He felt himself almost close to tears again as he listened to his brother pray. When he had finished the prayer Julie and Desmond both repeated Amen in unison. Jesse said it quietly, mostly to himself.

James gestured to Desmond and Jesse, "Eat up. There's plenty more. I'll warn you that we don't always eat quite this well, but I figured that if my prodigal brother has returned, then the least we could do was slay a fatted calf."

"Looks like chicken to me. You sure you killed the right animal?" Jesse responded with mirth in his voice.

James laughed out loud, "Same old Jabber I remember," and then more seriously, "Although I guess you're not the kid I remember anymore, huh?"

Jesse paused in the act of scooping mashed potatoes onto his plate, "No, I guess I'm not. But you don't seem like you spend all your time in libraries anymore either."

"We've got a lot to catch up on, I think."

Desmond listened to this exchange and took it upon himself to refill everyone's beer. He then raised his mug, "Journey's end and new journeys beginning."

The others raised their mugs as well.

"To being home." Julie said.

"To family." Jesse said.

"Next year in Jerusalem!" James said. Julie leaned over and punched him. He laughed. "To life!" he said. They all drank deeply and then dug into the food. The travelers ate ravenously. James ate but mostly watched the others. He brought the rest of the food out from the kitchen and smiled as they devoured the rest it. There was little conversation. "I guess the food on the road isn't so great then?" James asked. They all murmured in agreement.

Once the meal was over James produced a bottle of brandy from a cabinet near the table. He poured everyone a small glass. He swirled his around in the glass for a few seconds watching as the red liquid sloshed around, releasing its aroma.

"So, I imagine you have some questions," he said.

"I have a few, yeah." Jesse answered, "Although really they mostly boil down to one. What happened?"

James took a sip of the brandy and looked at his glass for another moment. Finally, he said, "That's a long story and not always a particularly happy one. You sure you want it now or would you rather get some rest first."

"Are you stalling?"

"A bit, yeah. It's not a real crowd pleaser and honestly, I don't like telling it. Hell, I don't like thinking about most of it. I guess I was just hoping to have this night without having to get into it." He took a sip of the brandy, "But if you want it now then you deserve to hear it."

Jesse took a sip of his brandy and thought about it. Before he could respond Desmond asked, "How did you know I was coming?"

"Dylan said you would be. He got the clothes too."

"How did he know?"

"That youll have to ask him. That's his story to tell."

"Did he leave because he knew we would be here today?" Jesse asked.

"I don't know, but If I had to guess, then I would say yeah, probably. But Dylan does things and doesn't really explain them to anyone. I just know that I trust him and what he says."

Jesse nodded and polished off his brandy. James poured him some more.

"I can sleep another night without knowing what happened, James. I don't need to know so bad that it can't wait a bit. I'm glad for a night without any awfulness."

"Agreed. Don't forget that you owe me a story too. Dylan may know what has happened to you, but I don't, and I would like to know. Tonight, let's just put that all aside and be together."

"Sounds like a good plan." Desmond responded, downed his brandy and shook his glass at James who laughed and refilled it.

"Oh!" James said suddenly, "I nearly forgot. Dylan also brought this."

He got up and went into the other room. When he came back holding a case. Julie and Jesse looked at it blankly, but Desmond's eyes grew to the size of saucers.

"Is that..." he said, unable to finish the thought. James flipped the case open and inside was a beautiful brass horn polished to a gleaming shine.

"Do you play?" James asked and then saw that all three were staring at the horn.

"How could he know?" Desmond asked quietly, never taking his eyes off the horn.

"Sometimes he just knows." James said and handed Desmond the horn.

Desmond took it and removed it from its case. He picked up the mouthpiece and attached it to the horn. He put it to his lips and played a few experimental notes.

"It's been a long time." Desmond said apologetically.

"Go on, play something." Julie said.

Desmond took a deep breath and began to play. He was rusty at first and missed a lot of notes but gradually his fingers began to remember, and the halting notes soon melted into music. He closed his eyes and let the music that had been in him all this time come pouring out. The room filled with the sounds of jazz and old ska songs that he had not played in years. Jesse and Julie were mesmerized. James left for a moment and came back with a guitar. He listened for a little while and then began to play. Desmond's eyes never opened, and he never stopped. Soon they were following each other through songs they both knew and songs they did not.

After a while Desmond took the horn from his lips. He looked at it for a long while. Jesse and Julie broke into applause and stopped only when they saw the tears streaming from his eyes.

"I thought," Desmond began to say and his voice cracked, after a moment he composed himself and went on, "I thought that part of me was gone. I thought I left it out on that highway. I... "

Jesse went to hug him, but Desmond waived him off. He then raised the horn to his lips and began to play again. James joined in on the guitar and they played for what seemed like ages. When Desmond lowered his horn again, they were all in tears.

"I'm looking forward to meeting this Dylan fellow, I think." Desmond said.

"I imagine he's looking forward to meeting you too." James said.

"Well, I don't know about anyone else, but I think I'm ready for bed.

The dishes can wait until morning." Julie declared. They all agreed. After clearing the table, they said their goodnights. Julie and James went to their bedroom and Jesse and Desmond retired to their rooms in the loft.

They were all asleep within minutes except for James. He lay awake holding his wife and wondering how his brother was going to react to the story he had to tell. He was not sure if he could stand losing his brother so soon after finding him again. Eventually he drifted off. He dreamt of the music that had filled the night and his life. It was a good dream.

CHAPTER TWENTY-THREE

"C'mon, wake up."

Jesse opened his eyes and blinked blearily. For a moment he could not remember where he was. He sat bolt upright when he realized there was someone standing over him. The person was standing in front of the window with early morning sunlight streaming in behind him so that Jesse could not make out who it was.

"Good morning!"

This time Jesse recognized the voice as that of his brother James. The realization brought him all the way awake. He still was having trouble accepting that he had found his long-thought-dead brother.

"Good morning." he mumbled.

He had been dreaming about his mother and the house he grew up in. In it he and his mother were chasing each other around the house in bright midday sunshine, laughing. When she finally caught him, she had tickled him into fits of laughter. The tickling morphed her carrying him on her shoulders toward the gate of their farm. It was suddenly night and he was begging her to not open the door because there were monsters on the other side. She did not react and continued to advance on the door. By the time she reached for the handle he was begging her to stop. She flung the door open and standing on the other side were Desmond, Julie, James and Dylan. He had immediately felt relieved. Dylan had opened his mouth to speak and before he could say anything, James had woken him up.

"Well, aren't you a ray of sunshine this morning?"

"I've been on the road for a while and was living in a tent before that. This might have been the most comfortable bed I've ever been in, sorry if I wasn't in a hurry to leave it!"

"C'mon, put some clothes on and let's go for a walk before the others wake up. We need to talk, just the two of us."

"Ok."

Jesse got up and pulled on the clothes he had been given the previous day. Despite being half asleep, he relished the feel of clean clothes. James had gone downstairs while he got dressed. After he came down and used the bathroom his brother had two mugs of coffee poured.

"Real coffee?"

"Yup. Traders from out west come through with the beans. I have a little cream and sugar, if you want."

"No, thanks."

"Great. Let's go."

He led Jesse out the door and down the street. There were a fair amount of people up and moving about. Jesse wondered if anyone here slept in.

"Farmers. The fields around here are all communal, so people work in shifts. Everyone works at least one week in the fields a month."

James took a left at the end of the street and Jesse realized they were going back the way they came the previous night. As they rounded another corner, the gate appeared and was wide open. Several people were heading out and a few were milling about the entrance. As they passed through it, almost all of them greeted James warmly and welcomed Jesse. Once they left town, James led Jesse up one of the small hills to the south. There was a gazebo at the top. James went in and sat down. He motioned for Jesse to sit as well. He sat and looked down at the town. He could see the bustle as people headed to the fields. Smoke had begun to rise from some of the chimneys. He sipped his coffee, which was delicious, and marveled at how idyllic it all seemed.

"It looks too good to be true." He said after a few moments.

"Doesn't it?"

"Is it?"

"Too good to be true?"

"It feels like it sometimes, but no, it's true. It's not perfect by any means, but it's a better way than most."

"Is it because of Dylan?"

"Partly."

"Julie said people think that you are all in a cult here."

James laughed. The sound sent Jesse back to when he was five and trying to impress his brother. His laugh was deeper and more resonant, but he could hear echoes of his twelve-year-old brother in it.

"We're not a cult. Just trying to be a community rather than a collection of people. Most folks are stuck in the old way of doing things and keep trying to get an economy going again. They're interested in alliances and power and politics. We still bring our goods to harvest days in other towns usually in trade for things we don't have, it's just that here we try and share things."

"Isn't that communism?"

"Yeah, I guess. Everything has to be an ism in way or other, I guess. We don't have secret police though." He chuckled, "Anyway, does it matter? We're not bothering people with how we do things. I don't know if it's better or worse than anything else, but it works for us."

"Sorry, didn't mean to put you on the defensive. I guess when you've spent the last few years mainly begging for change, the idea of people sharing food seems like it must have a catch."

"Oh Jesse..."

"Hey, sometimes that's life. So, you said you had a story to tell me?"

"Yeah, I guess I do."

James sighed deeply and looked down at the town for a little while, gathering his thoughts.

"Julie and I were married here, in this gazebo. Dylan married us."

"He's a minister?"

"Close enough." He paused again before going on, "Look, Dylan asked me to leave most of this to him. He wants to be the one to explain this all to you, and I owe him that much. But some of it you need to hear from me."

Jesse nodded. He felt the same irritation he had the previous night when James told him Dylan was not there. For all that, Dylan had told people to withhold things from him he could have at least had the decency to be there when Jesse arrived.

"Mom died that night. She was chasing after me and fell into a washout and broke her neck. She died suddenly and without any pain."

Jesse took this news in as much stride as he could. He knew his mother was dead. He had known for years. In a way it was a relief. He was afraid that she had been torn apart by Changed, or worse, had become one herself. To hear it put forth so matter-of-factly still stunned him. He felt tears welling in his eyes and put his face in his palms for a minute. He let out one great sob and then forced the tears to stop.

"I knew she was dead," he said, "And I guess I'm glad to hear it wasn't the Changed. But there was a part of me that held out some hope, ya know?"

James was looking up at the mountains and said, "Yeah, I do."

"So why did you run off?"

James looked at Jesse for a long moment. Jesse felt like he was trying to gauge what his reaction would be, which was exactly what James was doing. After a moment, James shrugged and said, "I ran off because Dylan asked me to."

"What?" Jesse nearly yelled. He had gone through a million scenarios in his head and had conjured up a thousand reasons for his brother leaving. That was not one of them.

"What do you mean he asked you to?"

"I mean that he told me I needed to go with him and explained why. He made a good case and I decided I would."

"But..why?"

"He's going to explain that to you."

"What? No? I don't want him to explain it to me. I want you to explain to me. Why this guy asked you, a twelve year old kid, to run off with him and you just up and went, apparently getting Mom killed in the process?" He was shouting by the end. He immediately regretted blaming his mother's death on James. Especially since it sounded like it was Dylan's fault to him.

"Ok, I deserved that, and I understand why you would say it. But I'm going to say this just once. What happened to Mom was neither my fault, nor Dylan's. There's no reason for you to believe that, so all I can ask is that when Dylan gets back, you give him the benefit of the doubt. If not for his sake, then for mine."

"And why should I give you the benefit of the doubt for anything? You abandoned me, your seven-year-old brother, remember? Jesus Christ." He stood up and walked around the gazebo.

"Because I'm still your brother. We're family and we're together now. Look, Dylan will.."

Jesse cut him off, "And where the hell is Dylan? Can't someone give me a goddamn straight answer other than 'wait for Dylan?' You know I've been taking beatings for him? That son of a bitch Reverend Jordan has been telling lies about what happened that day. I've been telling the truth and getting my face rubbed in gravel for it. I'm getting really tired of having my face rubbed in gravel."

"I'm sorry I wasn't there Jesse. I'm sorry you had to grow up alone. You may not believe me, but I'll never forgive myself for that. But you're not alone anymore. And you won't be ever again. I can promise you that. As for Dylan, you need to hear the whole story and he's the only one who can tell you that. All I ask is that when the time comes that you listen and then make your judgments."

Jesse turned to his brother. He saw that James sincerely believed what he was saying. As he looked at him, he mentally transposed the full-grown James for the twelve-year-old version. Jesse sat down heavily on the bench and exhaled. His anger was spent. He had stuck to his story for years because he believed in the truth. Deep down he also believed that there was something magical about Dylan. If he was able to believe that, then he could believe that there was a good reason that he had to grow up like he did. He would do as his brother asked and reserve judgment. At least until he talked to Dylan.

"So, what happened next?"

"Next?"

"After you ran out. I guess Dylan caught up to you?"

"Oh, yeah. Yes, he did. We had a place to meet, but he had not counted on Mom running out after me. He found her and together we buried her. We then set off together heading east."

"How did you not get attacked by the Changed?"

"The Changed don't bother Dylan."

"Why not?" Jesse had guessed that years ago but never could guess why.

"He'll explain that."

Jesse sighed.

"So you headed east?"

"Yup. And we spent the next nine years walking the old highways of what used to be America."

"Why?"

"To understand what needs to be done."

"What needs to be done?"

"To save the world."

"Huh?"

"That's about all I can tell you, Jabber. The rest Dylan will explain. I know your life has sucked. I know you turned to booze and spent most of the time miserable. I can only tell you that living rough for years wasn't much of a picnic either. I like to think Malice and Julie are my rewards for that."

Jesse thought about that for a while. He had spent the last few weeks on the road and while he enjoyed some of it, he could not imagine living like that.

"I guess we both had pretty shitty childhoods."

"Yup."

"Well then, I guess we're going to have to see if we can make things better for ourselves."

"Amen."

"Your wife is hot."

"Isn't she?"

They broke into fits of laughter and hugged each other. Jesse knew he was being given a second chance and did not want to throw it away over bitterness. He just hoped Dylan had some pretty convincing things to say for himself.

Together they walked back to the house and made breakfast. Julie and Desmond woke up to the smell of bacon and the sound of laughter coming from the kitchen.

CHAPTER TWENTY-FOUR

Desmond dreamed about his wife and son. They were unusually happy for him. Usually when he dreamt of them, the dreams were at best melancholy and at worst horrifying. When he woke up, he felt better than he had in years. He wondered if it was the comfort of the bed or the music or the release he had felt since the tunnel.

He sat up and stretched. The sounds and smells that drifted up to him made him smile. He stretched again, then sat back down on the bed and picked up the horn. He looked at it for a long time running through old fingering exercises that he had half forgotten.

"It's almost too good to be true." he said quietly to himself.

He thought about that for a moment and started to get anxious. It really did seem too good to be true. They knew he was coming, they'd given him a horn, fed him, gave him a comfortable bed, and reunited Jesse with his long thought dead brother. They did all this in the name of a man who had summoned Jesse. A man who was not here when they arrived. He wondered if this was all some sort of elaborate trap, a way to get them to let their guard down. He could not think of what possible reason anyone could have for that. He didn't have anything resembling an enemy in the world. He had gotten into the occasional scrape but that was about it. Jesse did have one, he realized. Father Jordan. Jordan would have the resources to do something like this but no motivation that he could think of. If Jesse was too much of a problem, then he imaged Jordan would just have him killed. He certainly had no compunctions about having him roughed up. This town being a trap didn't make much sense to him.

It felt more like a sales pitch.

If they were trying to get people to live here and sleep in comfortable beds and drink beer, then he was all in. That did not strike him as something they would need to recruit for. That was the kind of thing you would just have to advertise, and people would be beating down the door. He had lived in a tent for the better part of the last twenty years. There would be no reason to be circumspect if you wanted him to live a better life.

It was a sales pitch, he decided. They needed Jesse and him for something. More likely they just needed Jesse, but he was part of the pitch.

These people, nice though they might be, are hiding something and it was something important. As he got dressed and went downstairs, he resolved that he would be on his guard for both him and Jesse.

"So, tell us about Malice." Jesse said between bites of eggs and toast, "Like, why is it called Malice? Your wife was a bit tight lipped about it."

Julie coughed and swallowed hard before saying "Hey, I told you. I made a promise!"

"Alright, alright, don't choke. So why is it called Malice?"

James answered, "This place was some sort of resort that had been abandoned when we found it. Dylan thinks it might have been designed for people to live in these cabins for a day or two and then have the company that owned the place build them one. There were fifteen cabins built surrounded by a large fence. The gate in the fence had a sign over it that read 'Mt. Alice' but the T and the period were missing, so it just read M Alice. The sign is actually hanging in his cabin. We just thought it was ironic given what we wanted to turn this place into, so we kept it. We meant to change it at some point but after people started to trickle in and it was too late."

Desmond laughed and shook his head, "Somehow I expected some deep meaning to the name."

"We like to think of it as meaningful," James replied, "The idea is that you leave any malice at the gate."

"It does seem sort of," Jesse paused for a moment, searching for the right word, "Idyllic."

"Like I told you this morning, we made the place with an idea in mind. We wanted a place without cynicism where people trusted and helped one another. It's possible even in this post-Change world. It doesn't have to be Julie's Dad's wild west or your refugee slums. Tell you what, it sounds like Dylan won't be back today so why don't you wander around and meet some of the folks and you can make up your own mind?"

"Sounds like a sales pitch." Jesse said casually.

Desmond looked at Jesse a bit surprised. He had figured Jesse would be too numb from reuniting with his brother to look at things objectively.

"I guess you could say that, although I'm not trying to sell you anything. This is where and how we live. I will be upfront in saying that I hope you stay," He turned and looked at Desmond, " You too, Desmond."

Jesse had not really thought about that. He was still thinking of this as a trip, a visit, and that he would eventually return to Silver City and his previous status quo. Hearing his brother ask him to stay caught him off guard. He could not think of a single reason he would want to go back to Silver City, he had to admit to himself. He was ruminating on this when Desmond responded.

"I appreciate that James. I haven't given much thought to the idea of pulling up roots, but I guess anything is possible. I'd like to see this paradise you've created before making any decisions."

James and Julie both laughed.

"It's not paradise," James responded, "Not by a long shot."

He was about to expound on that, but Julie cut him off, "We have our problems just like everyone else. Drought one year, too much rain the next, fires, sickness, and so forth. I guess the main difference is that everyone is sharing the abundance when we have it and sharing the scraps during the lean times."

"Communism." Desmond replied.

"Of a sort," answered James, "Although we have an elected council, and we have town meetings once a month or so to make decisions."

"That's not really all that different from what other towns do. Wellersville had a mayor but still provided a common place for all the locals to bring their wares, the only folks who went hungry were the people who didn't bring anything to the table. Seems like more of a philosophical difference than a practical one."

"You're partly right. But that's still a big difference, if you ask me. People here are living, not just surviving. There's a future here." retorted Julie.

"Now that," Desmond said thoughtfully, "is something you don't hear people talk too much about."

"No, you don't." James said, "And that's really at the heart of what we're trying to do. It's been thirty years since the Change and people still don't think about the future. They think about tomorrow, and where their next meal is coming from. Silver City keeps building more walls as people emigrate there, but all the walls are filled with are slums and tent cities. We want to get society back to a point where they no longer have to worry about survival. Like it used to be."

"That's a noble goal, but easier said than done. This isn't a big town you got here. How many people?" Desmond asked.

"About 150."

"One hundred and fifty people. That's a drop in the bucket, even if you're all working towards one goal."

"Well, take today and explore around town. Meet some folks. See what they have to say. We'll talk more about it tonight. For now, I'm tired of looking at you and my brother when I could spend time looking at my wife who I haven't seen in almost two months."

They all laughed at that. Jesse and Desmond agreed to leave them alone for the day but would be back for dinner. After they left, Julie and James cleaned up the kitchen.

"He's right you know. It is a drop in the bucket. I wish we could tell him the rest of it." Julie said as they finished drying their breakfast dishes.

"Dylan should be back tomorrow."

"I know. But I don't like keeping secrets."

"Me either. I mean, he's my brother, and I can't even tell him why I never came back for him. It makes me sick just thinking about it."

"How do you think he's going to react when Dylan talks to him?"

"I honestly don't know. Hell, you know him better than me at this point. How does it seem like he'll take that kind of news?"

"I wish I knew."

"Well, no sense in worrying about it. I have faith in Dylan, and I have faith in my brother." He sighed and was silent for a minute. Eventually he shrugged and said "It's in God's hands now. So, I imagine you have a lot of bruises from your journey."

"I feel like one big bruise."

"Care to show me?"

He grinned at her. She grinned right back, and they went off to their bedroom so she could show him the scars she picked up on the road.

CHAPTER TWENTY-FIVE

Jesse and Desmond walked down the main street of Malice looking at the houses. They were mostly cabins, similar to the one Julie and James lived in. Beyond the cabins there were other houses and a few buildings that looked like they had once been used as storehouses. A larger building at the end of the road Desmond recognized as an old movie theater. He imagined it was now the town hall. There was a marquee on the front of the building that had a date and a time listed under the title "Next Gathering".

They were admiring the building when they heard barking behind them. As they turned, a beautiful collie ran up to them and jumped up on Jesse. The dog began to lick his face playfully. Jesse, who's initial reaction had been terror, began to laugh. He had never had a dog and had not spent much time around them. The dog's rough tongue tickled his face as it slobbered on him. A man came jogging up the street after the dog.

"Grendel! Grendel! Get down!" the man shouted. When he got closer the dog turned and leapt in his direction. The man turned and threw a rubber ball he was holding. The dog went tearing down the street after it. The man smiled at Jesse and Desmond. He stood about 5'8 with thinning hair and glasses. Jesse guessed he was in his late forties. He had a round face with large eyes hidden behind the glasses. He took his glasses off and began to clean them with a rag from his pocket.

"Sorry about that. He's utterly harmless and just about the friendliest dog I've ever met."

He put his glasses back on and proffered his hand first to Desmond, then to Jesse. As they shook, he said, "My name is Michael Simonon, most people call me Mick. You must be James's brother and his friend. Jesse and Donald, was it?"

"Desmond."

"Desmond!" he cried, "I apologize. James told me that and I got mixed up. Names are not my strong suit, I'm afraid."

The dog came running back and dropped the ball at Mick's feet. Mick picked up the ball and put it in his pocket. "Grendel! Sit!" he said. The dog looked at him with a very expressive look that implied he had absolutely no comprehension of what the man was asking. After a couple more requests to sit went ignored Mick gave up and said, "Fine. Stand!" The dog continued to stare at him. He laughed and said to Jesse and Desmond, "See? He obeys my every command."

Jesse laughed and knelt down to pet Grendel. The dog immediately started to lick him again.

Desmond asked, "Grendel?"

"Named for a mythical beast from a book called Beowulf."

"I've read it," Desmond responded, "Can't say your dog seems much like a mythical beast."

"Not a scary one at any rate," Mick responded with a wink, "I figured since this town was called Malice when there is actually a lack thereof, I would name the dog in a similar opposite fashion."

"He's great." Jesse said happily.

"I am very fond of him." He leaned over and scratched Grendel on the rump. "So how are you gentlemen finding our little slice of heaven?"

"It's different, that's for sure." Desmond answered.

"That it is. That it is."

"How long have you lived here?" Jesse asked.

"Almost since James and Dylan started it. I was one of the first who found himself drawn here."

"Drawn?"

"I like to think so. I was living in a town to the north and one day I woke up and decided that It was time to move on. I packed what I could carry and set out that same day. A few weeks later I ended up here and have been here ever since." He also added, "If you ask around most folks have a similar story."

"So you were summoned somehow?"

"I don't know if summoned is quite the right word, nothing so overt. I didn't like where I was living much and as I said, one morning it just felt like the right time to go. Even as I wandered, I didn't feel like I had a destination or that I was being pulled anywhere. One day I crested that hill just like you did, and it just seemed right. It felt like this is where I was supposed to be. That's about the best I can explain it."

"I think I understand. That doesn't sound so unusual." Jesse replied sounding almost relieved.

"Right, it really doesn't. That is, until you talk to other folks here and realize everyone has the same story."

"You mean everyone else..." Desmond began.

Mick finished for him, "Woke up one morning with the urge to go, found their way here and felt at home. Correct."

"That doesn't seem weird to you?" Jesse asked.

"Oh, sure at first it did. But the more time you spend around Dylan the less strange other things seem."

"How so?"

"I'll just say that Dylan is special. I imagine you know that though. You've met him before."

"When I was younger, yes, but I don't know how much of that I might have imagined."

"Really? And yet all this time you've stuck to your guns. Even when it got you in trouble with Jordan's disciples. Why change now?"

Jesse looked surprised.

"I'm on the town council. Before Julie was sent to find you, Dylan and James told us about you. He asked us to let him be the one to talk to you, but I will say this, faith is important. Don't lose your faith now."

Jesse started to say something but another voice from down the street cut him off. A diminutive Latino woman was walking down the street calling out.

"Mick, you leave our guests alone! And for God's sake, get that mutt away from them before he slobbers them to death!" the woman yelled.

"Gentleman, I'd like you to meet my wife, Guadalupe."

The woman ambled up to them and whacked Mick on the shoulder, then turned to look at Desmond and Jesse. She appraised them both from top to bottom. She was only about five feet tall but well-muscled and solid. She looked like a farmer to Desmond.

"So, you're the two who poor Julie had to go traipsing about God knows where to find." She said in such a way that implied that Desmond and Jesse should feel terrible about it all.

"I guess we are, my name is Des..."

"I know full well who you are." she said cutting Desmond off, "You're old but I think we'll find something for you to do. You," she said turning to Jesse, "Are far too skinny. We're going to have to fatten you up some."

Jesse looked at Mick for some help and he simply shrugged and winked at him.

She gave a loud humph after a moment and said, "Well, if you're half the man your brother is you should be ok."

"And you want me to leave our guests alone?" Mick said laughingly.

"I know you, mister. Leave somebody alone with you for ten minutes and you'll start boring them to tears with your stories."

"We were just saying hello, and my stories are not boring."

"Well, Desmond here might like them, he's old like you. If you start in with Jesse, he's likely to head right back out the gate!"

Desmond and Jesse both chuckled.

"You know some people are impressed when they find out I was a baseball player. But never mind that, why are you here? Aren't you supposed to be in the fields today."

"Oh, I see, you love me so much you wish I was somewhere else?"

"You know what I mean!"

This time Guadalupe winked at Jesse and Desmond. Jesse imagined they did this a lot. It was clear to him they loved each other very much. They also seemed happy to him. It struck him that they, like his brother and Julie, did not have a sense of world weariness to them. They did not seem to be expecting the worst at all times consciously or unconsciously. He had met so few people who did not seem resigned to hardship that it was hard to not look at them as being in denial.

"Anyway, enough of your nonsense, old man. I'm here to find these two," she waved her arm at Jesse and Desmond, "Dylan's back early."

They walked through the streets following Guadalupe. Mick walked along with them as Grendel danced playfully around. Jesse was nervous. He had not thought he would be at this moment, but now that it was here, he felt like something heavy was in the pit of his stomach.

As he grew up, he always imagined he would meet Dylan again. The scenarios that had played out in his head were nothing like what was now happening. When he was very small, he always hoped Dylan would come riding back into town having married his mother. During his teenage years he largely gave up on Dylan or his family ever returning, but he could not help but harbor the wish that Dylan would come back and take him to where his family was. After he had begun looking for answers in the bottom of a bottle, he sometimes thought he would see Dylan again and Dylan would just walk by and not recognize him. He did not understand why this man who he had only known for a couple of days when he was seven was such a large figure in his imaginings, he only knew that he was.

Now that he was finally going to see Dylan again, he felt both shame and anger. James had answered some questions but not enough. Jesse needed answers now and was tired of people not being straight with him. That anger was butting up against the feelings of abandonment that he had come to define himself by. Jesse thought he could feel the battle as if it was being fought in his stomach.

Desmond put his hand on Jesse's shoulder as they walked toward the gate and gave him an encouraging squeeze.

"Moment of truth, kiddo. Don't worry, I'm right beside you. Let's see what this guy has to say for himself."

Side by side they followed Guadalupe out of the gate and south towards one of the fields. On the far side of the field a small group of people had gathered. He could hear laughter coming from them and as they got closer, he saw him. He was older and he had a full beard the same straw color as his long hair. He had on well-worn denim jeans and cowboy boots. A loose fitting black and grey plaid shirt hung open revealing a tighter black t-shirt underneath. He rocked easily back and forth on his heals with his hands in his pockets as he laughed at something the tall man next to him had said. He looked to Jesse like a man who was comfortable with himself and his role in the world. His guitar was slung over his back.

When Dylan caught sight of them, he broke into a huge grin and raised his hands up and out like he wanted to hug them.

"Jesse! Desmond!" he cried out in the voice that Jesse remembered so vividly.

"That him?" Desmond said very quietly to Jesse.

"Yup."

"You never told me he was an old hippy."

"What the hell is a hippy?"

The group of people who had gathered around Dylan parted as Jesse and Desmond arrived and walked up to Dylan. Dylan was beaming at them.

"Welcome to Malice! I'm so glad you both decided to come."

Jesse wanted to say so many things but all he managed to do was croak out, "Thank you."

"Thank you. Glad to finally meet you, I've heard quite a lot about you." Desmond said and offered his hand to Dylan. Dylan took it with both hands and shook it.

"I know you've had a hard trip and there is a lot I need to talk to you both about and not very much time, I think. If you wouldn't mind, I'd like to speak with Jesse alone for a bit? That ok, Jes?"

"Er, yeah, that's ok." Jesse stammered. He had expected Dylan to be more effusive and less to the point and felt off balance.

"Fine by me." Desmond responded.

"Excellent. Jesse, let's take a walk."

He clapped Jesse on the back and motioned with his hand towards the hill with the gazebo on it where James and Jesse had talked that morning. The people that had been standing with Dylan as they arrived started to filter away. As the man who had been standing next to Dylan began to walk away Dylan exclaimed, "Oh!" and put his hand on the man's shoulders.

"Desmond, have you met Stu?" Dylan said and then turned back to Stu, "Stu, this is Desmond Hibbard, your father."

Desmond stared at the man Dylan had called Stu. His first instinct was to lash out at Dylan. It seemed like a cruel joke. He felt his hands curl into fists and began to visualize the violence that he was suddenly very capable of performing. He started to say, 'how dare you' but he did not get any farther than 'how'. He found himself looking at Stu's face and realized that he was looking at his wife's eyes. They were the same size and shape and even the same color. The more he stared the more the features revealed that this man could very well be his son. He looked to be about the right age.

"How?" he said again but with less anger. He struggled to believe that this was his long-lost son but he couldn't deny the evidence before him. More than that he instinctively understood that Dylan was a truth teller. He had no idea why he believed that, but he did, with absolute certainty.

"My father is dead." Stuart said. It was clear from his tone that he did not believe the man in front of him was his father. He did not have the evidence of memory to go by.

"Oh, I think if you two compare stories you'll find some similarities. I realize this is quite a bomb to drop on you both and I'm sorry. I tried to think of a better way to let you know but sometimes I think you just have to throw stuff out there. Please, talk. Jesse and I will be back in a while."

He put his hand on Jesse's back and motioned again toward the gazebo. Jesse had been staring at Stu and Desmond and barely noticed Dylan's gesture. Dylan said very quietly to him, "I think they will need some time alone. Best we attend to our business while they attend to theirs." That snapped Jesse out of it and he turned to walk with Dylan.

"My son," Desmond began and then paused to compose himself and then continued, "My son disappeared on a highway near Chicago. He was just a little over one year old."

Stu looked at him for several long moments and then said, "I was raised by a woman who was not my mother. My mother handed me to Tanya when I was a small child and told her my name was Stuart. My mother then, with a group of others, tried to hold off a swarm of Changed. Tanya was sixteen at the time and ran with me gripped to her chest for hours. She tried to find my mother in several refugee camps but never did. This happened outside of Chicago."

Desmond realized he was crying. He could not help himself and truthfully did not want to. He did not know exactly what had happened after he was knocked unconscious, but he could not deny the logic of what Stu had said. He took a deep breath and said, "Your mother's name was Frances Hibbard. You were born a year after we were married. Your full name is Stuart Cliff Hibbard. Her maiden name was Cliff. My name is Desmond Leslie Hibbard. I was knocked unconscious by a stray bullet the night your mother was killed." He pointed to the scar on his head.

Stuart felt overwhelmed. He had always assumed his father and mother were dead. Logic told him thatthis man standing before him, openly weeping, could not possibly be his father. He had lived in Malice long enough to know that logic did not usually have anything to do with what happened. Dylan always said that faith was the key to everything, and he had not led Stuart wrong yet. If Dylan said it was true, then that was enough for him. He felt tears forming in his eyes.

"I think we have a lot to catch up on," he paused and looked into Desmond's eyes to confirm what he was already starting to accept as the truth, "Dad."

"I looked for you." Desmond managed and then embraced his son in a hug. They remained that way for a while.

When they finally broke Stuart smiled at his father and said, "Come back to town. I live with Tonya, I think she would like to meet you."

"I would like to meet her too. I have a lot to thank her for."

Together they walked back to town.

CHAPTER TWENTY-SIX

Jesse and Dylan walked in silence for a while. Jesse was waiting for Dylan to speak. He had questions he wanted answered but was too overwhelmed to ask. When they got to the gazebo, he expected Dylan to stop but he kept going. They walked into the woods on the far side of the hill.

The country here was beautiful. Jesse had spent so much time in the city that he had forgotten how truly gorgeous the world could be. The trees around them were tall and straight. The scent of pine and sap were overwhelming and wonderful. The crunch of dried needles below his feet brought him back to his childhood. The assault on his senses was a comfort and gradually as they walked the knot in his stomach gave way. He began to feel at peace.

They began to climb another hill and after a while the trees gave way to a clearing at the top. In its center, was a fire pit with some large logs arranged around it as benches. Wood for an unlit fire filled the pit. Dylan pulled something out of his jacket and lit the kindling. While he was doing that Jesse took in the view. From this spot they could see for miles. All of Malice and the valley it rested in could be seen, as well as a river parallel to the fields that he had not noticed before. It was a breathtaking vista with the mountains behind it as a backdrop.

"Amazing isn't it?" Dylan asked.

"It's wonderful."

"I come up here a lot. It's peaceful. Helps me clear my head. I thought it would be a nice place for us to talk."

"As good as any."

"I imagine you have some questions."

"A few."

"All I ask is that you hear me out and then I'll answer whatever you want as best I can."

"Ok."

Dylan sat on the ground and leaned against one of the log benches. Jesse went and sat on the log opposite him.

"First off, I owe you an apology."

"An apology?"

"It is my fault your mother died."

That caught Jesse off guard. After what Dylan had said about that man being Desmond's son, he expected a lot of things from this conversation. An apology was not one of them. Certainly not an apology for his mother's death.

After a moment Dylan went on, "I made a mistake that night and your mother paid for it. I guess you could say I miscalculated. I did not think she would follow James like she did. I made another mistake that night as well, but we'll talk about that in a minute."

"James said my mom fell and broke her neck. He also said it wasn't your fault and I should give you the benefit of the doubt."

"Your brother is the forgiving sort and God bless him for it. I had thought I would get to the gate faster than she did and that I could convince her to stay with you while I went after James. It didn't work out like that and your mother died because of it."

"So, why did you want James to leave with you in the first place?"

Dylan picked up a stick and poked the fire with it. There was a cool breeze and the fire felt good on Jesse's skin. He watched the flames dance as he waited for Dylan to answer. Finally, he did.

"Because I guessed wrong about God's will."

"God's will?"

"Yes."

"It was God's will that you kidnap my brother and run off into a night filled with monsters?"

"Nope."

"Then..." Jesse began but Dylan cut him off.

"It was God's will that I kidnap you and run off into a night filled with monsters. I got it wrong and that was my other mistake."

Jesse was getting mad, "You were supposed to kidnap me? God told you to kidnap me. I trusted you then and for years have looked at you as some sort of savior and what you are telling me is that God told you to convince me or my brother to run off with you. Are you out of your mind?"

"You have every right to be mad Jesse."

"Your Goddamn right I do."

"I only ask that you hear me out."

"Why the hell should I?"

"Because you've believed in the truth all your life. You have kept faith for these past years even when it caused you trouble. You kept faith even when you did not understand what it was you had faith in. Because minutes ago, you saw your best friend reunited with a son he had long since given up on."

"How do I know that was true?"

"Because it was, and I believe you know it."

Jesse had no response to that. He did believe it. He did not know why, but he knew it had been the truth.

"I'll make a deal with you. Let me tell you my story and then if you want to go back after I am done you can. I will not bother you again. Like I said, all I ask is that you hear me out."

Jesse stared at him for a long time. Finally, he said, "Ok. Let's hear it."

Dylan poked the fire again and took a deep breath. As he exhaled, he thought back to that day that felt like it was so long ago.

"When I woke up, I was in a record store..."

The record store was in Warrensburg, Missouri. I was terribly hungry and thirsty, and I had no memory of how I got there. I didn't even know my name. I guess I still don't. I had memories of colors and light and pain but nothing that made any real sense to me. At the time I was delirious, barely coherent. I went out the front door of the store and was nearly blinded by the light outside. I distinctly remember feeling like I had not seen the sun in years. Across the street was a supermarket. I stumbled in there and found some bottled water. I drank deeply and almost immediately threw it back up. After that I drank more slowly and found some canned food. Gathering it all I went back to the record store. After eating a can of beans cold and drinking some more water I fell asleep and slept, for how long I don't know.

The next few days passed in that fashion. I would wake up, scavenge for food and water, and then retreat back to the record store. It's hard to describe what it felt like. I guess feral would be the best word. My mind had regressed to a point where I was only aware of my basic needs and impulses. I was little more than a wild animal. I think if some hand had not been guiding my actions even at that point I probably would have starved or died of thirst shortly after waking up.

I'm not really sure how long it was before I started to get some sense of awareness back. It was a long slow process. My sense of self and ability to think beyond simple thoughts like 'hungry' or 'thirsty' was really that last thing that came back. Once that happened, I began to wonder things like 'Who am I?" and "Where am I?" I began to expand out of my tiny world of the record store and supermarket. I explored the town some and found other stores. Most of them were in shambles either from age, or looting, or the Changed. I couldn't really tell. One store was a newsstand that still had some yellowed papers in the back from around the time of the Change. As I stared at them it was like a switch went off in my head. I actually remember seeing the symbols coalesce into words and words into meanings. As a sensation it's hard to describe. The best I've come up with is that it was similar to when you have a cold and are congested and you turn your head just the right way and your sinuses clear for a moment and suddenly you can breathe again. That's what it felt like, like the sinuses of my mind unclogged. I gathered up all the papers and pretty much everything else I could carry from the newsstand and took them back to the record store. Coming back was the first time I was able to read the sign over the store. It read 'Droge's Hot Wax'.

I spent the rest of that day reading everything I could. I was able to piece together what had happened. I had no idea how much time had passed. I guessed from the yellowed papers and the rundown look of the town around me that it had been a while. I guessed about five or six months at the time. It turned out to have been about fifteen years, but I had no way of knowing that. I honestly started wondering whether I was the last person alive.

There was no one around that I could find. There wasn't even a trace of people having been there recently. It was a ghost town. Over the next few days, I began to explore more hoping for some sign of people and found nothing. The other thing I didn't find were Changed. The papers and magazines talked about barricading yourself in at night, so I locked the door of the record shop dutifully as the sun set. In all my time there, I never saw a single Changed. I doubt this is still the case though. I think they were repelled from the town while I was there.

Despite the lack of interaction with other people, each day I recovered a little bit more of my humanity. I would remember things like how to use a can opener or what a microwave oven was. It seems strange now, but I really was a tabula rasa, a blank slate. Believe it or not, despite my place of residence it was weeks before I remembered what a record was. It was another week before I was able to figure out how the battery-operated players the shop had in the back worked.

That was probably the happiest day of those times. The first record I played was 'Highway 61' by Bob Dylan. The opening drum beat and the first line of the song 'Like a Rolling Stone' was like magic. It hit me with the force of all that's good about people in one burst of sound and emotion. I wept like a child. The chorus certainly was applicable to my situation, with its questions about how it feels to be all alone. It was the first human voice I'd heard besides mine. I must have played that record a hundred times before I started playing anything else.

I played every record in that store at least once. I greedily absorbed every sound, every voice, every note. Somehow the music made me feel real, less fractured, less like a ghost. Dylan's words were the ones that stood out to me though. He sang about being a complete unknown, and that's what I was.

I started looking for some record of my identity. When I woke up, I was naked. I had no wallet, or passport, or dog tags. I found nothing in the record store either. I thought I might have been the owner for a while until I found some papers in a desk in the back that had a photocopy of Peter Droge's driver's license. The same man on the license photo was in a bunch of framed pictures behind the counter of the shop. I looked nothing like him, so I assumed I was not the 'Droge' of Droge's Hot Wax.

I searched for days and found nothing. Eventually I gave up looking. The answer may have been in the town somewhere, but I didn't have the wherewithal to find it. It occurred to me that if I really was the last person on earth, I didn't need to know who I was. It wouldn't matter. For the time being I was happy to wander around town and listen to records.

On one of my wanderings, I found my guitar. I was exploring some of the houses in a neighborhood outside of the main part of town. There were some woods that I imagine had once been behind the houses but had surged back to the fore in the absence of people. Small trees had grown right next to the houses, in some cases right through porches or into windows. Lawns that had once been well trimmed had been given over to veritable jungles of tall grasses and bushes. The pavement of the road that went down the street was cracked in places from roots that were run wild. It was beautiful.

I had made several trips to the area before. Most of the houses were empty of provisions With nothing but time on my hands I was systematically working through each building. I was always careful to look at any pictures on the walls, in case I happened to turn up in one. It never happened.

The house I was looking in was made out of brick and stood two stories tall. A tree had fallen and collapsed part of the roof, so it was more treacherous than normal inside. The floor creaked loudly with each step I took as I prowled around the living room. There was a painting hanging over what used to be a sofa. The paints had run in the rain and melted into a swirl of colors. I'm not sure what drew me to it but as I stood admiring it, the floor beneath me gave way. I think it was because of the lack of roof. The floor simply wasn't built for years of rain, I guess.

The fall knocked me unconscious. I don't know how long I was out, but it was dark when I woke up. I had not brought a flashlight with me, so I found myself in a pitch-black room with a throbbing head. I tried to feel my way around the room in order to get outside and ended up with nothing but more bruises. Eventually I gave up and went to sleep on the floor.

That night was when the dreams started.

In my dream, I was walking through a desert. I could feel the sand under my feet, and the heat of the sun beat down on me. My mouth was dry from lack of moisture. All around me was the quiet emptiness of sand. I kept walking in one direction and eventually saw something off in the distance. As I got closer, I realized it was a tent and I began to hear music coming from it. As I approached, I heard someone singing 'Like a Rolling Stone' and playing along on a guitar. The voice was incredible. The only way I could describe it is that it was the voice that every song was written for. Eventually I got to the flap of the tent and paused listening to the music. Abruptly, it stopped and the voice called out, 'Well don't just stand out there, come on in."

I entered the tent to find a person sitting there. At least I think it was a person. Its face was hard to see even though the tent was brightly lit. It was as if it kept changing, never staying with one set of features. Whichever way you looked it was different. Sometimes it was old, sometimes young, sometimes it was Asian, and sometimes it was Indian. The strange thing was that it never actually seemed to morph into different faces, it was just as if it was every face at once. It was both male and female, sometimes one and sometimes the other, sometimes both, and sometimes neither. Its voice was the same way changing pitch and tenor with each word while never seeming to change at all. "I'm glad you're finally here," the being said, "Please, have a seat." It was sitting cross legged on the dirt floor with a guitar in its lap. I sat across from it in the same fashion. It smiled and began playing the guitar again. I recognized the music this time as 'Highway 61 Revisited". It began to sing the song and sang the opening lines. It stopped abruptly after it sang the line about God wanting killings done on the highway, and said conversationally, "Things used to be much easier back then." After a few moments it went on.

"I'm glad you finally got here. I've been waiting a while. You have some work to do. I've given you some time to get back into fighting form, but that time will end soon. You'll know when. For now, I just want you to know that I expect things of you. Here, take this as a token of my appreciation for your efforts in what is to come."

It stood up and handed me the guitar. It was as beautiful in the dream as it is in real life. After it handed it to me it touched my hand and spoke once more, "You are not the only one left."

I woke up in the basement sometime the next day. There wasn't much light in the room even at that point. What light there was shone through the hole in the floor I had made when I fell. It came through as a dusty beam of brilliance and landed on the guitar. It was hanging from the wall. The light glinted off its polished enamel body and made it look like it was glowing. I went over and picked it up and just stared at it for a while. I wanted to tell myself that I saw it when I fell down, but I knew there was no way I could have seen it in the darkness. I didn't understand how it was I dreamt of the guitar, but I didn't much care at that point. It was as lovely an instrument as had ever been made. I slung it over my back and moved a workbench that had been against the wall to the middle of the room and climbed out of the basement.

Once I was outside of the rotting house, I sat down on the curb and took the guitar off my back. As far as I know I had never even touched a guitar before. I sat with it in my lap enjoying the weight and the size of it when finally, I strummed the strings with my right hand. As my hand touched each string, I experienced a revelation like when I found out I could read. Each note felt like suddenly being able to breathe again. I put my left hand on the fretboard and without really thinking about it began to make chord shapes and play notes. Soon my fingers were flying over the strings. I tried to remember the songs I had listened to on the records and found that if I just opened my mind to the song and relaxed, I was able to play it. It wasn't simply playing back the notes I had heard; I was able to put my own touches on them. I simply knew how to play.

I played for hours sitting there on the curb. I played till my fingers bled and my muscles ached. I sang till my voice was hoarse. When at last I looked up it was night again and the stars were illuminating the world. I took the guitar back to the record shop and went to sleep with my hand resting on its body.

I knew the guitar was a gift from the person in my dream. I didn't know why it had been given to me, but I knew that it was good. I knew that it was pure. It was a sign of faith from it to me. I knew that by accepting the guitar I had formed a covenant with that person and that they had work for me to do.

I spent the next few days listening to records and playing along with them. I was learning the words to the songs. I immersed myself in music. I think I once told you that I learned the songs I knew when I was younger, which was in essence true. Although I was physically in my twenties I was completely born anew. No trace of who I had been still existed. I may have known how to play the guitar before I lost myself and was playing off sense memory, but I don't believe so. I believe I was given the ability by the man in my dreams as a way of conveying the message he wanted me to spread. And so, I learned songs and played. My fingers became calloused and grew stronger and I was able to play even more nuanced songs. Eventually my body caught up with my gifted ability.

After that first dream, they no longer took place in the desert. In the second dream, It was sitting by the side of a road. We were on one of the roads that led away from Warrensburg. I walked over and sat down next to them. It told me it heard me playing and said it sounded wonderful. It's funny how conversations fade into memory, and you forget things, but with them I remember everything it said almost like it's burned into my mind. Even the most casual greeting. As we sat there, we watched the sun set and finally it said, "People always said rock and roll could not change the world, but they were always wrong. Music has always been a catalyst for change. You folks down here never spent enough time looking at the little things. Music, rock and roll especially, always had the ability to inspire. If one song inspires one man to go out and feed one hungry person, then has not music changed the world? Music in all its forms is at its core an expression of love, and as was once said, all you need is love. You will be changing the world with music my friend. I want you to always remember the way you felt when you started listening to those records. That feeling is what I want you to give others. It will be your mission to inspire people and make them remember how to hope for the future."

It got up and walked down the road.

I woke up with that idea glowing brightly in my mind. Music could change the world and it was going to be my job to change it. I had no frame of reference at this point to think this sort of dream was weird or to question anything. I was little more than a babe in the woods. This being came to me when I slept and told me what that it needed me. That was enough.

I met them for the third time sitting on the steps of your house. When I found myself dreaming, I was walking up the path to your gate and then passed through. It was sitting on the bottom step with its legs crossed. It's strange shifting face broke into a smile when it saw me. It beckoned me over and tapped the step inviting me to sit next to them.

"The time is getting close. You will need to go soon," it said, "But not yet. Before you go out into the world again you should understand that world."

When it said that, my mind filled with images. I can't really describe what I saw but suffice to say it was a vision of pain and misery. It was the world before the Change. It was filled with starvation, poverty, degradation, but most of all sadness. In the vision, the people I saw weren't really people, they were more like outlines of people. Some were filled with a very bright light, a few with a darkness that seemed to absorb light, but most had no light at all. They were like shadows.

Once the visions receded, it put his hand on my shoulder. The feeling of overwhelming horror and sadness went away at its touch but it was a moment before I was fully recovered.

"People are capable of the most wondrous things and all that is needed to fuel their fire is love. Love one another, have compassion, empathy, truly see each other. That is what is important. Years ago, a man explained this in the simplest of terms. People listened. Some still listen but most lost the message. They lost it in details and rules that were put in place to somehow govern love, as if that's possible. Love is the function of your spirit, your soul. That is what it does. Words in a book hold no power over it."

He paused for a moment.

"What can prevent the spirit from its purpose is placing your faith in those trivialities. Love is what matters. So many forgot this and eventually their spirits shriveled and died. They lost their ability to love, to hope, to dream. A body without its spirit is simply a shell. This absence of spirit is not like dying. It is a kind of undeath. The body becomes something else, a mindless thing. A thing that abhors light because a spirit is brighter than the stars. These husks see the light and they are filled with longing. They know in their rudimentary thoughts that they are missing something and that the light coming from people is what they long for. All trace of what they were is gone."

"This plague swept the world and what is left is people who have not forgotten that spirit for good and for ill. Many still teeter on the brink of losing themselves. That is the world in which you now live."

He got up and walked a few steps towards the gate before turning and looking at the house. He waved me over and compelled me to look where he was pointing. In the window on the second floor stood a child. He smiled and waved at me. I waved back and the dream faded.

I understood it was talking about the Changed. They aren't zombies or monsters. They are people who have lost connection with their souls. I still did not understand how I fit in to what he was talking about. The idea of bringing hope to people through music made sense to me but I still didn't see what it had to do with the Changed.

In my fourth dream it all became clear.

It was several weeks before I dreamed of it again. During that time, I got myself ready to leave. I knew on some level that the next time I saw them, it would be sending me forth for whatever purpose it had in mind. Scrounging around town, I found a bag and some spare clothes. I also raided the music store nearby for all the guitar strings I could find. A lot of them had rusted but there were more than enough good ones. I stuffed everything I thought I would need in a bag and then waited. During those weeks spring ended, and summer began.

On the first really hot night of summer I dreamt of it again. It was sitting on the ground with its back leaning against a gate. The gate had a sign over it that said 'Mt. Alice'. As in the other dreams I was walking up to them when it began. It waved me over and gestured towards the town that was visible behind the gate.

"Pretty place," it said. I looked at the town and nodded. After a moment it motioned for me to sit beside it again. The pattern had become familiar by now. Once I was seated, it patted my knee and smiled at me.

"It's time for you to begin your work. Though there is a plague on earth there is also a cure. As always with humanity the path to salvation is there if you choose to find it. As it has before, the redemption of humanity comes in the form of a person. Unlike before, this person is purely of earth and is not divine. Their life will begin as a test. They must be put on the path to the wilderness. While they are facing their trials, you will be preparing the way. You are tasked with opening the minds and hearts of people so that they may accept their deliverance. If this person perseveres over the obstacles that will be mounted against them then you must find them on the far side of that wilderness. It will not be easy. But do not be afraid. Place your faith in love and you will succeed. I believe in you. Will you do as you are asked?"

"I will." I responded.

"Thank you." It said

"Who am I?" I asked.

"You were Changed but have been restored. Your spirit has been cleansed. Who you are is a question only you can answer."

With that I woke up. I knew what I had to do, if not exactly where I needed to go. I had been Changed and then was Changed back. That was why I had no memory of who I was. I had lost myself into that nightmare and was rescued. My faith will never waiver again. I was being asked to open people's hearts and given the tools to do it. It did not matter who I was before, only that I had been given a second chance.

I left that day. I strapped my guitar to my back and walked down the road I had seen in the dream. I didn't know where I was headed but I had faith that I would be guided to where I needed to go. I walked all day that first day without seeing a soul. I hadn't traveled much beyond Warrensburg before then and found myself marveling at nearly everything I saw. The long lines of cars, the sheer number of deer in the fields, and the way nature had reasserted its dominance in places where people were no longer occupying.

I felt like an explorer traveling through places no one had gone before. I guess in some ways that was true. There were very few signs that people had been there in years. I was rediscovering a small part of what used to be America. It was exhilarating. It was like being a child again, which in a lot of ways I was.

I walked until past sunset. Finally, once the sun had disappeared from the sky, I made camp. This consisted of making a small fire, heating a can of beans, and unrolling a sleeping bag. I was exhausted but nearly bursting with excitement. After I finished my dinner, I laid down in my sleeping bag and looked at the stars. I could see them very well in Warrensburg but out on the plains it was different. There were no buildings in the way so the whole sky was an open map before me.

I first heard them when I was halfway between wakefulness and sleep. I dismissed the sound as something out of the early stages of a dream and started to drift off again. Then I heard it much closer. It was a moaning and shuffling movement. I sat up and looked around. It was hard to tell where the sound was coming from. Soon I realized that was because they were coming from all sides. I could feel fear rising in me. I had not seen a Changed up to that point. All I knew of them was their nature as I was told in my dreams and what I had read in old papers and magazines. Everything in those magazines described them as monsters that relentlessly sought to destroy humanity. As terror threatened to overwhelm me, I began to think of the dreams. They had laid out a path for me and I was now following it. It would have been a waste if I died on my first night. I decided that I would place my faith in the hand that was guiding me.

I picked up my guitar as the first one came into the circle of light given off by the dying fire. Another appeared opposite the first. More stepped into the light in a circle around me. I couldn't say how many were outside the light. It was impossible to tell but the air was filled with moaning. Part of me was expecting them to descend upon me at any moment but they didn't. They simply stood there moaning and staring at me with those shriveled husks of eyes.

I do not know why they stopped. It could be the hand of God or it could be my nature as a Changed who returned to humanity confused them. After what seemed like hours, I decided to play the guitar. I had picked it up as a potential weapon but that did not seem to be necessary. And so, I played.

I started with a song from Highway 61 called 'Just Like Tom Thumb's Blues'. As soon as I started to strum the guitar the moaning quieted. When I joined the guitar with my voice even the residual moaning stopped. They stood stock still around me in the quiet evening. It was almost as if they were listening to me. Halfway through the song they began to leave. By the time I finished there was no trace they had ever been there. I sang another song partly to calm my nerves and partly to make sure they were gone. After the second song I sat listening for a while and eventually drifted off to sleep.

Most of my encounters with the Changed went like this. They won't harm me. They rarely come near me and if I play and sing, they go away. I don't understand why. I may be the only person on the planet who can sleep under the stars without hiding behind a fence.

The next day I moved on. I walked the highways feeling no particular pull in any direction. I just let my feet decide where to take me next. It was the end of my second week that they took me to a farm.

As sundown approached, I walked to the gate on the farm's fence and found myself even more nervous than I had been the first night with the Changed. I had never met another human being and after the Changed I had no idea how they would react. I hoped I could trade some songs for a meal. It was the idea of eating something cooked and fresh that got me past the fear I felt. Summoning all my willpower, I rang the bell that was hanging by the door.

I was just about to ring the bell a second time after about two minutes when a voice called out telling me to hold my horses. It was another minute before a small slot on the door slid open to reveal a pair of older looking eyes peering out at me. "What do you want?" the eyes asked. I told him that I wished for a place to stay and maybe a hot meal. I could play the guitar as payment. The eyes stared at me for a while and then the slot on the door closed again. Moments later, I heard the sound of boards being moved and the door being unlocked.

Standing by the door when it opened was a man in his late forties dressed in jeans and a t-shirt. The man looked me up and down for a moment and then held out his hand to shake mine.

"Name's Neal." He said before adding, "Most folks just call me Diamond. Might as well come on in. Not going to reach anywhere else before they come out."

He waved me into the complex and securely closed and fastened the door when I went through.

"Who might you be?"

I felt stunned for a moment. I realized that I had no name. In my dreams one had not been used and I had not needed one when I was on my own. I stammered for a moment buying time and finally said, "My name is Dylan. Dylan Droge. Pleased to meet you, Mr. Diamond."

Diamond took me in and fed me. We spoke for a while of the state of the world. He was a small farmer who lived on his own. Once a month he would take his surplus into the nearby town of Morningside. Other than that, he spent his time in solitude.

We talked about his parents who had died in the Change and about his life since. He told me that he thought he was probably happier than he would have been if the Change had not happened. He had been in college and was studying to be a lawyer. His mother had wanted him to go. His real love was farming. He loved the land and working with living things. I asked him if he was ever lonely and he thought about it quietly for a long while. Finally, he said sometimes he was but mostly he was not. He would like to have met a good woman but never felt the burning need for companionship.

He brought out a pipe and lit it up and began to ask me questions about my life. I did not see any particular reason to lie so I told him the whole story. He was silent for a long time after that. When he finally spoke again, he said, "I believe you. But most people will not." Then he asked me to play for a while, so I did. I played and sang late into the night. Sometimes he joined me and sometimes he listened. When I was done, he told me that my music was the nicest thing he had heard since before the Change.

"Hope is a rare thing these days," he said, "It's something most folks have boxed up and put up on a shelf like a wedding tuxedo. A nice idea from a better time but not something so very useful anymore. Your singing makes me want to go get it down from the shelf and try it on again."

After that he showed me to my bed. I was asleep almost as soon as my head hit the pillow. I dreamt of the town I then thought of as Mt. Alice again. Only this time there were people living in the cabins and building new ones. In the dream, Diamond came up and greeted me and thanked me for the invite.

The next morning over breakfast I asked him if he believed in God. He said he surely did and added that my story strengthened that belief. He went on to say that he wasn't much for church. His parents had gone to a big church with lots of people where the minister talked a lot about some people were ok and others weren't. He never saw how that sort of thing made sense with the Beatitudes. I didn't know what he meant by that at the time, so I just nodded my head a lot. I've since come to realize it was a lot like what I'd been told in my dreams. He went on for a while in this fashion and then took a serious tone.

"You need to watch yourself with that story of yours. Prophets have a tendency to come to a bad end. You may be out there setting the stage for some sort of second coming but people ain't all gonna like that."

He was right. In all my wanderings there are people who greet me with warmth and happiness and some who do not, like Father Jordan. People are so invested in their own version of things that they feel threatened by someone else's.

I left Diamond's place that day and got back on the road. Before I left, I told him about Mt. Alice and asked him to join me there. He said he would think about it. I told him that when the time came, he would know. He laughed and smiled at me. He told me either I was completely crazy or someone very special. I guess he decided the latter as he was one of the first people to arrive in Malice.

That's how things went for me. I would wander around, sometimes staying at a farm or a town, sometimes sleeping under the stars. I would meet people and play my guitar and sing. I felt more like a bard than a prophet. The music always had an effect on people. Usually for the good, although sometimes it would be more than people could bear. In instilling hope for the future, the music forged a link to the past. It was too much of a reminder of what they had lost.

I would dream on occasion. Never as vivid as those first dreams but often with a direction or a road or the name of a town. I was walking a path of my own, but I always had a guide. I met a lot of the folks who live in Malice today during those days.

It was one of those dreams that led me to your farm.

I had been heading to Wellersville to ask around and see where to find you when I saw the swarm as it attacked. Without them I would have walked right past. I began to play to get their attention. Once I had that I knew they would leave and so they did.

That night was also when I made my mistake. I had interpreted my dreams to mean I was to take you onto the road and to live as I did. I also thought that the one I was meant to find was your brother. I had a lot of reasons but mostly it was because I thought he was special. He was quiet and introspective and smart. I also thought he was the child I saw waving in the window in my dream. I had been on the road for a few years and I wrongly assumed that the child I saw had grown up some rather than seeing him as he would be when I met him.

And so I talked to your brother and told him that it was my mission to take him on the road with me to prepare him for his destiny. Your brotherhad read a lot, so he was receptive to my message. We decided that he would leave from the town and I would follow him. You know what happened next.

I spent the next decade on the road with James. We wandered the country from end to end and met many people. I have played for thousands over the years. I have seen both oceans and I have seen that people are ready and waiting for the next change to come.

CHAPTER TWENTY-SEVEN

"This just seems so impossible." Desmond blurted out. He was sitting at Stu's kitchen table waiting for his son to finish making coffee. They had come here after stopping by to talk to James and Julie. They had been just as surprised as Desmond and Stu although they more readily accepted the news than Desmond had. He imagined that living in a town that seemed to readily believe in magic would do that to you. "Oh, he's your long lost son, is he? Ok. So, what's for dinner?" Desmond thought to himself. Soon he would meet the woman who raised his son from the night he lost him. He just could not wrap his brain around any of this being true.

Stu walked over with a mug of coffee and Desmond took it gladly. Stu pulled out the chair across the small table from Desmond and sat down.

"Yeah." he said.

"James and Julie didn't seem all that surprised." Desmond was trying to make conversation and finding that he had a lot to say but could not make himself say it.

"James was on the road with Dylan for years. I imagine there isn't much that surprises him."

"This Dylan guy. Everyone here talks like he's Jesus. Sort of feels like a cult."

Stu laughed, "Yeah, I could see that. A lot of the neighboring towns think we are a cult. It's not the case though. He isn't Jesus. Doesn't claim to be either. The only thing I've ever heard him call himself that was out of the ordinary is prophet."

Desmond whistled.

"He thinks he's a prophet?"

"Near as I can tell, he is a prophet. He knows things before they happen, and he's spent the last fifteen or so years preparing the way for someone. At least that's what he says he's been doing."

"That doesn't seem crazy?"

"It does at first but the more you talk to people here and the more you spend time around him the less crazy it seems. I mean, here you are, my long lost father. You arrived in the company of the person Dylan has been waiting for. Maybe it was meant to be, I don't know."

They sat in silence for a while sipping their coffee. Finally, it was Stu who broke the silence.

"Tell me about my mother. Please," he asked.

"She was a wonderful person. Beautiful, smart, thoughtful, kind. She was a little older than me. I met her in Boston during her senior year at Boston University. I was playing in a band that had been hired for a party she was at. After our set she introduced herself. She was studying foreign policy and hoped to go work for the United Nations." He barked a laugh at that. He knew his son would not have much concept of foreign relations, or the UN, or even college. Things certainly had changed.

"You played music?"

"Yup. I played horn in a few bands. Mostly ska and jazz outfits. That was how I earned my daily bread. I was looking for more steady work after we were married and you came along, but I never took to 9-5 jobs well. She paid for most things with a job she had gotten as a supervisor at a call center. About a year or so after you were born, I started gigging heavily again because she got laid off. That was when the Change hit."

"I wish I could have known her."

"I do too, Stu," he paused, "Hey, do you prefer Stu or Stuart?"

"Either is fine, er, Dad."

Desmond found himself unable to speak for a minute after hearing that. Stu gave him a meaningful look and smiled. He had accepted the new paradigm even if Desmond had not.

"Dad." Desmond said wistfully and found himself smiling, "I didn't think I'd ever hear that said to me. I looked for you. I did."

"I know. I also understand the impossibility of the task. I don't blame you. I'm sorry that this is really the first time we're meeting, but I'm thankful for this chance."

"I am too."

"More coffee?"

Desmond looked into his mug and realized he had finished it as they spoke. He handed it to Stu for a refill.

"Tell me about yourself." Desmond asked.

"Welp, as I told you I was raised by Tonya. We lived in a town west of here on the other side of the mountains. When I was younger, we moved around a lot. She was able to work as a seamstress to earn our food and put roofs over our heads. The trouble was she is a lesbian. People were ok with a white lady raising a little black kid in the face of the Change, but lesbians still weren't overly accepted. The combination of those two things made people awfully uncomfortable. She mostly tried to keep it a secret. I was too young, obviously, but I imagine you remember that the world wasn't a very safe place for homosexuals right around the Change. She had lost her lover to a pack of misguided bastards who were acting on orders from that TV preacher. That's why she was on the highway that day. She was trying to get away from folks like that."

"Where was she headed?"

"Seattle," a voice said from the kitchen doorway. Desmond turned and saw a smallish woman about his age with long silver hair standing there. She was wearing a green sundress that reminded him, jarringly, of the dress his wife wore their last day in Boston. He stood up to greet her. Across the table, Stu got up as well.

"Hi, Mom." he said.

"So, Robbie at the gate told me your father was here?"

"Yup. Tonya this is Desmond, Desmond this is Tonya."

Desmond held out his hand to her. She took it and shook it tentatively.

"You believe he's your father?" she asked Stu.

"Dylan said he was. His story matches up with mine."

"Also, you look like him."

"Do I?"

"You do."

"I guess I owe you a debt Ma'am." Desmond said when they paused.

"I guess I owe you one as well."

"How do you figure?"

"You gave the world a fine man in Stu over there. And you gave me the privilege of raising him. The circumstances may have been terrible, but my life has been better for it. So, thank you."

"And thank you for saving him. And for believing me to be his father, I guess. I know how strange this must all seem."

"In this town? We eat breakfast cereal that's stranger than that."

Desmond and Stuart both laughed.

"Did he tell you how we ended up here?"

"No Ma'am, he did not."

"Please call me Tonya."

"I will, thank you."

"Tell the man, kiddo."

"Had the same dream. We didn't actually realize it for a few days, either. We were living in Hill City on the other side of the mountains. Mom had a customer stop by the name of Alice and I made a Mount Alice comment. Mom stared at me for a while and later told me she had dreamt about a place with the same name. The compulsion set in after that. The feeling of restlessness and time-to-go-ness that you'll hear just about everyone here talk about."

"That's bizarre."

"If you think that's bizarre, ask Dylan about his dreams sometime."

"I think I might just do that."

Stu poured his mother a cup of coffee and she sat at the table next to Desmond. They talked about the years since the change and about the years before. After a while, Stu got up and prepared some dinner for them. Tonya explained that he was by far the best chef in town. They ate the meal together and slowly the weirdness began to fade from Desmond. He stopped trying to wrap his brain around the synchronicity of it and just accepted that he had found his long lost son. As they ate, the joy he felt welling up threatened to overwhelm him. He had stopped thinking much about the future a long time prior and suddenly found himself filled with hope that there may be a better tomorrow.

He decided at that dinner that he would be staying in Malice. He hoped Jesse would also be staying. He still felt like some of the people were trying to sell him on something but that no longer mattered. Malice felt like a good place to him. He hoped that whatever Dylan had to say to Jesse was ok because he truly believed these people meant what they said. In the end what made the decision for him was that meal. It was a family meal. As much as he cared for the people in Silver City, and Jesse, this was his son and the woman that raised him. If they would accept him, he wanted more than anything to be a part of their lives. Tonya had also been telling the truth about Stuart's cooking abilities.

After dinner Tonya went down to the basement and came up with a bottle of wine. It was a sweet dessert wine she had been saving. Together they laughed and drank, and Desmond felt a hole in his heart heal.

It was after they finished the wine that they heard the shouting.

CHAPTER TWENTY-EIGHT

Brother Lydon had had enough. He was tired of being on the road. He was tired of sleeping in worn out bunk beds in rooming houses. He was tired of eating soup and having to be friendly to people who had nothing for him but thinly veiled hostility. He hated having to try and spread Father Jordan's word to people who could not care less if they tried. He wanted to find Jesse and this Dylan person and drag them back to Silver City or kill them if they resisted. He no longer cared. Father Jordan had said that Dylan was the Antichrist and he would be very pleased if Lydon could end the threat to humanity. It did not seem like the kind of job that Father Jordan's holy hands should be used for.

They were marching towards Malice. He had guessed wrong for the last time. There was nowhere else to go. According to the people he had spoken to in Black Horse there were very few farms in the area so if they had come this way, then Malice was the only option. The person had also suggested that Malice was run by a cult. That clinched the deal for Lydon. That had to be where they went. It had all begun to make sense to him. The Antichrist would have a cult around him and Jesse would be a member. He hoped the people who had been listening to this false God could be brought back to the light but if they couldn't he would consider ridding the world of them.

The thugs that had come with him were ready to do violence in the name of God. He had not trusted them for most of the journey but after so many weeks on the road they were as ready as he was to return home. Every time he spoke to them, they either glared at him or flinched from him. He took the glares to be their hatred of Jesse and the flinches were their fear of him. That was good. They should be afraid of him. He was filled with the holy fire. He had become Father Jordan's flaming sword in this war. He smiled.

They crested a hill as the sun began to turn red in the sky. Before them was the town of Malice. He could see the mountains behind and the fields and hills that surrounded the town. He did not appreciate the beauty although he thought it ironic that such evil would find a place that looked so pure.

"The easier to draw flies into their unholy web." he said aloud.

"Pardon?" asked Angus who had walked up next to him as he surveyed the scene.

"Pardon what?" Lydon replied.

"You said something. I thought you were talking to me, I guess not." Angus shrugged.

"I said nothing." Lydon insisted. He did not realize he had spoken aloud.

Angus gave him a sidelong glance and shrugged. "That's Malice."

"I know." Lydon replied sharply. "It would seem prudent to wait until all the people have returned from the fields before we go down there."

"How come?" Angus asked.

"So that we aren't attacked from behind." Lydon responded curtly.

"Attacked? Why would we be attacked? I thought we were just looking for two guys?" Angus wondered.

"We are, but this is their lair! These are not mere townsfolk; these are people who have come here to worship at their black altar. We must be careful now!" His voice was rising in volume as he spoke.

"Ok, ok, relax. Looks like they're mostly back. I'd say another half hour and we should go."

"That would be acceptable." Lydon said, calming down slightly.

"Did you have a particular plan of attack?" Angus asked.

"We will walk through the front gates and declare our purpose. That should be enough to cow them. If not, we will take up arms and purge them of this earth." Lydon responded.

"You want us to shoot up the town?" Angus exclaimed, surprised.

"It may be necessary but not until we have come face to face with the beast himself."

Angus nodded and walked back to relay this to the rest of the men. He had come this far so he would see it to the finish, but he would not start shooting up a town. He would take care of Lydon himself if it came to that. The man was obviously crazy. He realized none of the other men cared but he did. He had been having dreams the last few nights about this town and this Dylan person and was having second thoughts about the whole thing. The dreams made him feel good when he woke up. They reminded him of home and better days. They made him feel exactly the opposite of what Brother Lydon made him feel.

He had been working for Father Jordan for a while and wanted to buy into what he was selling but never quite felt sold. Guys in the church like Lydon had always made the message seem off to him. The fact that the church needed to fairly regularly have him rough people or send messages did not do much to convince him of their cause. He did appreciate the hot meals and a roof over his head though. He was not one to look that sort of thing in the mouth. The world being as it was, he did not know what else he might be good at. Since the dreams had started however, he had been wondering if he might not be good for something besides cracking skulls and looking intimidating. He thought he might make a good farmer and he was certainly ready to give up the gray walls of Silver City. He looked again at the vista before him. It was as pretty as it was in his dreams.

As the last of the townfolk passed through the gates Lydon stood up and said, "It's time." The all the men got up and began to walk toward the town. Lydon walked next to Angus and began to speak about readiness and how they had God on their side. He quoted scripture and talked about the Antichrist. As Angus watched despairingly, Brother Lydon worked himself into a frenzy. He turned, hoping to see the men had reached the same conclusion that he had about Lydon and saw nothing but grins and smiles. He was beginning to believe this would end badly and he did not know if he could stop it. He took out his pistol and made sure it was loaded with grim determination.

CHAPTER TWENTY-NINE

"You are the next change, Jesse."

He had stayed silent while Dylan told his tale and now he did not know what to think. Nothing in his life had prepared him for someone to tell him they were a prophet who used to be a monster but was then sent by God to kidnap him. He was completely at a loss. Dylan looked at him expectantly and he felt completely empty.

"I don't know what to say."

"It's a lot to take in, I know. "

"A lot to take in? Yeah, you could say that. It's not every day someone tells you they're a prophet. Probably even rarer for someone to tell you they're your prophet."

Jesse got up and walked around the campsite for a few minutes. It was getting dark and he knew they would have to go back soon. Finally, he took a deep breath and sat back down across from Dylan who had not moved or spoken.

"You're wrong you know. There's nothing special about me. You made a mistake."

"No, Jesse, I haven't."

"If I was some sort of ... whatever you think I am... wouldn't I know it? Wouldn't I somehow sense that I was different?"

"I don't know. I had thought you might sense something, but I know only what I've been told."

"Told. In your dreams. By God."

"Yes. Jesse have you not seen enough by now to understand that there are greater forces at work here?"

"What? What have I seen? When I was seven my family disappeared.

I saw a man change into a monster and back again. I bounced around for most of my childhood and young life before discovering that a bottle had more answers than anyone else. Or did you mean more recently? Like when my long lost brother's wife showed up and angrily dragged me across the countryside before getting stuck in a room full of people who killed themselves in a burned out town, followed by crawling through a pitch black tunnel to avoid certain death? Or did you mean the part where my friends long lost son shows up? How about when the crazy guy told me he meant to kidnap me and not my brother, BECAUSE GOD TOLD HIM TO?"

Jesse's voice had risen to a yell and now he sat there panting. He felt spent. He had no more anger left to give. The disillusionment was too much for him. He wished he had a bottle with him.

"All those years you would never back down from Father Jordan. You said it was because it was the truth. That's fine but everyday people take the easy way when they know the truth is the harder path. They will tell people what they want to hear because that is how the world works. But not you. You stuck to your guns and it got you beaten more than once. Why do it? Why stick to the story?"

"Because it was the truth. Because, I don't know. Because. Just because."

"How do you know that it didn't happen just as Father Jordan said it did?"

"You mean his faith bringing him back? Because I was there. It was his bullshit faith that caused him to change in the first place."

"How do you know?"

"You were there. You saw him screaming and carrying on."

"Right, but maybe it was his faith that Changed him back."

"It wasn't."

"Why not? Seems as reasonable an explan..."

"It just wasn't! You know it as well as I do."

Dylan's eyes met Jesse's.

"Then what was it?"

"I don't know."

"That's not true. If you didn't know then, you wouldn't have fought so hard to say that it wasn't his faith. So, tell me what it was that turned him back."

"It was you! Ok? It was you. With your playing and singing. I don't know how but it brought him back." Jesse shouted.

Very quietly Dylan responded.

"No Jesse. It was you."

Jesse stared at him blankly. Dylan was no longer looking at him he was looking up at the darkening sky.

"It wasn't me. It was you with the music." Jesse answered eventually.

"My music can give people hope. It can inspire people. It can make them dream again. It can do a lot of things, but it cannot reverse the Change."

"Then how?"

"It's you, Jesse. You've always had the ability. That's why God sent me to prepare the way. It's why I was sent to find you. And sometimes I think it's why I found your brother instead. I said I made a mistake, but I think I was supposed to. I think the wilderness you were to experience wasn't ever supposed to be the actual wilderness."

"So." Jesse felt blindsided, "What am I supposed to do? If I did change him back, then I don't know how

I did it. Are you saying I'm the second coming or something? At least I have the right initials if that's the case."

Dylan laughed.

"I had thought of that, but no. I don't think you're the second coming. That's something else. I think your job is to bring the world back. God works in mysterious ways as they say, but I think the Changed plague was designed to clear the world of clutter. Spiritual clutter, moral clutter, societal clutter. Now that the clutter is gone someone has to rebuild what's left and make it something better. That's you."

"Rebuild the world."

"Yup."

"How? You say I can turn people back from the Change but how? And how will that rebuild the world? Won't that just bring back people who Changed because they were messed up in the first place?"

"I think that when you change people back, they will be like me. Blank slates. But I don't really know."

"Why not? Why don't you know? You seem to know everything else."

"I know what I've been told, Jes. No more, no less. But I have faith that we are on the right path."

"Faith. that seems to be your answer for everything."

"Well, what other answer is there? When I go to bed at night, I have faith that morning will come. When I open my mouth, I have faith that my voice will come forth. We do what we do because we have faith that we are doing the right thing. You came all this way because you have faith in me. I traveled where I did because I have faith in God. The message I was given was simple. Love and faith. With those two things the world can be Changed and that's why you and I are here today."

"This all seems so insane."

Jesse leaned back and looked up at the stars. They were beautiful at night out here. He realized that it had gotten dark.

"Oh crap." He said when he realized that night had fallen, and they were a ways away from town. "We have to get back before..."

"Before what? The Changed show up? Look around you."

Jesse looked around the edge of the light given off by the fire and saw them. The whole campsite was surrounded by Changed. They weren't moaning or moving. They were just standing there silently. Jesse felt dread descend on him.

"We're ok, Jes. They won't harm us. They won't come near me."

"What about me?"

"They won't come near you while you're with me. I've spent a lot of nights outside the walls of towns. Your brother and I walked across the country sleeping outdoors most of the time. I don't really know why but they won't come any closer."

"You brought us out here so that this would happen, didn't you?"

"I brought us out here because I like this place, but this was part of it. I wanted to see if you could change them back into humans."

"I can try I guess but I don't know how."

"Believing that you can is a good start."

"Easier said than done."

"I could play some, if you like."

"Yes. Please."

Dylan began to play, then after a while he began to sing.

He sang about dreaming beneath a desert sky.

Jesse got up and walked closer to the Changed. He could not believe he was trying this. As he stood there he thought of his mother. He thought of his brother and of all the horrible things that had happened in his life. The idea that it was all part of some plan to get him to this point terrified him. He could not get over how Dylan believed it all. He had dedicated his life to the idea that Jesse was some sort of savior.

He looked at the Changed and had no idea what to do. He listened to Dylan playing and tried to picture what had happened when he was a kid. All he could remember was all those people singing and then seeing Jordan shift back. From the moment it happened he knew it was not anything Jordan had done. He had always believed it was Dylan who had done it.

"But that's not true." he said quietly.

If he was going to be honest with himself, he had never truly believed it was Dylan. The realization hit him like a bolt of lightning. The idea filled his mind and his senses. The long-repressed memory came firing to the surface. He remembered the scene from his childhood. Dylan walking toward the Changed Father Jordan slowly playing. People joining in the song. And he remembered focusing on Jordan and believing he would change back. The picture of him changing back had formed in his head before it had happened and he had faith that Jordan would turn back, and then he had.

Jesse shook his head to clear those thoughts. He focused on the Changed directly in front of him. He met the hollow sunken eyes. He imagined the skin filling back in and the eyes seeing more than light and shadow again. He thought of Dylan and James and Julie and Desmond. He thought of all the sacrifice and horror that had led to this point and he believed that it was more than happenstance. He let go of his notions of how the world worked and he let go of himself. He believed that this Changed was more than a monster and could be a person again. He closed his eyes and prayed.

Nothing happened.

He looked over to Dylan who didn't half his playing, he only nodded encouragingly.

Jesse closed his eyes and tried again. He tried to push through all the pain and anger that lived inside of him and find that small space under the weight of years where he kept a light of hope. He focused on that pinprick of light imagining it as coming out of a keyhole in the dark. He picked himself looking into that tiny hole and as he did he felt his skin break out in a cold sweat. The hair on his arms and neck stood up. The air around him started to feel alive.

A sudden shift in the air caused him to open his eyes. The Changed in front of him opened its shriveled mouth as if to moan but no sound came out. The mouth began to open wider. Jesse shuddered when he felt something happen. He was not sure what, but for a brief moment he had a connection to the thing in front of him.

Then it happened.

The Changed eyes began to raise in their sockets. The gray pallor started to change hue. The dry blistered skin began to turn pink. Slowly, the Changed filled out in size and in the time it took Jesse to take a deep breath it was gone, replaced by a man.

The man met Jesse's eyes and moved his mouth as if to say something and then his eyes rolled back in his head and he passed out. Jesse caught him before he hit the ground. Dylan stopped playing and rushed over to help. The man weighed almost nothing. Together they brought him over by the fire. Dylan had a canteen and unscrewed the top and held it to the man's lips. His eyes opened and he took a drink. Dylan pulled it away before he could drink too much.

Dylan went over to his bag and took out an extra set of clothing. With Jesse's help, they got the man dressed. The clothes did not fit well but they would keep him warm. As they watched, he tried to speak but could not.

After a few moments he closed his eyes and fell asleep.

"You did it, Jesse."

Jesse could not respond. He just stared at the man sleeping by their campfire who had once been a monster. He did not know what to say but he felt something new within himself. He felt a sense of purpose.

Eventually he held his hand out to Dylan. Dylan took it and shook it. "Thank you." Jesse said.

"Don't thank me. I was only doing what I was asked."

"Thank you, anyway."

Dylan smiled and nodded.

"You're welcome. We should take him back to town."

"Yeah, that would be for the best."

That was when they heard the gunshot and the scream float in on the wind.

Dylan looked in the direction the sound had come from.

"Time's up." he whispered.

CHAPTER THIRTY

As the sun began to dip below the mountains to the west Brother Sidney Lydon and the seven men he had begun thinking of as his soldiers walked up to the gates of Malice.

There were two men manning the gates. They were sitting on stools watching Lydon and his men as they strolled up. They each had hunting rifles strapped over their shoulders. Robbie Helm and Levon Robertson had been there most of the day and had been looking forward to locking up and being relieved by the night shift. Both men were in their early twenties and had spent most of their lives working on farms. Neither of them were very suspicious of strangers. They would ask the men their business and point them toward the bunk house and then let whoever was on the list for taking care of guests know they had arrived. They did not expect trouble. It was out of the ordinary for such a large group to arrive but not unusual enough to set off alarms.

Brother Lydon walked up to them with Angus right behind him. The rest hung back and spread out.

"Greetings!" Lydon said in a tone that was over the top friendly.

"Good evening and Welcome to Malice." Robbie replied, "Looking for a place to stay the night?"

"Absolutely. My friends and I have been on the road for a while. So, this is Malice?" he looked around as he said it, "We've heard a lot about it."

"She's a great town. We're always glad to have guests. Cutting it pretty close though! Getting dark out."

"Yes. It was a long walk from Black Horse."

"Black Horse?" Levon asked. "Where are you headed if I may ask?

Most folks who pass through here are on their way to Black Horse and the pass."

"Well, in point of fact, we were headed here. We're looking for someone."

Robbie and Levon glanced at each other. They were both starting to feel uneasy and were unsure how to react.

"Two men actually. One is a young man named Jesse Chapin," his face twitched a little as he said Jesse's name, "And another that currently goes by the name of Dylan Droge."

"What's your business with them?" Robbie asked.

"Oh, I'm an old friend of Jesse's and I work on behalf of someone who would like to meet Mr. Droge."

Robbie and Levon both looked at him for a moment. There was something unsettling about the man. They did not like the way that the men had spread out. Something was wrong here.

It was Levon who spoke, "Well, I don't know that first guy you mentioned. Dylan's not in town at the moment. So, why don't I take you over to the bunk house and Robbie here will fetch the people on guest duty." He turned and addressed Robbie, "Rob, go get Paul, I'm pretty sure it's his night to feed folks." Robbie nodded. Paul Headon was the man who functioned as the town's sheriff and walked through the gates. As soon as he was out of view of the men outside, he broke into a run.

Levon turned back to Lydon and smiled at him. "Why don't you follow me, and we'll get you settled."

Lydon slapped him across the face. Levon had not been expecting the blow and it spun him around. Lydon raised his hand to do it again and Angus caught his arm.

"What the hell are you doing?"

"Get your hands off me." Lydon said and pulled his arm free from Angus's grasp. Levon had turned back around and went to pull the rifle off his shoulder. As he did so he heard six loud clicks from behind Lydon. He saw that each of the men had pulled a gun and they were all pointed at him. He tossed the rifle aside.

"What do you want?" he asked.

"I told you what we want. I know they are here, and I am tired of playing nice with you heathen. I do not care about you or your pissant little town. Turn Chapin and Droge over to me and we will leave first thing in the morning. Now, let's all go inside, close the gates, and you can fetch them for me."

"I told you, I don't know any Jesse and Dylan isn't here."

Lydon slapped him again.

"Do not lie to me!" he shouted.

"What the hell is going on here?"

They all turned their attention from Levon and saw a large blond man standing in the gate. He was almost 6'3 and thick with muscle. In his hands was a shotgun. Standing next to him was Robbie with his hunting rifle.

"You must be the guest committee," Lydon said with an acidic drawl.

"My name is Paul Headon. I'm the sheriff here. Who the hell are you and why do you have guns pointed at one of our citizens."? His voice sounded like it was coming from deep within him. The citizens of Malice had no real need of a sheriff, but they had people pass through who needed to be reminded that some behaviors were not acceptable. Headon served as a very effective reminder.

"As I told this gentleman here," Lydon said, and waved dismissively in the direction of Levon, "We are here for Jesse Chapin and Dylan Droge. We do not want any trouble, but we will not be denied in this. We have been sent by God's chosen on this Earth, Father Jordan, to retrieve these men."

"That's nice. That lunatic preacher holds no sway here. So, here's what's going to happen. You and your men are going to drop your guns in a little pile over there. You're going to come inside, and we'll take you to the bunk house where you'll spend the night and in the morning, you will be on your way. You can go back and tell Holy Joe to leave us alone."

Lydon's face went apoplectic at the insults to Father Jordan.

"You will not insult him, you will not!" Lydon screamed.

"I can and I will. Now, let's get rid.."

Lydon cut him off and pointed at one of his men. "You. Shoot him."

"Wait!" Angus shouted but it was too late. The man Lydon had pointed to, Lou Niko, did not hesitate. He leveled his pistol at Headon and fired. The bullet hit him in the shoulder, sending him spinning to the ground and his shotgun flying away from him. Robbie ducked as the shot was fired and then went right over to Headon as he hit the ground.

People had started to come when they heard the shouting but now at the sound of a gunshot they came running. Desmond, Stu, and Mick were among the first to arrive.

Desmond recognized Lydon the moment he saw him.

"You?" he blurted out.

"That one, he is Jesse's friend, grab him." Lydon shouted. He turned to Angus, "You. Give me your gun."

Angus stared at him, "What? No." He started to say something else when Lydon kicked him in the groin. The blow stunned him and he went down hard. Lydon pulled the gun from his holster, walked over and grabbed Levon by the collar. He held the gun to his back.

Three of the men advanced on Desmond. Desmond pushed his son behind him and stared the men down.

"Whoa, now let's all calm down. What are you doing here?"

As he spoke, Mick circled around to where Headon's shotgun had landed. Robbie was still standing between the men outside the gate and Headon, who was groaning on the ground. One of the three advancing on Desmond stopped and turned to Robbie.

"Drop it." He said in a tone that implied he meant business, "And you, get away from the shotgun."

Mick froze. Robbie, who honestly did not know if his rifle was even loaded, tossed it away but did not move away from Headon.

The remaining two had reached Desmond. One of them grabbed him roughly by the right arm and Desmond hit him on the chin with his left. The man stumbled backwards stunned. Before Desmond could turn to the other man, he was pistol whipped across the face. This dropped him to his knees. The man he had hit recovered himself and raised his gun to hit Desmond. Stu leapt into him knocking him to the ground, sending the gun flying to the ground.

"Stop!" shouted the man who had hit Desmond. He was standing over him with his pistol a foot from the back of Desmond's head.

Stu stopped. The man he tackled kicked him in the stomach. Stu doubled over. He got up and kicked Stu again.

"That will be enough of that." Lydon shouted. "You will turn Chapin and Droge over to us now or there will be consequences."

It was Mick who spoke, "What do you want with them?"

"They will be brought to Father Jordan. God's justice will be done."

"God's justice? Are you insane?"

"You live here with the Antichrist and you ask if I am insane?"

"The Anti-what?"

"You debase yourself in the eyes of God consorting with the Devil!"

"You think Dylan is the Devil?" This time it was James speaking.

"I know he is the Devil. He has blinded your eyes to his evil. I am here to save your souls, if they can be saved!" Lydon was shouting again.

"You are misguided my friend." James replied calmly.

"Do not speak to me with your forked tongue. If you say another word this sinner will pay the price." He jabbed Levon in the back with the gun for emphasis.

Behind him Angus had gotten to his knees.

"There's no need to shout so much. You wanted me and I am here."

The voice came from behind everyone. The gunmen spun and looked into the darkness beyond the arc of the gate's spotlights.

Dylan and Jesse emerged with a man hanging limply between them.

"At last." Lydon hissed.

CHAPTER THIRTY-ONE

Lydon's eyes met Jesse's.

"I told you it was not over between us." he growled.

"You really are a loyal dog, aren't you?" Jesse shot back.

"I have had enough of your insults!" Lydon yelled.

"Ok, let's all calm down." Dylan said placidly, "James, Mick, please come take this man and get him to a bed. He is not well." The formerly Changed man stared blankly at the scene before him.

Mick and James both took tentative steps forward, their eyes on the myriad of guns on display.

"Do not move." Lydon spat back.

"Mr. Lydon, I am willing to cooperate with you, however this man needs medical attention, and I will see that he has it." He nodded at James and then turned to Headon, "Paul, are you ok?"

Headon who had managed to sit up, nodded. Robbie was next to him applying pressure to the wound.

James and Mick came forward and took the man from Jesse and Dylan and brought him back to the crowd that had gathered. They handed him to two of the younger folks who left with him. Once the man had been carried away Dylan turned back to Lydon.

"I would ask that you let Levon go. If you feel the need to point your gun at someone then by all means let it be me." Dylan said calmly.

"You're trying to trick me. I can feel it. Get on your knees. Both of you." Lydon nearly shouted.

Dylan got down on his knees and motioned for Jesse to do likewise. Behind Lydon, Angus got to his feet.

"So, what is it you would have us do, Sidney. Would you have us go back to Silver City with you? Is that what it will take for you to leave these people alone?" Dylan asked.

Lydon was clearly unnerved by Dylan's cooperation. He had built the man up to be a monster and he was not behaving as such.

"You speak as if you have a choice. I will not stand for your devilry. You will be bound and gagged and led back like the beast that you are." Lydon growled.

"I will do as you ask. But why do you need Jesse? It would seem to me that Father Jordan would prefer to see the back of him." Dylan asked.

"He will be brought back to denounce you. Your lies will be exposed, and he will come to see the true glory of Father Jordan's miracle." Lydon replied.

"He's wrong, you know. Father Jordan's return from the Change was a miracle, but it was not his miracle. He is a convincing man, though; I do not blame you for following him." Dylan said, his tone never wavering.

"He is your enemy on this earth, and he will send you back to the pit." Lydon replied, bordering on manic at this point.

"I'm sorry that you cannot see the truth, Sidney." Dylan said.

"I will show you truth!" He shouted and shoved Robbie aside. He raised his gun toward Dylan.

At the same moment, a low moan came from the darkness beyond the edge of the town's light. The men still standing on the perimeter spun and a group of Changed emerged.

As Lydon raised the gun, Angus dove for him. He hit him just as he fired. Behind them the men fired into the group of Changed. The men who had been holding their guns on Desmond and the crowd turned at the sound of gunfire.

Wasting no time, James grabbed the gun hand of the one who was covering Desmond. He wrenched the gun free and then punched him. That stunned him long enough for Desmond, who had risen from his knees, to land a haymaker. He went down in a heap.

Stu kicked the legs out from underneath the man closest to him. He dropped his gun as his legs whipped out and he landed flat on his back, knocking the wind out of him. Guadalupe who had been standing nearby picked up the gun and pointed it at him.

The four closest to the Changed kept firing and the Changed kept coming. They turned to run and were grabbed. The Changed dragged them out of the circle of light. The sound of screams split the night.

Angus and Lydon wrestled on the ground for the gun and there was another muffled shot. Lydon sat up as Angus dropped off him holding his side. Lydon turned and saw Jesse flying at him. Jesse had gotten up and charged the moment Angus had tackled him.

Before Lydon could get the gun up, Jesse dove into him. His shoulder collided with Lydon's jaw with a sickening crack. He landed on top of Lydon and the pistol flew out of his hand. Jesse sat up with one knee on Lydon's chest and raised his fist. He brought it down with all the hatred and frustration he had left and felt something break in his hand as he connected. Lydon went limp after the blow, unconscious.

Everything went quiet after that. For a moment Jesse heard nothing but the low moans from the darkness and his own heavy breathing.

"Jesse?"

He turned to see Dylan still kneeling. He had a hand over his chest, and he was covered in blood.

"No." Jesse whispered and scrambled off Lydon to get back to Dylan.

He got there just as Dylan slumped over. Jesse caught him before he hit the ground and cradled him in his arms.

It was like a spell had been broken and the people of Malice began to move. They secured the remaining gunmen including Lydon and went to help Angus and Headon. A small crowd began to gather around Jesse and Dylan. Julie and James put their hands on Jesse's shoulder and Desmond knelt beside them.

"It's finished for me, Jes. My job is done." Dylan said, weakly

"C'mon Dylan, you'll be ok. You must have a Doctor here." Jesse could feel his eyes getting wet.

"Nah. My journey's over. I got a second chance and made the best of it. Now it's your turn. You have the hard job. All I had to do was play guitar."

"I can't do it alone."

"You're not alone. These people are all here to help you. And remember, you have God on your side."

He closed his eyes and died in Jesse's arms.

Jesse removed the guitar strapped to Dylan's back and laid him down. He handed it to James.

He looked at each of the people around him in turn. Julie, Desmond, James, Stu, Mick, Guadalupe and Tonya were all there.

"He brought me here to ask me to save the world." Jesse said with a small laugh. "I mean to do it. Will you help me as you helped him?"

It was James who spoke. "We will."

"Then we'd better get to work."

EPILOGUE

James and Jesse carried Dylan back to his house and laid him on his bed. The house Dylan kept was spare of amenities. There was a record player and a lot of records. Everything else was bare bones. They covered him with a sheet and then locked the door behind them.

As they stood outside Dylan's house, Jesse asked, "Did he tell you what I'm supposed to do?"

James nodded. "Yeah, he did. That guy you brought back with you; he was a Changed wasn't he?"

"Yup."

"I have to admit I wondered if it was true. I spent years with Dylan, and I saw some pretty amazing things. I had dreams about Malice before we found it and about people who would later arrive here. Things were never normal with him. But the idea that my chatty little brother was supposed to save the world seemed farfetched."

"Still does."

"Yeah, it still does."

"I don't know if I can do it. It seems so immense. Folks like Father Jordan are still out there. He's not going to stop. He thought Dylan was the Antichrist. He's going to think even less of me."

"We'll be ready for him. This town and the people here aren't an accident, Jesse. God drew each of them here for a purpose. You talked to Dylan, he told you about his visions. None of this is a coincidence. Malice was created to help you fulfill your purpose. See, the thing of it is not just that we have faith in God and each other. It's that God has faith in us."

"I hope so." He looked at Dylan's guitar slung over James's shoulder. "Think you can play that as well as him?"

"No, but I can certainly try."

"Do you think the stuff he said about music changing the world was true?"

"I do. I saw it in action. When he played it brought people hope and joy. It pushed the darkness away."

"So is that how we're going to save the world. Faith, Hope, and Rock and roll?"

"Works for me."

"Me too."

They headed back to the gates to help out.

The next day Lydon and his men were sent on their way. Angus who was badly wounded was allowed to stay. They had kept them tied up in Stu's basement that evening with a guard on him. The town's doctor, Ian Barre, looked in on Lydon and did his best to set his jaw. There was little he could do and did not think it would heal well enough to be functional again.

Once he was done with Lydon he checked in on Angus and Paul Headon. Headon's wound was not bad. The bullet had gone clean through his shoulder. It had glanced off the bone but nothing too damaging. Angus was not quite as lucky. Barre bandaged the wound and did what he could. He did not know if Angus would live through the night but guessed if he did that he would recover.

Julie, Desmond, Stu, and Mick escorted Lydon and his men out of the gate and down the road. They did not give them supplies or their weapons back. Lydon was delirious with pain from his shattered jaw and had to be half carried. They walked in silence until they reached the top of the hill where they would leave them. Julie broke the silence.

"I don't really care what you do from here but don't ever come back. If you want, take him back to Father Jordan and let him know that he and his kind are not welcome here. He is a relic from the world before the

Change. Things are different now and his time is done. The world doesn't need fake holy men who hide behind thugs and psychopaths anymore."

They watched as the men led Lydon away on the road towards Black Horse.

"Think they'll drag him all the way back to Silver City?" Stu asked.

"Yeah, I do. I also don't think we've seen the last of Brother Lydon." Desmond answered.

"Maybe not." Mick said, "But Julie's right. They're relics of a world that really is gone. I don't think we have much to worry about even if they do come back."

"I hope you're right." Desmond responded.

"Did any of you notice how those Changed just grabbed those guys last night and then disappeared?" Julie asked.

"I guess in all the confusion I hadn't thought about it but yeah. That's pretty odd." Stu said.

"I think Dylan was right. Maybe we do have God on our side." Julie responded.

"That's an encouraging thought. Especially if it's our job to save the world." said Desmond.

They turned and walked back towards Malice.

The day of the funeral the sky was as clear and striking a blue as anyone could remember ever seeing. The air was crisp and smelled sweetly of pine forests and mountain lakes.

The town gathered by the gate as Jesse, James, Julie, Mick, Stu, and Desmond carried the coffin from Dylan's house through the town. Grendel followed them quietly making low whining sounds.

Once they reached the gate, the coffin, which had been built the previous day by several of the townsfolk, was taken from them by Guadalupe, Tonya, Paul with his good hand, Levon, Robbie, and Ian.

Together they left the town's borders. They had not seen any

Changed since the night Dylan died. No one was sure exactly but a few around town had put forth the notion that whatever kept the Changed from attacking Dylan had been shared with them when he died.

They carried the coffin for a while and eventually handed it off to another six. This was how Dylan traveled from the town he had helped create to his final resting place atop a hill, surrounded by pine trees.

A grave had been dug the previous day. The casket was placed next to the hole and opened. James walked up and placed a record on top of Dylan's body. It was Highway 61 Revisited by Bob Dylan. Once the record was placed, he closed the casket again. He turned and addressed the town.

"We, better than anyone, know that this body is just a shell. Dylan's spirit has gone to his reward. There is no denying that he touched all our lives and changed us for the better. Today his work is done and ours begins. He prepared a path for all of us, not just my brother. His promise to us was that he would give us the chance to make a better world. Our promise to him is that we will not waste this chance we have been given."

He took the guitar off his back and began to play. The song was familiar to everyone there. After a few moments, they all joined together singing an old Bob Dylan song about the times changing. It was the first hymn sung at the dawn of a new era.

THE END

**Spotify playlist of songs
that inspired the book**

ACKNOWLEDGEMENTS

First and foremost, I'd like to thank my wonderful wife Jennie. Not only did she do the cover art and book design, she encouraged me every step of the way during the writing and editing process. Without her, there would be no book.

I would also like to thank my fellow Oddities; Nick, Shasta, Marcella, Pat, and Steve. Their help, support, and drive made this book possible.

Eric Dellinger provided the graphics for the Kickstarter as well as the amazing video. I cannot thank him enough for his friendship and encouragement down through the years. I don't know what I'd do without him.

Trapper Schoepp wrote and recorded an amazing song out of my raw lyrics. For that I will be forever grateful. His grace in allowing us to make a record and put it out with our kickstarter helped make a dream come true for me. I cannot thank him enough. His music will always be an inspiration.

Music is the soul of this book and so many artists make up its playlist. Thanking them all would be impossible, but a few stand out. Jesse Chapin was named after Jesse Malin and Harry Chapin. Malin has been my musical north star for years, opening up so many different doors. Harry Chapin was the other namesake. His music and activism has been both an inspiration and a balm in hard times.

Joe Strummer, a mural of whom led me to Jesse Malin. Pete Droge who recorded my favorite song and inspired a 3000 mile journey. Tom Petty, Paul Simon, and so many others. The Mighty Mighty Bosstones, even wandering in the desert as they are, have been the most important band of my life. Woody Guthrie and Bob Dylan who both provided a blueprint and a mythology for the core of the story.

They're listed in these pages, but I'd like to thank all of the Kickstarter backers, who had faith in the book and generously aided in its creation. I do not take that support for granted.

Very special thanks to Amelia and Gabriel Brick for general awesomeness. Kristin and Bernard too.

Everyone in the local writers community who has helped me along on my journey from dreaming of seeing my writing in print to publishing my first novel. There's too many to name, but Maria Masington who ran the open Mics at the Newark Arts Alliance that helped set me on my course. David Shoemaker was a friend first and then a writing peer has been an inspiration. Weldon Burge, Joanne Reimbold, Phil Giunta, Danielle Ackley-Mcphail, Mike McPhail, and so many more who have supported me and Oddity Prodigy Productions.

Special thanks to Greg Schauer who edited the novel and whose encouragement has meant so much.

My family were my first readers. My mother Bonnie, my brother Jeremiah, and my father Stephen, who provided my first review, calling the book "credible." Love you all.

ABOUT THE AUTHOR

Jacob Jones-Goldstein, founding member of Oddity Prodigy Productions, is an internationally published author, journalist, and editor. His short stories have appeared in anthologies and magazines such as 'Plague of Shadows' from Smart Rhino Press, 'Beach Pulp' from Cat & Mouse Press, and Lovecraftiana from Rogue Planet Press. His novella, 'The Last Summer', is forthcoming from the Systema Paradoxa series of Espec Books.

He has edited the previous volumes from Oddity Prodigy Productions 'Scary Stuff', 'Beneath the Yellow Lights," and "Bright Mirror." He is hard at work on their next anthology, "Where Legends Walk."

In addition to fiction, Jacob writes about music for his personal site, ShoutingStreet.com, and has covered the Philadelphia 76ers for several online publications. Beyond writing and editing, he hosts popular podcast "The Scary Stuff Podcast", plays Magic the Gathering, Disc Golf, and way too many board games.

He loves comic books, movies, exploring, cats, family, friends, Joel Embiid, Tyrese Maxey, and his wife, Jennie.

Visit our favorite comic shops and bookstores!

CAPTAIN BLUE HEN

After he crashed landed on Earth and saw his favorite stuffies torn from him, The CAPTAIN swore to protect stuffed animals everywhere and create the most amazing comic book and pop culture buying experience this side of the Mississippi. For nearly 40 years, Captain Blue Hen Comics has been your one stop shop for all your pop culture and nerd needs, and we don't plan on stopping anytime soon!

www.captainbluehen.com
302.737.3434

DAYS OF KNIGHTS

The Days of Knights game store has a huge selection of Board & Card games, Magic the Gathering, YuGiOh, Pokemon, RPGs D&D and Pathfinder, Sci-Fi, Miniatures, Warhammer 40K & Bones, Tarot, Chess, Mahjong, and much more! Friendly staff in a business that's been on Main Street in Newark, DE over 40 years!

www.daysofknights.com
302.366.0963

Also available from
ODDITY PRODIGY PRODUCTIONS

SCARY STUFF
Horror Anthology

A tribute to the classic style of horror published in comics from the 60s and 70s, Scary Stuff is at heart a love letter to the kind of scary stories we grew up on.

$18.95 paperback

BENEATH THE YELLOW LIGHTS
Urban Fantasy Anthology

The new collection of short stories from Oddity Prodigy Productions captures that feeling of magic on city streets, just out of the corner of your eye. Join us as we take a walk, Beneath the Yellow Lights.

$18.95 paperback

Order at your local bookstore
WWW.ODDITYPRODIGY.COM

www.ingramcontent.com/pod-product-compliance
Lightning Source LLC
Chambersburg PA
CBHW071139180726
48291CB00007B/2262